The Midnight Unicorn

Published in the UK by Scholastic Children's Books, 2019
Euston House, 24 Eversholt Street, London, NW1 1DB, UK
A division of Scholastic Limited.

London – New York – Toronto – Sydney – Auckland
Mexico City – New Delhi – Hong Kong

Text © Alice Hemming, 2019

ISBN 978 1407 19771 5

A CIP catalogue record for this book is available from the British Library.

Printed by CPI Group (UK) Ltd, Croydon, CR0 4YY
Papers used by Scholastic Children's Books are made
from wood grown in sustainable forests.

1 3 5 7 9 10 8 6 4 2

This is a work of fiction. Names, characters, places, incidents
and dialogues are products of the author's imagination or are used
fictitiously. Any resemblance to actual people, living or dead,
events or locales is entirely coincidental.

www.scholastic.co.uk

The Midnight Unicorn

ALICE HEMMING

SCHOLASTIC

For Simon, Clara and Tom,
with all my love and thanks.

FAR AWAY

IN A

MAGICAL LAND...

the bridge with their broods. One had an infant strapped to her back and the other held a child by the hand. Five more children walked or tottered along behind. The families were off to gather the first new berries of the season. They would each make a pie at the end of the day and if any berries were left over after baking, they would box them up to sell at the market. The hedgerows were so laden with fruit that they could pick blackberries all morning and never exhaust the supply.

Some of the older children minded the younger ones; the others got to work, although the purple stains around their mouths and the lack of fruit in their baskets gave them away.

The sweet, orangey smell of wild bergamot blew on the breeze. Time passed quickly, with singing, joking and city gossip. The women wondered about the price of goat's cheese at the dairy stall, whether this warmer weather would last, and why the queen's brother had left Essendor so suddenly.

They were so engrossed in their chat that they barely noticed one of their youngest break away in search of his own entertainment. An old willow tree with an inviting Y-shaped trunk stood close by. The little one climbed up with fearless agility. He inched along a bough which hung over the river below. On another day, all may have been well, but today the wind was blowing in

FAR AWAY

IN A

MAGICAL LAND...

CHAPTER ONE

THE SNAPPED BOUGH

The city of Essendor stood on a hill, a stone castle at its summit. Small but sturdy houses were squeezed into every available space and stone steps twisted and turned down the hill. One warm day in early autumn the red swallowtail flags fluttered on the turrets of the castle. A new queen, just married, sat on the throne and there was a celebratory feel in the air. Bunting hung in the market square where some street performers had attracted a crowd.

An arched bridge led through a gap in the city's walls and across the river to the fields beyond. Two young mothers crossed the bridge with their broods. One had an infant strapped to her back and the other held a child by the hand. Five more children walked or tottered along behind. The families were off to gather the first new berries of the season. They would each make a pie at the end of the day and if any berries were left over after baking, they would box them up to sell at the market. The hedgerows were so laden with fruit that they could pick blackberries all morning and never exhaust the supply.

Some of the older children minded the younger ones; the others got to work, although the purple stains around their mouths and the lack of fruit in their baskets gave them away.

The sweet, orangey smell of wild bergamot blew on the breeze. Time passed quickly, with singing, joking and city gossip. The women wondered about the price of goat's cheese at the dairy stall, whether this warmer weather would last, and why the queen's brother had left Essendor so suddenly.

They were so engrossed in their chat that they barely noticed one of their youngest break away in search of his own entertainment. An old willow tree with an inviting Y-shaped trunk stood close by. The little one climbed up with fearless agility. He inched along a bough which hung over the river below. On another day, all may have been well, but today the wind was blowing in the wrong direction or the stars were not aligned as they should be. The brittle bough, which had held fast all summer, snapped.

The sound of a branch splintering and a piercing shriek alerted the mothers. They dropped their baskets and rushed to the source of the cry, trying to piece together what had happened.

The child had fallen six feet and now clung on to a rock protruding from the steep bank above the river. He was just two summers old.

He saw his family looking and cried out in anguish. As the mother panicked, her eldest child began to scramble down the bank to retrieve him. But the descent was slow and the little one's pink fists could not hold on. His grip loosened and he tumbled down the bank, head over heels in a sickening acrobatic display. He vanished under the water as the movement of the river turned him on to his stomach and carried him along.

The mother gasped as if winded and the elder sister screamed, "He can't swim!"

The older children raced along the river, trying to keep up with the little boy as he tumbled along in the river's current. The mothers followed, making sure that the younger ones were with them – they didn't want to lose any more of their number. For a few yards, trees and overgrowth shielded the boy from view, then a little further along, the ground level dropped and there was a gap allowing access to the river. By the looks of things, anglers – possibly poachers – had fished there in the past. The families scrambled through and looked frantically up and down the river. The boy should have reached this point by now. His mother stared into the flowing water, holding on to her friend for support. The child was nowhere to be seen.

But then, from behind them, came a cry. A powerful cry, from a healthy little boy. There he was on the bank, shivering behind a bush, wet through but unharmed. His mother rushed to him, hugged him tightly to her chest, stripped off his clothes and wrapped her shawl around him. He was mottled and red from the cold and would soon be covered in bruises, but he was still able to cry lustily. His mother's embraces and some blackberries from the basket soon soothed him.

The woman looked around for someone to thank. It was inconceivable that her son, who was unable to swim, could have made his way to the side of the rapidly flowing river and clambered up the steep bank. But there was no rescuer in sight.

"Who pulled you out?" she asked the child.

"'Orse," said the little boy. "'Orse with a 'orn." He indicated on his head where a horn might be found.

The two women looked at one another questioningly.

"A unicorn?" whispered the mother in disbelief.

The boy nodded. "One 'orn."

"Was the unicorn silver?" asked the friend, who knew a thing or two about such animals. "With a spiralling horn and a flowing mane?"

The boy shook his head. "Like midnight."

"A midnight unicorn," whispered the mother to her friend. And louder into the empty woods, "Unicorn, if you are here, thank you for saving my child!"

From that day, he was known as the Boy River. His story spread quickly across the city and he enjoyed some fame, which was soon forgotten. But the Boy River never forgot that he was the first to set eyes on the Midnight Unicorn of Essendor.

FIVE

YEARS

LATER

CHAPTER TWO

THE PROTECTED CITY

There were the usual daily grumbles. Sometimes the crops failed. The price of goat's cheese remained high. The local tavern shut too early on a Saturday. But overall, this was a happy time for the inhabitants of Essendor, and bigger disasters were averted. Three straw-thatched cottages burned to the ground in the night but all the inhabitants escaped unhurt. A wolf was seen creeping into a field of sheep but not a single animal was harmed. Foreign invaders approached from the Island of the North but were thwarted at Essendor's gates.

And always there were reports of a mysterious unicorn,

with sparkling jet fur and a shimmering white horn. Many of the spectacular rescues took place in the dead of night, which gave the creature its moniker. To the inhabitants of Essendor, their protector was known as the Midnight Unicorn.

Every day, the king and queen looked down on their subjects and smiled. Their city was protected and their people were happy. What was more, the royal couple had good news of their own.

The queen was to be blessed with a child.

THE SIGN

Nanny selected a speckled brown hen's egg from a bowl on the side. It had been gathered this morning by the kitchen hand.

What the queen needed was a good, nourishing breakfast to give her strength and to help the baby grow. The cook here couldn't be trusted – he was an imbecile who served all manner of strange things for the royal breakfast, like bread and fruit. Nanny would just have to make it herself: a bowl of scrambled eggs with lots of butter and ground white pepper.

Nanny cracked the egg into a bowl. The clear white slid out of the shell, complete with not one, but two, rich yellow yolks. Nanny stared for a moment. A double-yolk. She had not seen such a thing for some time. All the better for the queen: a lot of the goodness in a hen's egg came from the yolk. She reached for another egg and cracked it alongside the first. Four yolks now bobbed in the bowl. Two eggs, each with two yolks? This was highly unusual. Nanny clapped her hands to her cheeks. "It's a sign!" she cried. "A sign, as clear as day."

The kitchen hand and the scullery maid came rushing in to see what all the shrieking was about. Nanny held out the bowl of unwhisked eggs and smiled broadly. "The queen is expecting twins," she announced.

EGG ON THE DRAPES

Queen Bia did not take the news well. In fact, she threw the bowl of eggs across the room from her dressing table. "I do not want eggs. I do not like eggs. I am not unwell, I am simply with child. And I am *not* expecting twins!"

The lady's maid sidled into the room with her head lowered and began scraping egg from the bed drapes. The king threw her a sympathetic look and cleared his throat.

"Nanny did say that it was quite clear. Two yolks, twice in a row."

"Ha!" said the queen. "I am not taking the word of a servant on such matters. This is all silly superstition."

"She is not a servant, my love. She is my trusted nanny. And she has been right about many things over the years. She predicted the death of the old footman, Bourke, do not forget."

"Bourke was one hundred and twelve! I can assure you that my breakfast menu has no connection whatsoever to my unborn child. It was not even my breakfast of choice."

The king paced up and down the bedroom. "I know she can be old-fashioned but it would be unwise to ignore such a clear sign. Nanny has some experience in such matters. She cared for me and my six siblings from when we were just babes in arms."

"This is the woman who told me not to play the piano while I am with child, as it will make them too flighty!" complained the queen. "I will not accept servants' fancies; I need to consult someone I trust. Send for my sorcerer."

THE SORCERER

The young sorcerer, Maneo, was a favourite of the queen. Nobody knew quite where he had come from but it was well known that he had served his apprenticeship with a great master. When he was ready to practise on his own, he came to Essendor. News of his prowess in the magical arts soon reached the royal court. He was different to the old seers and magicians who set up homes in the south of the city. His spells were experimental but precise. He cured a mute woman who had not spoken for seventeen years. He transformed a billy goat to a nanny goat, which gave the creamiest milk for miles.

The queen summoned him to cast spells for her pleasure. He permanently freed the roses in the royal garden from pests. Now they bloomed all year and rivalled any in the kingdom. To mark the king and queen's anniversary, he turned the water in the castle fountain into the finest champagne. Queen Bia quickly gave him a place within the royal court, including his own quarters and all the specialist equipment he needed.

There was something about Maneo's manner that pleased the queen. Others at court flattered her and told her pretty lies, but Maneo was not like that. He may have been a sorcerer but he dealt with facts.

Right now, he stood looking dispassionately at the queen's newly pregnant belly. His face was young but his eyes were old and he might have been handsome if only he had smiled. He had a very small pointed beard and wore a floppy yellow hat with a black feather tucked into its brim – his only frivolity. He carried a wand that was black and fine, like a switch. Right now, he turned it over and over with his slender figures.

"There are certain spells I can cast to protect you and the newborn. Would you like me to proceed?"

The queen nodded and smiled. She enjoyed watching him work. Maneo looked to the ceiling, hands raised on either side of his head, and began to mumble – a string of unintelligible sounds that grew louder until he was almost shouting. He swished the wand around him, creating a sparkly sheen in the room, like dust caught in a shaft of sunlight.

"This charm of protection will last for six new moons – enough to take you through your confinement. As long as the birth takes place in this room, then your health and that of the newborn is guaranteed."

"Thank you, Maneo," said the queen.

Maneo inclined his head towards her. "And would you like a guard to watch over you and the new baby?"

The king nodded. "Yes. That would put all our minds at rest."

This time Maneo took the black feather from his hat, threw it in the air and pointed his wand towards it, his arm extending swiftly. There was a screech and a blaze of blue light in the corner of the room. The king and queen both jumped at the sound and then laughed, embarrassed.

A large bird with black feathers, a black beak and a flash of white at its throat perched on the washstand. A raven. The sorcerer approached the bird, which seemed perfectly tame, and ran a long pale finger lightly along its head and back. The raven did not appear to mind his touch.

"This is Corvus. He will sit in the corner of the room to watch over you. He will not disturb you and does not require food or water. If you leave the window open then he will attend to his own needs."

"The fresh air will be welcome," said the queen.

The king raised his eyebrows. "An . . . unusual childminder."

"Not at all," said the sorcerer. "Ravens make excellent guards. They are highly sensitive, intelligent communicators and display great loyalty."

Right now, the raven did not appear to be doing any communicating. He nestled his head under his wing and closed his eyes.

"I like him," said the queen.

"If he pleases you, my dear, then we shall keep him. But

Maneo, we invited you here with a specific question," said the king. "There has been a suggestion that the queen may be carrying more than one child. Can you confirm or deny this?"

Maneo shook his head slowly and steepled his fingers. "Alas, this is a skill I do not possess. I have practised alchemy and potion making but I cannot predict the future. The craft of fortune telling is less precise than my own. It requires a level of intuition and faith that I cannot claim. For that you need a seer."

THE SEER

The seer from the town was brought to the queen's bedchamber that very afternoon. She was old: older than anyone else in the city. No one could remember her as a girl apart from the old footman Bourke, before he had passed. It took a long time for her to climb the steps of the south tower. When she entered the queen's chamber she stood still for some time, regaining her breath. She looked out of the window, beyond the city's walls, and shook her head in amazement. "Such a view you have, from the very top of the castle. I have never climbed so high. Not even in my youth, when I would think nothing of ascending the Grey Mountain."

She paused, remembering. "I would strip as naked as the day I was born and bathe in the waterfall up there. Not a soul to see me apart from the birds."

Corvus cawed and the seer coughed, a hacking cough that went on for some moments. The king smiled politely. "Can we get you anything? Some sweet mint tea, perhaps?" He pointed to the silver teapot at the queen's bedside.

The seer shook her head, still coughing, and continued staring out of the window. "From here, I have the view of a bird. I can see the city laid out below us." Her coughing eased and she raised a hand. "I can also see the future coming. It is a dark cloud. Great change is on its way. And where is the Midnight Unicorn? The creature has not been seen for some weeks. Will it be there to protect Essendor in our time of need?"

She turned and stared at the queen.

Queen Bia said nothing, but gazed out of the window as if she too could see the dark cloud.

The king nodded. "And so ... can we attend to the matter at hand? The royal baby – or babies."

The seer nodded. She walked to the bedside and unlaced the

queen's outer robes, placing her hands on the gentle swell of the queen's belly.

"I will need your wedding ring," said the seer. The queen twisted the narrow band of gold from her ring finger. She handed it to the seer, who threaded it on to a long green silken thread.

"What?" said the king. "We bring this woman all the way up here and she performs the old ring on a string trick? Anyone can do that! Nanny did it on my mother. The string swung back and forth and she knew I was a boy."

The seer spoke quietly. "Anyone can make a lucky guess. Sometimes, the signs need someone who can actually read them."

The queen narrowed her eyes at her husband. "Yes, let the seer do her job."

The king slumped into a chair and said nothing more. The seer dangled the wedding ring over the belly of the queen. It remained motionless. Then the seer began to hum – a strange, low sound like a lullaby. The ring began to move, slowly in a circle, and then faster, turning round and around in a clockwise direction.

"A daughter," said the seer, her voice barely above a whisper. "A strong and healthy daughter."

The ring stopped moving and the queen smiled at her husband. "A healthy daughter. Just the one."

The seer put her crooked finger in the air for silence. "Wait!"

The ring on the thread started moving again, circling in the opposite direction. The motion was barely perceptible but gradually grew quicker, as it had done the first time.

The seer nodded. "It seems the signs were true. There is another daughter. A twin. Her voice is not as strong as the first, but she is there. They are growing alongside each other."

The queen sat up in bed and held her head. "No! It cannot be true! I do not want it to be true!" This time she threw her teacup on the floor, which didn't make nearly as much mess as the egg had done.

The lady's maid swept up and reported back to Nanny and they both shook their heads and smiled. It was natural for any woman to be worried about her firstborn. And of course that worry would increase with a multiple birth. "She will soon get used to the idea and see this for the blessing it is," said Nanny.

The lady's maid nodded. "The queen has been on the throne for five years. It is about time she produced an heir. Two at once can only be a good thing."

As the queen's belly grew in size, few would have doubted that she was carrying more than one infant. And the queen seemed happy now, stroking her swollen stomach in rhythmic circles. She insisted on continuing with her active lifestyle, pottering around in the rose garden, singing, playing the piano and even swimming well into her third trimester.

"Who are we to question the habits of the royal family? They often act in stranger ways than this!" Nanny said one day, pursing her lips.

"And all this activity will keep her fit for the birth," said the lady's maid.

"Queens do not have to worry about that. She will have the most experienced women in the city in attendance. I for one will make sure I see these babies safely into the world. And, of course, she is tall. Tall women have twins easily. I predict it will be like shelling peas for her."

THE BIRTH

It was not quite as easy as shelling peas.

The pains started when the queen was in the rose garden. She had insisted on rising as she wanted to see her new yellow roses. They were a new species named after her – Bia – a deep yellow the colour of the double egg yolk and with the scent of nasturtium and lemon.

"The scent is best in the mornings," she insisted, and so, while the sun was barely peeping over the horizon, her lady's maid accompanied her carefully down the stone steps of the south tower and into the rose garden. There were maybe fifteen varieties of rose in bloom: red, pink and white, but it was the special yellow ones that drew the queen. She buried her face in the blooms and drank in their aroma.

As she straightened up, she gasped and said a few unqueenly words.

The lady's maid offered an arm to steady her.

"Is it birthing pangs, Your Majesty?"

The queen nodded, breathing steadily through her mouth and confirming the maid's worst fears. Why, oh, why did this have to happen now? She had never attended a birth and was unsure how long the whole procedure took. Would she have to deliver twins right here in the rose garden?

"We need to get you back to your bedchamber, Ma'am."

The queen shook her head. "No. I want to give birth here, where the air smells sweet and I can look upon my favourite blooms."

The lady's maid was a little flustered. "What about the charm of protection, Ma'am? The sorcerer said that it was put upon your royal bedchamber alone."

"I have a feeling that all will be well with the birth. These roses are charmed by the sorcerer himself and I could not be in a sweeter location." The queen bent over as a new wave of pain washed over her.

The voice of the lady's maid grew higher and panicky. "It would not be seemly, Ma'am! Anyone might walk into the rose garden." Right now, she was hoping that someone *would* walk into the rose garden and rescue her.

"Help, someone, help! The queen is in labour!" she cried eventually. Windows all around the courtyard banged open and courtiers in their nightcaps flooded to the rose garden to assist. A messenger was sent to the south of the city to instruct two wise women to attend the royal bedchamber.

The king, nanny and the lady's maid bustled Queen Bia back up to her bedchamber in the tower, stopping on every seventh stair for the pains to disperse.

The lady's maid needn't have worried about the babies rushing into the world because the labour was a long and drawn-out affair, which lasted all day and into the night. Corvus the raven perched, alert and unblinking, on the washstand.

The queen couldn't forget about the blooms of her yellow roses and repeatedly requested to see them. Eventually, the king sent for the gardener, and ordered him to cut every yellow bloom from the fronts of the bushes. He came back with armfuls of the flowers, which were placed in vases and bowls around the queen's chamber.

As soon as the queen smelled the roses, her mood improved and she was calmer. "Care and Joy," she muttered. "The perfect flowers for my newborns."

From then on, the birth proceeded smoothly. Any doubts about the sorcerer's protective spell were negated when, around midnight, two healthy twin girls came into the world. One baby was long and strong, with a birthmark on her left cheek and a full head of hair. The other was smaller and bald, but still healthy and hungry. The queen lay in bed with one baby at each breast and the king came in to meet his daughters. Delighted, he took each one in turn and held them proudly. "Heirs to the kingdom! Which is the firstborn?"

"The taller one," said the queen.

"Then she shall be heir," said the king.

"But in this kingdom, the law states that twins may rule together if the first is willing."

"Time alone will tell if that is a good idea."

The queen nodded. "I am worried for my daughters. Like the seer, I can feel the dark cloud approaching. What will it mean for this next generation?"

Nanny tutted and smoothed out the sheets at the bottom of the bed. "Don't you worry about all that now, Your Majesty. One thing at a time. Firstly, these children need names."

The king smiled. "We already have names prepared. All we have to do now is decide which name belongs to which daughter."

"I can guess that one will take your mother's name—" said the nanny.

"No!" said the queen. "We shall call our firstborn Alette, meaning Truth. Her sister will be Audrey, meaning Strength. For Truth and Strength are surely the greatest gifts we can bestow."

News of the twin princesses spread quickly through the city, though their names were not released at this point.

"We will know when the time is right," said the queen. "When I am sure that my children are safe."

The news was celebrated in many different ways across the kingdom. Two royal babies after a five-year wait was happy news indeed. Near to the castle there were street parties, with jugglers and banners and roasted chestnut sellers in the streets.

Further out in the kingdom there were fairs and fetes. Some used it as an excuse to open long-kept bottles of blackberry wine and fall down drunk in the street.

But in a far-off corner of the kingdom, by the rocky west coast, there was one who did not celebrate the news. A message had been sent to the queen's brother.

"This is not what I had hoped for," he said to his messenger. "I had hoped that childbirth would take her, as it does so many women. And two babies..." He shook his head. "But the infants can be taken care of. Yet while the queen is weakened . . . and the Midnight Unicorn has not been sighted for some time . . . well, this may be the perfect moment."

CHAPTER THREE

THE BOY RIVER

The Boy River was now seven years old. He had not grown up fearful of the water as one might expect. Instead, he spent all his time down by the riverbank, just outside the city walls. He trapped crayfish and freshwater mussels, which he sold to the noblemen in the city for a good price. His body and limbs were tanned deeply from the sun. He was normally without shoes and his feet had grown a hard layer of skin which protected him from the sharp stones on the riverbed.

River spent all his time outdoors and grew to know the

seasons, the changes in the clouds and the wildlife around him. Some said that he had a special gift – that he could talk to the animals – but River denied this. If you spent time with them, watching them, then you would know their ways too, he told people.

On this summer afternoon, the air was thick and motionless. River stood knee-deep in the water, which didn't smell too good. He checked his crayfish trap. Empty. A sheen of sweat glistened on his forehead. A dragonfly passed but didn't make a sound. The whole place seemed quieter than usual, as if the heat had stifled the sounds of the riverbank.

River waded out of the water and sat on the bank, legs stretched out straight. His shins itched as they dried in the heat. He opened a cloth bag and took out the dried sausage his mother had packed to keep him going until dinnertime. He bit off a chunk of the dark red meat and chewed, enjoying the saltiness. A little bird, a wren, came to join him, perching on his knee. Her tiny claws scratched a little but she was almost weightless. River knew this bird well. She often visited him out here and shared some crumbs from his luncheon. River wasn't sure she would enjoy the spices in the sausage but he picked out a tiny globule of fat and held it out to her. This meal would sustain her for hours.

He watched the wren peck at the fat and continued listening to the oppressive silence. Something was wrong today. His instinct made him look out into the hills. A dark shape moved into view on the horizon, on the top of the hill. Was it a man? A group of men? An army. River knew straight away that these were enemies of the city. Enemies of the queen.

He thought of her, lying on her bed with the twins. Princesses perhaps, but still small and vulnerable like his new baby brother. He had to get a message to the castle. He could run, but it was three miles or more and all uphill. And when he reached the castle, would they listen to him – a poor boy? All that time, the army would be drawing closer.

River leaned close to the little bird on his knee and whispered. "Will you help me, mistress Wren?" The bird cocked her tiny head to the left in a gesture that surely meant, *What would you like me to do?*

River rummaged in his pocket and pulled out a fluffy thistle head, which he handed to the wren. He pointed to the highest turret of the castle. "Take this and fly straight to that window up there – the queen's chamber. Tell her of the danger. An enemy approaches."

The bird cocked her head again and, in a split second,

launched herself skywards and sped off in the direction of the queen's tower.

Not everyone would understand such a message. Some would chase a bird from their chamber as if it were a pest. But River had heard about the queen's deep connection with nature and he felt sure that she would understand.

A WREN'S WARNING

The queen sat at her dressing table, cutting the ends of her rose stems with a pair of silver precision secateurs. If she could not be in her beloved garden then she could at least tend to the flowers in her chamber.

She inspected the water in the vases. It was growing cloudy. She would ask the lady's maid to change it when she next attended her. The queen would not call for her now, as she was enjoying a precious few moments alone with her thoughts. For the whole of her confinement, she had found it hard to get a minute to herself. People surrounded her constantly, telling her what to eat, how to exercise and how to look after the royal heirs.

At this moment, her babies slept soundly in a single cradle

below the open window. Nanny had told her that this was not good for them. The draught might give them a chill and they should not share a cradle, for how would they ever learn to be apart? But, said the queen, why would they ever need to be apart? She loved to see them curled up together like this, as they would have been inside her. Queen Bia knew only too well what could happen when sibling ties were severed.

Nanny also told the queen that she should sleep when the babies slept, and to transfer milk into a bottle for someone else to do the feeding. It was unseemly for a queen to breastfeed. But the queen ignored all this advice. She would feed her own babies as nature intended and she would not sleep in the day, otherwise when would she get anything done?

Today she was not getting much done anyway. In this unbearable heat the mere act of snipping the rose stems was exhausting. She snapped her secateurs closed, and took out a fan from the drawer of the dressing table. She wafted the fan around her neck, which helped for a time.

Corvus stood on his perch, head beneath his wing. He was free to come and go and sometimes at night she would hear him take off, giant wings flapping. But during the day he kept watch. He may look as if he were asleep but one eye was always alert to danger. Nanny said she would never have a raven as a pet, especially near the children. "They are harbingers of death!" she said, never one to mince her words. But Corvus was not the queen's pet. He was her guardian; her protector.

A sound at the open window drew her attention. A small brown bird fluttered into the chamber. It did not seem distressed as one might expect from a bird that had flown inside inadvertently. Instead, it flew past the cradle and Corvus to the queen's dressing table, taking tiny hops towards her. It had something in its beak which it dropped in front of the queen. She picked it up. It was purple and downy. Part of the flowerhead of a spear thistle.

The queen turned it around between her finger and thumb. A message. Not from the bird itself, but from another party. Whoever had sent this knew that she was familiar with the language of flowers. She tried to remember, what did thistle mean? Nobility, of course. But also, a warning. The queen felt a sudden fear, deep within her chest, that made her catch her breath. A warning. An intruder.

The little bird flew warily to Corvus. The raven stirred, lifted his head, shook his feathers. He eyed the smaller bird, who opened her beak wide. She churred and chattered, her tiny chest reverberating with the effort. Then the wren hopped to the open window and took wing, fluttering away to the sky.

Corvus turned to face the queen and flapped his wings noisily. He cawed and screeched, waking Alette, who began wailing. That awoke Audrey, who joined in the cacophony. The queen rushed to her babies and scooped them up, one in each arm. "Husband," she cried. "Husband!"

The king burst in and rushed straight to the cradle, thinking that something was wrong with the babies. But the queen pointed to Corvus. "The bird is disturbed. It is a warning, I know it."

The giant black bird turned to face the king, opened its beak wide, cawed and then gave voice to a noise that sounded very much like "Danger!"

DANGER

There was no doubting the bird's message. The queen faced the king, distraught.

The king was confused. "An army? Invading conquerors? But who? We would have heard of such a threat."

"No," said the queen. "The danger is not to our city. If it

were, it would be easier for me. You know that I love my people. Until now, they were my only children and I would do anything to protect them. And I still want to protect them, but on this occasion, I fear that it is my presence that is causing the danger." She began throwing garments into a travelling case. "We must escape now."

The king screwed up his features, concerned. "But, my love, this is a mere bird. Are we going to drop everything and just leave at his word?"

Corvus cawed indignantly and the queen sprang to his defence. "I thought you were the one who was fond of signs! Anyway, Corvus is not a mere bird. He is an enchanted raven, bestowed on me by my most loyal sorcerer to protect us. I suggest we act upon his word instantly."

The king sighed.

"Look," said the queen. "He may be wrong, in which case we will come straight back to the castle and never trust his word again. But if he is right, then we will be glad we acted."

"But I am concerned that you are not fit to undertake a long journey."

"That may be so, but I am even less fit to fight."

"I do not understand," said the king. "Who do you think this invader might be? An army from a far-off kingdom? Should we not stand fast to protect our people? Your subjects have always been so important to you."

The queen shook her head. "I told you, this is not a threat to the people of Essendor. This is a direct threat to me and my close family. This is someone who means me harm and wants the throne for himself."

"But you are a fair and just ruler. Who would presume to usurp you from your rightful place? And who would be powerful enough to do so? Will the Midnight Unicorn not protect us?"

The queen stopped packing for a moment and took both her husband's hands in hers. "I fear that it may be worse than enemies from a far-off kingdom. There is a chance it may be my brother."

THE ESCAPE

The king stood silent at the mention of the queen's brother. They had been married for five years and in that time she had barely mentioned him. They had been close as children, he knew that, but an argument in their adolescence had driven them apart.

Before the queen took her throne, her brother moved to another part of the kingdom and nobody spoke his name.

Now, in hushed tones, the queen told her husband more of the story. Her brother was a hateful and power-hungry man, who was jealous of her claim to the throne and wanted control for himself. Just before her coronation he had attempted to poison her and take the throne, but the plot had been discovered.

"My advisers told me then that my brother should die. This was treason and I should order his execution. But it was something I could not do. My own brother! We had been so close as children, sharing secrets and finishing each other's sentences. I could not have his blood on my hands. What a start that would have been to my reign. What a bad omen."

The king nodded, staggered that he was learning all this information for the first time.

"Instead of execution, I had him banished to a far-off corner of the kingdom. I hoped that I could forget him. I knew that I was more powerful than he was and that, all on his own, and far from the courts, he would not be a threat to me."

"And with the Midnight Unicorn protecting Essendor, he would not have been able to reach you."

The queen smiled sadly. "Exactly. But now I fear that the

unicorn will not be able to help. When we were younger, people joked that my brother and I could read each other's minds. And now I can sense him coming. He knows that I am weakened from the birth, and I know that he has been growing in power and waiting for the right time to attack."

The king looked out of the window and saw a dark shape on the horizon drawing nearer. "You may be right."

"My biggest worry is for the babies. My brother was next in line to succeed, but now Alette and Audrey come before him. He will want them dead."

"We must send the girls to safety," said the king. "They may be the kingdom's only hope for the future."

It was agreed that they should tell just two people. The more people that knew, the more chance there was of the plan leaking out to the wrong parties. So the king and the queen each called their closest confidant up to the chamber, and asked for their help.

For the king this was of course his old nanny. For the queen, it was Maneo the sorcerer. They both stood by the cradle, gazing at the infants while the queen told them the plan.

"If there had been time for a baptism then you would have been chosen as godparents, each responsible for one twin, but the latest events mean that there is no time for official ceremonies. We hope that you will each accept this responsibility nonetheless and keep our daughters far from those who mean them harm."

Nanny pursed her lips. "Let me take them both. I have experience of raising children. Not like this man of magic—"

"No. This is my instruction," interrupted the queen. "At this moment in time, the sisters are safer apart and the further apart the better. Maneo – travel with your charge to the west of the kingdom. Nanny – to the east. When ... if ... the time is right, we shall find you there."

The king took a plain wooden chest from the dressing table and unlocked it with a tiny brass key. He removed two red velvet bags and handed one each to Nanny and the sorcerer. "These bags are stuffed with gold coins. You and the babies should not want for anything. This should pay for whatever they need, whether it is food, shelter or staff."

"There is something else." The queen removed a silver pendant from around her neck. A circle, the size of a coin. She twisted the pendant and the circle snapped in two. It was, in fact, two necklaces joined together. She unwound the chains and handed one necklace to each godparent.

"I pray that all our family members will escape to safety. I pray that the girls will be reunited shortly. But I hand you these necklaces as proof of my love for my children. When they are old enough, they should wear these pendants every day so that, when the time is right, they will recognize each other again."

The queen reached in the cradle and drew out the sleeping Alette. She held her close and breathed in the scent of her head as she did her favourite flowers. She passed Alette to Maneo, who held her competently if coolly. Then she reached for Audrey, who gurgled a little and moved a curled hand to her cheek. To her, the queen whispered something that none of them could hear. Nanny reached for the baby expertly, tucking the blanket around her and holding the stray little hand close to her own body.

The queen had managed to stay composed throughout this exchange, but now that she'd handed over her babies she felt the pain physically, as if she were detaching limbs from her own body. Yet this was something she had to do. For the babies. For the kingdom. For her own peace of mind. When it was done, she turned from the nanny and the sorcerer, crying with great heaving sobs as she continued to pack essential items into a trunk.

The king placed a kiss on each of his daughter's foreheads and said goodbye, hoping that it was not for the last time.

THE TUNNEL

"Come with me," said the nanny. Maneo followed her down the steps of the south tower, across a courtyard and through a heavy wooden door. Then she bustled along the corridor and down a stone staircase until they emerged at one end of a busy kitchen, full of people and noise. Copper pots clattered, the fire crackled and pans bubbled. The red-faced cook sang a song that seemed to mainly consist of curse words and everyone shouted over it. The smell of a bird roasting over the fire made Maneo's stomach grumble. There was so much going on that you could have driven a pony and trap through the kitchen without anyone giving you a second glance. The kitchen hands barely noticed the nanny and the sorcerer, let alone the fact that they were carrying the two royal babies. Had they seen the bundles in their arms, they would have probably assumed that they contained firewood or ingredients.

Nanny led Maneo into the dry larder – a small square room lined with shelves. Onions and herbs hung in one corner and smoked sausages were strung up on the other side. The air was cool and pungent. Nanny pointed to a wooden crate behind Maneo. "Move that grain chest," she whispered.

The chest was half empty and Maneo pushed it easily to one

side, to reveal a wooden trapdoor. Nanny nodded to him to open it, which he did. "This tunnel leads to the back of the castle. Long ago, when I joined the castle staff, this was how deliveries were brought to the royal kitchen. I used it myself – standing out in the woods behind the castle to greet the carts. But since the new wing was built, access to the kitchen has been via the side door. No one, save the rats, has used the passageway for years now. I'd be surprised if they even remember it exists."

Maneo nodded. "It's perfect." He passed Alette to the nanny and stepped inside, down the stone steps. Nanny followed carefully with the babies, closing the trapdoor behind her. The sudden cold made them shiver and the babies started to cry in unison.

"Shhh, shhh, shhh," said Nanny, rocking them gently.

"They won't hear us out there in the kitchen," said Maneo. "We are well insulated down here. Besides, did you hear what a hullabaloo they were all making?"

Nanny made a sound that was something like agreement.

"Don't be alarmed," said Maneo, "but I am about to cast two spells and there will be some bright flashes."

Maneo cast his first spell. Despite the warning, Nanny jumped and both babies cried harder at the sudden flashes.

This was a spell of light, illuminating the whole tunnel with a flickering light of the sort you might expect from a dying candle. After the initial shock this gentle light seemed to soothe the babies somewhat.

The second spell locked the trapdoor behind them and, inside the larder, there were creaks and scrapes as the grain chest moved back into position. No one would find the trapdoor in a hurry and if they did, it would be locked.

"Now the spells are cast, let me take Alette," said Maneo, reaching for the baby. He held her at arm's length and jiggled her.

Nanny was horrified. "Not like that! Glory be. You'd jiggle her teeth out if she had any."

"This is not the time for childrearing advice," snapped Maneo as the baby started wailing again. "We must get these babies out as quickly as possible, crying or no crying."

There was just enough headroom in the tunnel for Nanny to stand, although Maneo had to stoop. It was cold and smelled of damp. Cobwebs covered the walls and ceilings. If somehow they got trapped in here, they would never be found. The steps led down for a time and then up, in a gentle V shape, as they travelled under the moat.

At the other end of the tunnel, Maneo pushed hard on the

trapdoor and it creaked open. They emerged into the woods and looked around, blinking as their eyes adjusted to the light. No soldiers. No enemies or even friends. Just an ordinary woodland clearing flanked by mature trees: a large oak, a pair of silver birches and a tall and slender sweet chestnut.

They were free.

"We need to cover our path. No one must notice how we escaped; we may need this route again one day. Stand back, Nanny."

Nanny stood her ground. "Just so we are clear, I don't accept orders from a nineteen-year-old, even if he happens to be the queen's favourite."

"Then I *advise* you to stand back."

Nanny huffed a little and shuffled a few paces away.

"I advise you to stand *well* back." Still clutching Alette, Maneo lifted his wand arm and began muttering a new spell. The wand sparked and a loud creak made Nanny turn. The tall chestnut tree swayed dramatically as if caught in a gale. It bent further and further to each side until the trunk splintered, sending shards of bark flying. The magnificent tree fell slowly, in a controlled manner, pushing through the leaves and branches of the surrounding trees until it was lying flat on the ground, right over the trapdoor to the tunnel.

Nanny looked neither surprised nor impressed. She wandered back over to Maneo and rubbed her hand over the bark of the fallen tree, tracing one of the horseshoe-shaped markings on its trunk. "Poor old tree," she said. "It had to die to keep us safe."

"The tree is not dead, Nanny. Merely resting until we need this route again."

Nanny nodded. "I fear that may not be any time soon."

"No," said Maneo, looking at his feet. "Now, Nanny, I wonder if it would be a good idea for you to put both the babies into my care for now. I can keep them safe with my magic."

"No chance of that! You heard Her Majesty! She said they were safer apart for now and I for one am sticking to my side of the bargain. Even if I think both the girls would be better off with *me*."

Maneo bowed his head. "Very well, but—"

Before he could finish his sentence, a twig cracked. Someone was watching them. Maneo looked around and saw a boy standing in the bushes. This was a child who clearly spent a lot of time outside. He wore a pair of short, ragged trousers and his feet and torso were bare. He carried a fishing rod and a cloth bag.

Still holding Alette, Maneo strode towards the boy and gripped his shoulder with his free hand. "What is your name?"

"They call me the Boy River, sir."

"And did you see anything?"

"I saw everything, I think, sir."

The boy did not seem scared. He held Maneo's gaze, and the sorcerer felt he could trust this child.

"Are you loyal to our queen, Boy River?"

At this, the boy nodded vigorously. "She is a true and noble ruler."

"The queen and her family are in grave danger," said Maneo. "Do you know these woods well?"

More nods.

"I need you to guide this woman and child out of these woods, quickly and quietly. Use the paths that no one else knows."

He released his grip on the boy's shoulder. "It is important that you do not tell a soul about this. Not now and not afterwards. Do you understand?"

"I do, sir."

Maneo believed him.

"My gratitude for your silence." Maneo one-handedly opened his drawstring bag and pulled out a small gold coin, which he handed to the Boy River.

Nanny gasped. "That is more than I am paid in a month."

"This is an important job and the boy deserves proper payment. The first thing we can do for these babies is to get them as far away from Essendor as we can."

"Thank you, sir." The boy put the gold coin deep into the pocket of his britches and turned around to begin his journey, beckoning to the nanny to follow him.

"Head to the east," said Maneo. "Take a cart or a coach that is heading in that direction. Tell them she is your aunty, or some other similar story. You understand?"

"They are safe with me, sir," said the Boy River, taking long strides through the ferns. The nanny bustled along behind him with Audrey in her arms.

"Farewell, Maneo," she called. "May the Midnight Unicorn protect you."

Maneo nodded and put a hand to his hat, but as he walked away, he muttered to himself, "I suspect that the days of the Midnight Unicorn are gone."

THIRTEEN

YEARS

LATER

CHAPTER FOUR

THE SORCERER'S DAUGHTER

Alette

Alette strode into the room and slammed the door. Her leather boots were plastered with mud, which she deposited in a trail behind her. She stood shivering by the empty hearth and wrung out her waist-length black hair into a rope, leaving a puddle on the stone floor.

Her father, Maneo, did not look up from his work. He sat at the scrubbed wooden table counting something small, like grains of rice, into the sample pan of a set of brass scales. It looked like a tedious task. Alette would have thrown in a handful of the stuff and hoped for the best. But the sorcerer was engrossed, counting out one tiny grain at a time.

"I have been worried about you, my daughter," he said.

"Worried about me? Worried that I might have been struck by lightning or swept away in the swirling torrents?" Alette laughed at the idea. She had been exploring these wild territories since she could totter on her own, turning pebbles in the brook and reaching for minnows. She could look after herself and her father knew it.

The sorcerer stood up and handed Alette a blanket. He spoke quietly, in a measured fashion. "I worry not for your safety in the storm, for what lightning bolt would dare to touch you when you are full of temper?"

Alette wrapped the blanket tightly around her hair and shoulders. Her temper had eased now.

"Where did you go?" her father asked.

Alette did not reply.

"Did you go to the forest?"

Alette raised her chin and looked him in the eye. "Yes, I ran to the forest. Then I ran to the river. I ran along the bank until the mud spattered my legs and then I stood by the water until the sound of the torrents nearly deafened me."

"Why?"

"To escape this place. This cold place that is my home, my schoolroom, my . . . prison!"

The sorcerer nodded.

"And I stood by the waterfall until the sound filled the empty silence in my head. The silence of being here. The clock ticking. The potions slowly dripping into their glass vessels. You – and the irritating way you clear your throat!"

Her father stared at her, as if trying to read her mind. "You adopted your changed form."

Alette nodded.

The sorcerer tightened his fists and the knuckles grew white. His voice still did not rise. "We have spoken of this. Of the danger."

"What danger? Not a soul saw me. Unless you count the forest creatures or the fish in the river. There is no one in this desolate place."

The sorcerer said nothing.

"I can't help it, anyway," said Alette.

The sorcerer shook his head. "You can help it. You have to help it. You must control this power and not let it control you."

He took a deep breath. "There is something else." The sorcerer could not read minds but sometimes he knew her too well.

"Yes."

"Well?"

"After I stood by the waterfall for a time, I was calmer. But I was hot from the running so I went to the river's edge to drink. I bent my head to the water and I saw a creature looking back."

"Your reflection."

"Yes. But there was another, next to me. She looked almost like me but not quite. I turned to greet her, but there was no one there."

"The water was agitated by the storm, no doubt. This distorted the reflections and made you see things that were not there."

Alette raised her eyebrows. She would not be fobbed off by this unlikely explanation. "I saw another. Another like me. This was not the first time and I know that she is significant. You cannot lie to me, I must know. Who is she?"

THE TWISTED DOUGH
Audrey

Usually, Audrey sang while she worked, but today, nothing was going her way so she didn't feel in the mood. She had burned a batch of currant buns, and put twice the salt in the usual bread recipe. Another batch of buns was now in the oven upstairs. Mother said that this time *she* would take them out when they were ready.

Rather than waste the ingredients, Audrey took the oversalted white dough and began to pull, twist and roll. She was known in the village and beyond for her decorative breads. In the window of the bakery were a round wreath and a tall sheaf of wheat, painted with egg wash and baked to a shiny golden brown. Her father used to joke that since Audrey has taken over the window display, no one shopped with their competitor. This was funny because there was no competitor. There were only fourteen families in Lullgrove and no other bakeries for miles around.

Audrey smiled at the thought and continued kneading and shaping the stretchy dough. She had promised to make something special for the midsummer celebration next week. She breathed in the smell of the warm yeast and hardly thought what she was making. But the shapes began to form... A hill. Houses. Stairs from the bottom of the hill, twisting and turning all the way to the top. A castle, with pointed turrets and flags flying. A city. It felt like a real place to her. Like somewhere she had been before. But something was missing...

"What do you think, Shadow?" she whispered.

"To whom are you talking now?" asked Mother, her voice echoing down the wooden staircase. Her ears were as sharp as ever.

"Oh, no one."

Her mother came down the stairs, red-cheeked and wearing a floury apron. She plonked the tray of loaves on the counter and a cloud of flour puffed up, obscuring her from view for a second. "You are getting too old for imaginary friends, Audrey. How many times do I need to tell you?"

"Sorry, Mother." Audrey lowered her gaze. Mother was usually so good natured and easy to please but she was irritated by any mention of Shadow.

Shadow had been there in Audrey's mind for as long as she could remember. She was as real to her as Mother and the memory of Father. Audrey spoke to Shadow at night when she was sad or lonely, sometimes asking Shadow for advice. There was no way she could give her up.

Shadow was speaking to her now, she felt. Sending her a picture. The message seemed to travel straight to Audrey's hands, which were working quicker than ever. She wetted the dough by dipping her fingertips in a small bowl of water. That would help the tiny pieces stick.

Mother dusted off her hands on her apron and came and stood behind her daughter. She placed her hands on Audrey's shoulders and gave them a tender squeeze. Then she gasped, staring down at the unbaked bread. "What is this?"

Audrey stopped and looked down at her creation. There was no doubt it was her best yet. Very lifelike, and those final touches had brought the whole scene together. A side view of two sleek horses, heads dipped and muzzles almost touching. No, not horses. Unicorns. A unicorn and her shadow.

Audrey's mother cried out suddenly and crumpled at the waist. Audrey turned to catch her a second too late. Mother hit her head on the floor with a soft thump. She had fainted.

THE TRUTH
Alette

The sorcerer gazed at the grey stone floor for half a minute. Then he sat at the bench across from where Alette stood and poured himself a goblet of wine.

"Alette. The truth-seeker. I knew this time would come," he

said. "I have never wanted to keep the truth from you and yet I fear it is a lot for you to hear at once."

Alette's eyes flashed. "I want to know everything."

"Then I shall tell you everything."

The sorcerer used his wand to light a fire in the cold grate and Alette sat near to its warmth, her hair still dripping. The sorcerer's tale transported her back to Essendor, thirteen years ago.

Alette watched the usually composed Maneo stammer over the information. She was not his own. Her mother was in fact the great Queen Bia and her father the king. This meant she was an orphan. Everyone knew about the death of the royal couple. Even Alette, cut off from civilization out here, had heard the story of how the Midnight Unicorn had deserted the city and they had died in suspicious circumstances soon afterwards.

Maneo continued. When her parents had sensed danger, the queen had entrusted Alette to Maneo, her most loyal aide.

Maneo was not of her blood but had cared for her for thirteen years. This made sense to Alette. Her features were different to Maneo's – rounder – and her limbs were sturdier. She had always thought that she had inherited her mother's looks but now she understood she was probably a combination of both parents.

But this was not the whole story. She knew there was a mystery over the death of the late king and queen – her parents – and their babies. Weren't there two babies? And who was the reflection in the water with whom she felt such a deep connection? She sensed it was not her mother.

"I have a sister."

Maneo nodded. "A twin." He told her how Audrey had been put in the care of the king's nanny.

The truth at last. Alette felt as if she were not in this room at all but back out by the waterfall, water roaring in her ears. Maneo was not her father. Her parents were of royal blood. Her parents were dead. She would never meet them. She had a sister. How should she feel about all this? Alette wasn't sure. It was too big for her to know what to do with it.

But Maneo had not finished his tale. There was more.

"I found out later what happened to your parents. Security in the city was not strong. The Midnight Unicorn had protected the city for so long that the people had forgotten how to fight off attackers themselves. There was an army, of course, but their role had become more ceremonial. But this time, the Midnight Unicorn did not come. The people were alone.

"The attacking army was small but well-organized. The

city's guards battled valiantly to keep them at bay but the attackers fought through easily. The enemy's soldiers surrounded the castle.

"Your parents, the king and queen, had already escaped. They took a separate path, out of the back gates of the castle, in an attempt to get away before the attackers arrived. But someone noticed them and sent word to the queen's brother. They were ambushed just a few hundred yards from the castle. They both died in the road that night as your Uncle Zelos stormed the castle and took control."

And that was the last hidden truth, now uncovered for Alette. Her parents had been murdered by her mother's brother. Her own uncle.

"How did they die?"

"We had gone by then, you understand, but I heard later that they were cut down by the swords of Zelos's henchmen. He himself was not present."

Alette was silent. She heard the voices in the night, smelled the yellow roses in the queen's chamber and felt the murder of the parents she had never known deep within her own heart. She tried to make sense of what this man who used to be her father was telling her.

"But I remember now – the royal princesses were killed alongside their parents."

"No. This was what your uncle wanted the world to believe. The news was announced: the queen was dead. The king was dead. The baby princesses were dead. If people knew that you were alive, then that would put your uncle's right to the throne into question."

A hot rage bubbled up inside of Alette, running right to her toes and fingertips. Now, she knew where to direct the anger that had always lived inside her. Towards her uncle – the evil King Zelos. She already knew of his reputation as a reclusive and stern man – and she had heard from Maneo how the kingdom had changed for the worse under his rule – but now she had real reason to despise the man.

Right now, however, the news of her parents' murder, even her royal blood, paled into insignificance beside the other piece of news she had been given.

"My sister. Where is she now?"

"I know not. It would have been dangerous to maintain any communication. I have not seen or heard of your sister or the nanny since we parted ways thirteen years ago."

Alette sat on the bench opposite Maneo, whom (she was

trying to process) was not her father. "You told me about my mother. You showed me a pencil portrait of her. You said that she died in childbirth. Who was that woman? A mere invention? Something to distract me from the truth?"

Maneo sighed. "There was a woman. For a year, I employed a wet nurse to look after you. After that, it was just the two of us. Father and daughter. We have not needed anyone."

"What happened to the nurse?" Alette tried to imagine how different their home might have been with a woman around the place. A mother. Would she have brought flowers inside? Maybe she had sewn baby clothes for Alette.

"She died. Of tuberculosis." The sorcerer's voice did not falter but Alette sensed strength of emotion that she did not normally hear from her father.

"I was going to tell you but I wanted to wait until the time was right. Until you came of age. Then, if it was what you wanted, we would find your sister and you could claim the throne together."

Alette said nothing. She scrubbed at her hair, drying it roughly, then went to her clothes chest and threw a few items into a travelling bag. She grabbed a hunk of hard bread and cheese from the side and threw those in as well. Then she picked up a sharp knife, a strong rope, a needle and thread.

"What are you doing?" asked the sorcerer.

"I have a sister. A twin sister. I am going to find her, then we are going to travel to Essendor to claim our right to the throne."

CHAPTER FIVE

HALF OF SOMETHING
Audrey

"How are you feeling, Mother?" Audrey wiped a warm wet cloth around her mother's tired face. "You are working too hard."

"Nonsense," said her mother. "I am quite well. I was just hot. And momentarily surprised."

"By what, Mother?"

"By your design. On the bread. It looked so real. Like somewhere I once knew."

"Like Essendor?" Audrey knew that her mother had worked there long ago as a nanny for a rich family. Her real parents.

Her mother nodded weakly. "How do you know what it looks like? Has someone been talking to you? Have you been there?"

Audrey laughed and shook her head. Her mother must be confused. The capital city was a good few days' journey from here. "Of course not! I didn't even know I was making Essendor. Maybe I saw it once in a picture. Or maybe it came to me in a dream."

Audrey's mother frowned, the vertical crease between her brows deepening. She struggled to get to her feet, and Audrey reached out a hand to help.

Her mother steadied herself on the counter and looked once more at the decorative bread. "How do you explain the unicorns? And why are there two?"

Audrey shrugged. "I don't know. I added them as a little amusement. They seemed to belong there. Of course – like the Midnight Unicorn of Essendor. Maybe I was thinking of that legend without realizing."

"Mmmm. Unicorns are not always a good sign. Some say that if you dream of unicorns, then you will soon be deceived," said her mother, making her way to the wooden steps.

Audrey was concerned. Should her mother be up on her feet again so quickly? "Where are you going?"

"To get those buns out of the oven. We don't want to burn another batch now, do we?"

Audrey watched her go and played absent-mindedly with the chain of her necklace. She pulled it out from under the collar of her dress to examine the pendant. It was made of a thick, dark silver, like pewter. The shape was odd: a teardrop but with one flat edge. It felt sturdy, yet the design was delicate. An engraved line followed the curve of the outside edge and branched off like a young tree. On the middle branch, like a single blossom on the tree, was a white stone with iridescent flashes. Precious opal, Mother said.

Audrey ran her finger along the flat edge. Why did the silversmith leave it straight rather than curved? It seemed unfinished. Like half of something.

She had often wondered about it. Her mother had told her that it came from her real parents, that it was precious and she should wear it always.

She tucked it back under her clothes. And for the very first time she wondered, was there another pendant? And if so, where was it now?

THE OTHER PENDANT
Alette

Alette ran her thumb over the embossed design. Maneo had told her that the necklace had belonged to her mother, which she supposed was true. But now she understood the whole story.

"My sister has the other half, doesn't she?"

Maneo nodded.

"Then that will be our proof. When I find the pendant that matches this one, I have found my twin."

"You cannot travel the kingdom far and wide looking for the other half of a silver necklace!"

"That is exactly what I intend to do."

"But you would have to knock on every door asking if they have seen anything like it."

"If that is what I have to do, then that is what I will do."

Alette made her way to the stables to prepare her horse, Storm, for the long journey ahead. The sorcerer followed.

Maneo stood behind her as she adjusted the saddle. "This is foolhardy, Alette. To leave in such a hurry. These things take preparation."

Alette shrugged in response.

"Why don't you wait until the light of the morning to leave? The moors will be dangerous at this hour. And in this weather – it may be dry again now but you know as well as I how changeable it can be."

Alette was fastening the stirrups and did not turn around. "What do I even call you now?"

"'Father' will still be adequate, if you do not object."

"But you are not my father. I no longer have to listen to a word you say. I shall call you by your given name."

"Sometimes, other ties can be more powerful than blood. The ties of commitment, loyalty, time."

Alette did not answer. She and the horse tossed their glossy manes in unison.

The sorcerer tried again. "Alette, do you not think that we should wait a few more years? When you are eighteen, you will be stronger. You will have mastered your craft. I was eighteen myself when I joined the royal household."

Alette stared at the sorcerer in disbelief. "A few years? You tell me this news and now you want me to wait five more years to find my sister?"

"Well then, can you wait five more minutes? If I cannot dissuade you, then perhaps you will let me accompany you. But I will have to gather a few things first. A map, at least?"

Alette mounted her horse and said nothing.

The sorcerer sighed. "I will protect you. Continue to teach you. If you are going to claim your right to the throne, then you will need good counsel. And good spells. Maybe now is the time to consider taking a wand. You could be a talented sorcerer if you applied yourself."

"I do not want to be a sorcerer. I have my own power without wands or spells. Together my sister and I will be strong enough to defeat our uncle."

"So will you let me accompany you?"

"I leave now. If you wish to follow then you can catch me up," said Alette.

CHANGE APPROACHING
Audrey

Audrey went upstairs to the bakery, where her mother was kneading the dough. She took half of it and started kneading opposite her.

"Why did it make you upset to speak of Essendor?"

"Upset! You are mistaken, child. Thoughts of Essendor do not upset me."

"Did something happen there? Long ago, when I was a baby?"

Her mother shook her head.

"Something with my birth mother?"

For a few seconds, her mother paused, fist sunk into the puffy dough. Then she carried on kneading. "It cannot do any good to rake over the past."

Audrey left her dough on the board, wiped her hands on her apron and stood at the open window. She looked out, past the village, over to the golden wheatfields that surrounded them. A little floating seed flew in on the breeze and she swept it from her cheek. "I feel that change is blowing in our direction." She half expected to see someone riding through the fields towards them. But there was no one there.

"Your place is right here in the village with me, Audrey. But maybe you spend too long cooped up in this bakery. The Harvest Dance is what you need, a chance to let your hair down with people your own age. You can dance all these silly thoughts out of your head! Speaking of which, are you planning to get that decorative bread of yours baked and ready, or are you going to leave it sitting on the counter?"

THE ROCKY MOORS
Alette

Alette left the house at a canter, wanting to put some distance between her and Maneo. She frequently travelled up to sixty miles in any direction around her home, although rarely came in this direction – east – because of the rocky outcrops that stood between their home and the rest of civilization. She urged Storm onwards but soon his pace slowed to a trot, and then a walk, as his footing became less steady and he started to climb.

Alette had grown up on these unpredictable moorlands and knew no other environment. She loved it deeply. She loved the way that, like today, the weather could change in a heartbeat. Now a chill early autumn wind blew in from the coast, transforming the mild afternoon into a gusty battle of a day. The sky darkened to grey and wind whipped her hair around her face. She tossed it back, pushing on with determination. She tasted the salt from the sea in the air. Storm fought his way bravely through the brownish purple heather. She knew he liked it here too. Storm knew her better than Maneo; they had similar temperaments and moods.

The rain came with virtually no warning. Heavy, soaking rain that blurred her vision. It would be over soon and there was no shelter to be found now. She kept on, pulling the hood of her riding cloak further over her face.

In fact she was glad of the rain. There was no room for the dark thoughts to creep in when she was out here, fighting against the elements. She didn't have to think about her dead parents or her twin or a plan for where she was heading. She simply had to press onwards – it was a question of survival.

But Storm seemed to be struggling. He was stumbling, losing his footing. The rain made it difficult to see and they had inadvertently walked into a boggy patch of land. Alette looked right and then left, but there were pools of water all around. She shifted her weight back in her seat and Storm took a couple of tentative steps backwards but then lost his footing and slipped sideways. One of his back legs sunk into a muddy pool. Alette tried to coax him in the other direction, but he panicked, his front hooves pawing uselessly at the ground and his ears flicking rapidly back and forth. He side-stepped in the wrong direction and his other back leg sunk into the same pool as the first.

Alette dismounted and slipped off Storm's right flank. She groped in her travelling bag to find the rope, which she tied around her waist and fastened with a bowline. She knew what to do – she would transform. In her transformed state she was much stronger and, if Storm calmed down, she would be able to pull him out.

But Storm was growing more and more panicky. He squealed loudly and reared round, nearly colliding with Alette. She stepped out of his way but then she too fell into the boggy trap. The ground put up no resistance and her feet sunk straight down until her legs were buried to the tops of her riding boots. Both she and Storm were stuck, on this desolate moorland where a person could ride for a day and not meet another soul.

A few minutes ago, Alette had not cared if she ever saw Maneo again but now she needed him. Had he followed them? She hoped so.

"Help!" she cried. "Help!"

SHOUTS
Audrey

Audrey heard the shrieking of a horse first. It was the sound that an animal only makes in real danger. She rushed back to the window, although as she looked out, she knew she would not see a horse. The sound was coming from inside her mind. Next, came the girl's voice. "Help! Help!"

It was so loud and clear that Audrey put her hands to her head. *Shadow is in danger.* The rational part of her knew that Shadow was a construct of her imagination, yet this felt so real.

Her pulse pounded in her ears, deafening her. It seemed to her an actual possibility that she might lose Shadow. She couldn't allow this to happen.

"Whatever is wrong, don't give up," she whispered. "Hold on. For me."

HOLDING ON
Alette

The rain had stopped but now the thick evening mist rose and swirled from the scrubland like smoke. Alette couldn't see even as far as Storm's hindquarters and she was growing cold and weak. She held on to the reins with numb, pink fingers but she was no longer trying to pull him, or herself, from the mud. She was just holding herself upright. Storm was shivering and blowing rhythmically through his nostrils but had stopped squealing. Maybe this was where it ended for both of them.

And then, another horse stood at Storm's side. A creature Alette recognized. Dark, with a white mane. This creature didn't sink into the bog, or twitch, or panic, but stood upright and calm as if it were floating above the ground.

And although it couldn't possibly speak, Alette heard a voice saying, "Hold on."

Alette found she could hold on. Just for a few more moments. She tightened her grip painfully around the leather reins, and she had just enough fight left in her to shout one more time.

"Help! Help!"

As she shouted, she lost sight of the black horse, which dissolved into the white mist. Then she saw a slim man, with a small beard and a dark gold floppy hat. It was Maneo.

AT THE BAKERY
Audrey

Minutes later, Audrey felt calmer. The danger had passed. She knew that, wherever Shadow was, she was safe. And for the first

time, Audrey realized with complete certainty, Shadow was real.
Shadow was looking for her. And she was drawing nearer.

THE NEXT MORNING
Alette

Maneo used a simple lifting spell to raise Alette and Storm out
of the mud and on to more stable ground. He led them to safety
across the moor, and they sought shelter at the only cottage
for miles around. The owner's wife looked kindly upon them,
especially Alette, who was half-frozen and covered in mud.

"These moors can be unforgiving," she said. She gave Alette
a warm bath, new clothes and milk and honey to drink, while
she laundered her muddy things. Even Storm received special
treatment from the resident groom. Alette got the impression that
they didn't receive many visitors out here.

In the morning, Alette was none the worse for her ordeal and
they set off again in an eastward direction. This time, Maneo didn't
question Alette's reasons for undertaking the quest, and Alette
didn't question his reasons for joining her. If nothing else, the map,
blankets and extra provisions he had packed would be of use.

The moor seemed in a better mood this morning, and looked like a different place. There were pretty yellow stars of asphodel scattered around, and it was easy to see where the boggy puddles were and which patches of land were safe to walk upon. Alette wondered how it could have seemed such a struggle last night.

They heard the trill of a whinchat and saw the fluffy white heads of cotton grass poking above the heather. When they passed a bilberry bush, Alette stopped for a moment, dismounting Storm and picking a handful of the dark blue berries. She popped them one at a time into her mouth, wincing at the tart but enjoyable taste. Maneo stayed on his horse, Silver, and declined her offer of a few berries. "Why did you not use your magic yesterday?" he asked.

Alette continued chewing. "I wanted to transform but I could not. My legs were stuck and I was weakened. And even if I had changed, I would still have been stuck in a bog."

"Will you not consider carrying a wand?"

"I do not want a wand. I am not a sorcerer and I have no intention of ever becoming a sorcerer. I have my own powers."

"Powers that are considerably weakened when you are buried up to your knees in boggy moorland."

"Yes. But that has never happened before and is unlikely to do so again."

Alette threw herself back on to Storm's back.

"The trouble with you, Alette, is that you do not stop and think," said the sorcerer.

"Thinking is overrated. What about feeling?"

"Feeling is overrated. I wonder sometimes if it will be your undoing."

Alette ignored him and urged her horse onwards. One way or another, this would be a long journey.

WAITING
Audrey

It was a quiet day but every time the door opened, Audrey's heart lurched. Would it be Shadow, here at the bakery? No, it was Madam Grey collecting her daily loaves and Farmer Donnelly with a special Harvest order. Audrey served them efficiently and politely as she always did but she found she had to force her smile more than usual.

"You look pale," said her mother. "Are you sickening for something?"

Audrey shook her head. She was not sickening. Just waiting. But waiting for what?

THE JOURNEY EAST
Alette

At the end of the second day, Alette and Maneo had reached a more populated region. It was a relief to join a proper road with inns and resting houses along the way.

At the first inn, Maneo took out a heavy red velvet bag and passed it to Alette. "I have been keeping most of this money since you were a baby. It is yours, from your parents."

Alette took the bag wordlessly.

"I have spent some over the years, but our needs have not been great. There is plenty left, although it will not last for ever."

Alette looked inside the bag, which was nearly full. She supposed she was rich. She waited for this knowledge to sink in but it did not mean much to her.

"I suggest that we take half each, for security purposes and in case we become separated."

Alette shrugged. "As you wish. Now I am tired. I am going to bed."

"Perhaps you should read a few pages of this before you sleep." Maneo held out an ancient book on the magical arts.

"You should not stop practising your craft simply because you are travelling."

Alette did not take it. "I've told you, this is not my craft. It is your craft. I like transforming but I do not enjoy potions, spells or charms. And you cannot tell me what to do any more."

The sorcerer sighed and withdrew the book. "You forget that your mother entrusted you to me. She would not want you to make yourself vulnerable in this way. She would want what is best for you."

"I know what is best for me better than anyone else. Better than my dead mother and definitely better than you. When I find my sister we will combine our strength and we will be too much for even the most powerful adversary."

"Still, if you are aiming for the throne, you should sharpen your skills. Your uncle is a powerful man—"

"But I have not yet begun my journey to the throne. I am trying to find my sister and until we track her down, I do not want to discuss this any further."

"And how are we to find your sister? You do not even know where you are going."

"You said that the nanny took her to the east. So I will ride with my back to the setting sun until I reach her."

"But there are countless towns and villages to the east!"

"I will find my sister, and I will know her when I see her. She will be like me."

The sorcerer shook his head. "You are not identical twins, remember. You are fraternal: born from separate eggs. She may not look like you. She was smaller than you as a baby. She does not share your mark."

Alette touched the oval-shaped birthmark on her left cheek. "She may not share my mark, but does she share my power?"

Maneo lifted his hands to shoulder height. "That, I do not know. Your power did not begin to show itself until a few years ago. It was impossible to tell when you were babies."

"Still, I will know her," Alette insisted. "When I look my sister in the eyes then I will know her."

AT THE BAKERY
Audrey

Audrey wrapped two round loaves in brown paper and handed them to old Madam Woodcroft with a smile. It had been a long and tiring morning but that was surely not the fault of Madam Woodcroft.

Another customer waited by the door. He was not a man she recognized, but this was not Shadow. He must be a traveller staying at the inn for a night or two. Perhaps he was here for the Harvest fair. He didn't look like the usual travelling sort: musicians, gypsies in their painted caravans – they were normally jolly sorts. Maybe he was a soldier, but he didn't look like a military type, either.

Madam Woodcroft left and the man approached.

He removed his floppy yellow hat and placed it on the counter.

"Two slices of the chicken and ham pie, if you please."

Audrey assessed him discreetly as she served him. Not old, but not young. He would have been handsome if only he had smiled. He had the look of a man of words. A scholar, perhaps, on his way to visit a grand library.

As he reached with slender fingers into a money pouch, Audrey spotted a girl outside with the horses. Audrey could see the back of her head – her long, black, tangled hair. His daughter perhaps, or a young wife. The girl turned and, through the window, Audrey saw a determined face and a distinctive oval-shaped mark on her cheek. She was young, just a little older than Audrey herself. And she looked lonely. Perhaps she would be at the Harvest fair and they would talk together. Audrey could show her how to make a dolly from a corn husk. Perhaps they would become friends! Audrey had never had a close friend of her own age.

Audrey accidentally caught the girl's gaze. The girl stared back, unsmiling, and Audrey lowered her eyes, embarrassed.

The traveller counted the coins out into her hand, then replaced his hat and nodded his thanks. Audrey wiped down the counter for a long time as she watched them walk the horses in the direction of the inn.

THE VERY FIRST VILLAGE
Alette

Alette and Maneo ate their picnic pie in Lullgrove village square.

"What do you think? Shall we stay at the inn for another night or continue on the road?" asked Maneo.

Alette spoke with her mouth full of pie. "Let's stay. We should check this place thoroughly, ask the right questions."

"It is unlikely that your sister will be found in the very first village we encounter."

"She is as likely to be here as anywhere else."

"But where will you start?"

Alette was only now beginning to realize the enormity of the task ahead of her.

"Will you know the old nanny if we see her?"

"Yes, I am sure I will remember her if she still lives."

"What do you mean, 'if she still lives'? Why do you say that?"

"Simply because it is possible that she has passed, through natural means or otherwise. Remember that Zelos's men were hunting us. She may not have been so adept at avoiding detection."

"But then my sister…?"

"Likewise, we cannot be sure what has happened to your sister. Thirteen years have passed, Alette. We simply do not know. You should prepare yourself for disappointment."

"I do not know about the old nanny, but my sister lives. I am sure of it. She appeared to me at the water's edge, remember? We should stay here for at least one night."

"I remind you that that the money in that velvet bag will not last for ever. It has lasted well but a few nights at village inns will exhaust it quickly."

"I remind you that you are not my father and it is not your money."

"That may be, but what is the plan if you run out of money?"

"If I run out of money, I shall sleep like a vagabond under the shade of an oak tree or I shall wash dishes in a tavern to pay for my board or I shall steal your spell book and learn to turn pebbles into jewels," said Alette flippantly.

"So you have not planned for unforeseen events?"

"I have not planned at all. But I will find my sister very soon and then we will not have to be concerned with such trivialities."

Maneo sighed. They finished the delicious slices of picnic pie and then made their way to the village inn.

THE DREAM
Audrey

Audrey sat up in bed. The clock showed midnight and her mother was asleep. The wind blew in the trees outside, sharp sudden gusts that threatened to develop into a storm. The occasional shower of rain hit the windows as if someone was throwing cups of water at the glass. It was not the sort of night that anyone would want to brave. Especially Audrey, who was not keen on the dark at the best of times.

But despite wearing only a nightgown, Audrey felt a strong

urge to venture outside. She pulled a thick cloak around her and stepped lightly down the wooden stairs, avoiding those boards she knew creaked. She walked through the shop and shoved her bare feet into the clogs by the door. She opened the door and was hit by the force of the wind, but she didn't feel it as she normally would. She closed the door as gently as she could behind her, battling the force of the wind, and stood listening to the night. The familiar lane looked so different at this hour, bereft of villagers and children playing. The sign of the pawnshop opposite swung rapidly and creaked. A faraway owl hooted and the moon lit up her hands, making them appear pale.

Audrey listened harder for a sound she knew would come. And there it was! Hooves on the cobbles. A galloping horse approaching. Coming for her.

She left the doorway and hurried along the lane, paying no attention to the shrieking wind. She broke into a run, desperate to greet the rider. As she ran, the galloping hooves sounded louder, almost as if Audrey herself were galloping.

The horse approached but as the creature emerged from the darkness, Audrey saw its outline and realized there was no rider. Also, this was no horse. Its sleek black body was muscular and its tail and mane swished elegantly, but on the creature's forehead, just above a white, oval-shaped mark, was a shimmering white horn, iridescent in the moonlight. A unicorn.

Audrey knew this creature. She felt as if she had always known her. In her dream, for this must be a dream, Audrey said one word. "Shadow?" The creature lowered its head.

Audrey wanted to run her fingers through the unicorn's fine mane. But as she moved, she realized that her arm was a leg. She had four muscular dark legs like this other creature. *She herself must be a unicorn.*

Shadow reared up and turned back the way she had come. Audrey was with her, trotting side-by-side, hips and tails level. Shadow increased her speed and they galloped together along the town's main streets. Not a single person was out that night. What would they have thought if they had seen two unicorns running together?

But the night belonged to Audrey and Shadow. They left the village and galloped through farms and fields that Audrey knew, but that smelled different tonight; the sweet smell of hay made her mouth water. The sounds of the autumn – the foxes barking and the powerful roar of the distant stags – didn't scare her any more; tonight she felt at one with these nocturnal animals. Through the fields and into the woods, the ground changing under their hooves. Softer now.

Shadow slowed. Was she making allowances for Audrey?

Then Shadow stopped all together and turned in a slow circle. Audrey followed her, nose to tail, and they turned in unison, like a dance. Twin unicorns in the moonlight, together at last.

When Shadow set off again, Audrey didn't know where they were going. She didn't care. She would follow this beautiful creature to the edge of the world. But they weren't heading out on a journey, they were heading home. As they passed the inn near the village, Audrey heard a voice calling out into the night: "Alette? Alette? Where are you?"

Shadow turned and galloped towards the voice, leaving Audrey behind. She could have followed but she was suddenly tired. As she stood there, breathing heavily, she felt her back straighten up and her view change. She shook out her arms and rolled her shoulders back. Audrey was a unicorn no longer. She was a girl, and her feet were cold.

BACK AT THE INN
Alette

At the inn, Maneo stood at the foot of Alette's bed. "What were you thinking? You galloped through a village in your changed form! Thank goodness I knocked on your door to say goodnight. Otherwise I wouldn't have known. Where would you have ended up?"

"I had a strong feeling that no one would see." Alette sat at the edge of her bed, fully clothed.

"A strong feeling? That is absolute madness!"

"But it is beside the point. The point is that she's here." Alette's face lit up. "My sister. And she shares my power, as I knew she would. I woke up in the middle of the night and felt her call to me. I met her in her transformed state and we went out together, running through the wind and rain."

Maneo shook his head. "Are you sure this was not a dream, Alette? You were alone when I saw you. I know how much you want to find your twin, but perhaps this is your mind playing cruel tricks."

Alette shook her head. "It was as real as I am talking to you right now. I had no idea it would be this easy! Right here in Lullgrove, the first village of the east. Who would have thought it? I shan't sleep for the rest of the night, for I am not going to risk missing her. At first light, I will leave this inn and find the girl that is my sister."

THE NEXT MORNING
Audrey

Audrey awoke to the sun streaming through the window. In the bakery, they were always up early. Hours before sunrise in the winter months. Outside, the wind had dropped. What a strange dream it had been.

She ran a hand through her hair. Although short, it was untidy this morning. Windswept and gritty. She left her bed and crossed the room to the washstand where she splashed water on her face to wake herself. Usually by this point, dreams began to drift away, completely gone by breakfast time. But today her mind wouldn't clear. Images from the dream played over and over again in Audrey's mind, mixed with the memory of the unsmiling girl in the bakery yesterday. Her long black hair. The oval mark on her face, and the similar mark on the creature's nose. The voice at the inn.

These were signs that Audrey couldn't ignore. She had to find that girl.

If the travellers had stayed the night in the village there was only one place she could be. The inn. Audrey did not waste time getting dressed. She put her riding cloak on over her nightgown as she had done the previous evening, and ran out into the cold, clear morning.

It took her six minutes to reach the inn. Panting, she reached up to the old wooden door and turned the heavy iron handle. And there she was – the girl from yesterday and somehow the creature from her dream – standing in the doorway.

Audrey spoke before she even knew what she was going to say. "Shadow? Sister?"

THE GIRL IN THE DOORWAY
Alette

"At least have some breakfast," said Maneo, as Alette gathered her things.

Alette looked at him as if he were insane. He had gone to his room to sleep but she had been up all night, staring out of the window at the stars and listening to the animals. Her eyes felt grainy and she was light-headed from lack of sleep but she was also full of energy, as if she could take off and run through the fields again. She splashed some cold water on her face and put on her cloak. "Can you not understand what I am saying? My sister is right here in this village. I know not if she lives here or is passing through. But I know I cannot let her leave."

Alette needed air. Space. She headed down the wooden stairs, trying not to clatter and wake the other guests. Maneo followed her, calling, "How will you know her, Alette? How will you find her?"

Why couldn't he leave her be? "I will know her." She walked across the shiny oak floor of the hall and headed for the door but it opened before she reached it.

A young girl stood in the doorway, blocking her path. The girl had a strange look about her. She was short and fine boned – probably a couple of years younger than Alette. She wore what appeared to be an oversized nightgown with a riding cloak on top, which made her appear even smaller. Her bare feet were pushed into leather clogs and she wore her hair short, like a boy's. She had a dusty look about her, as if covered by a fine powder, and her eyes were big, like a doe's.

The girl didn't move. Alette's first instinct was to shove her out of the way, but she resisted. The girl was staring at her, mouth slightly open as if she were trying not to yawn. What was wrong with her? Then she was saying something.

"Shadow? Sister?"

She reached forward and touched the mark on Alette's cheek. Her touch was cold, but Alette was so stunned she didn't even push her hand away.

The girl spoke again.

"My sister?"

Alette shook her head. This girl was not the same creature she had run with last night. "No. No. You are not my sister."

But the girl nodded. She moved her hand from Alette's cheek down to the chain around her neck and gently tugged. Alette's pendant swung out of her shirt. Then the girl reached to the necklace at her own throat. She undid the clasp at the back of her neck and held the engraved silver pendant up. Alette didn't move.

The two pendants fitted together and made a whole. A heart-shaped whole. And together, another design became apparent. The opals became sparkling eyes. And the engraved branches formed a long face with wide nostrils. A horse. Or a unicorn.

CHAPTER SIX

SHADOW

Audrey

Audrey could not take her eyes off her sister. She was beautiful. And so familiar to Audrey. She had met her before in the dream, of course, when they were unicorns. But now she understood. This was her twin. She was the secret Mother had been hiding from her.

She did not know how or why, but she was sure this was the case. Memories came back to her in a rush. She remembered a cradle. The lemony smell of yellow roses. The call of a bird . . . a crow? But she could not visualize their parents. Those faces felt distant to her.

Then there were their pendants. How strange that she should only recently have wondered if there was a second one.

A man with a small beard and a serious face came and stood behind Shadow. It was the man who had bought the picnic pie yesterday. What was his place in all of this? Perhaps her sister had also been adopted, like her. But why had they been kept apart?

Questions whirled in Audrey's mind, but right now all she wanted to do was to pull Shadow to her – to breathe in the scent of her hair. For there was no doubt that her twin was the imaginary friend who had been so clear in her mind for all these years. But Shadow seemed less sure. She pulled her pendant away and turned her face from her. Maybe Audrey shouldn't have called her Shadow. Of course, she couldn't really be called Shadow. She must have another name.

SISTER
Alette

"What is your name?"

It was strange to hear the girl's voice. She didn't sound as Alette had expected. A slight lilt in her voice marked her out as someone who had grown up in the east of the kingdom. So different to Alette's own, sharper, accent.

"Alette," she replied.

The girl repeated her name, sounding out each syllable: "Al-ette."

Alette didn't know what to say next. Her back, shoulders, even her tongue felt frozen. This wasn't how she had expected their meeting to be. The girl in front of her was different to her in every way. Her short chestnut hair, her pale eyes, her shortness, her thinness. How could she possibly be her twin?

Finally she managed to speak. "And you are...?"

The girl smiled warmly. "Audrey."

Of course she was Audrey. Alette knew this already.

"How old are you?"

"Thirteen," replied Audrey. "My birthday is the twenty-third day of the seventh month. Like yours!"

"But mine is the twenty-second day of the seventh month." Was this information wrong as well? Maybe they were not twins after all. Maybe somebody had made a mistake.

Maneo spoke for the first time. "Alette, you were born just before midnight, Audrey just after."

"But you look so much younger," said Alette.

Audrey smiled again. "I have always been small for my age."

"Remember you are fraternal, not identical, twins," said Maneo.

"How did you know I was here?" asked Alette. Audrey had not known her name. Had the king's nanny told her anything?

Audrey gripped Alette's arm. "I didn't know I had a twin. I didn't know anything. It was a feeling."

Finally, something they had in common. "I only found out myself a few days ago."

Alette pointed to Maneo. "This is my adoptive father."

Audrey looked, processing the information. "My mother – my adoptive mother – works in the bakery in the village."

That explained the floury look of the girl. So, unlike Alette, it sounded like she had always known she was adopted. But was she aware of her royal roots? It was time for a long conversation.

DISCOVERIES
Audrey

The three of them sat at a heavy wooden table in the inn. Breakfast would not be served for another two hours.

Audrey scrunched up her nose and scratched her forehead. "So you are telling me that I am a princess? From Essendor?"

"Yes," said Alette.

Audrey felt a rush of hysteria. She almost collapsed into giggles. She – a princess? This was surely not true. She searched her early memories, straining to recall anything that seemed regal about her surroundings. But all that came back to her was, once again, the scent of roses and a big black bird, cawing away.

"And you mean for us to reclaim our throne?"

"Yes," said Alette.

"Together?"

"Yes," said Alette, although she sounded slightly less sure this time.

Audrey shook her head. While the idea of having a twin was a surprise it was not completely unexpected. It made a lot of things slot into place in her mind. But the idea that she was of royal lineage? That her parents had been murdered when she was an infant? That the notorious King Zelos was her uncle? These ideas were too big and abstract for her to comprehend.

"But Essendor is such a long way away," is all she could manage to say.

"It is not so far. Just over two hundred miles as the raven flies," said Maneo.

Audrey paused, trying to let her brain catch up.

"Before I agree to anything, I must speak to my mother."

THE BAKER'S DAUGHTER
Alette

They all returned to the bakery, and the woman behind the counter rushed to Audrey. "Audrey, where have you been at this time of the morning? I thought at first that you had gone to the dairy for more milk but then I saw that the urn was full and I couldn't think where you had gone. There was no note. For an awful moment I thought you might have run away—"

The red-faced woman stopped mid-sentence as she saw Alette in the doorway. She drew her eyebrows together. Then she caught sight of Maneo, and gasped. "You. You haven't changed."

Alette believed that. Time had not changed her adoptive father in all the time that she had known him. It was not that he still looked youthful. It was that he had probably *never* looked youthful.

The woman put both hands on the counter, looking deeply concerned. Audrey went to her and put a hand on hers.

"Mother, I have found my sister. She has come to me."

"So I see," said the woman, raising her chin a little and directing her gaze at Maneo.

The sorcerer smiled slowly. "Hello, Nanny."

Audrey's mother bristled. "I have not been a nanny these past thirteen years. My name is now Madam Warner and I am the miller's wife ... widow. And Audrey's mother."

The sorcerer removed his hat and bowed low. "Madam Warner. My apologies."

Audrey's mother ignored him and turned to look at Alette. Her face softened. "You must be Alette... You always were the bigger child... And so like your uncle in looks, but with your mother's height." Madam Warner brushed Alette's hair away from her face. "I see that the birthmark has not faded."

This was the second time today Alette had been manhandled by a virtual stranger and she didn't like it. She jerked her head away.

But still, she took the words in. Alette was like her uncle Zelos. This was something Maneo had not mentioned.

Madam Warner addressed Alette and the sorcerer

together. "Tell me – both of you – what do you want? Why are you here?"

Alette did not know where to start but Maneo stepped in. He knew this woman, after all. She tried and failed to picture them both as part of a royal household.

"Audrey, you may have noticed you are different from other girls?" said Maneo.

Audrey nodded slightly, barely moving her head. Alette wondered why she didn't speak.

"Alette tells me you share some of her powers?"

Audrey looked up at her sister, as if surprised by this. "Did she?"

Alette nodded.

"What powers are these?" Audrey's mother looked sharply at her daughter.

Audrey said nothing.

Maneo continued: "Your magic will be different to Alette's. She has been with me all her life. She has learned – to an extent – to control these powers but yours will be raw and difficult to control. If you come with us, you must let me help to guide you."

Audrey stayed silent, the confused look stuck on her face. Wasn't she going to speak, wondered Alette.

Madam Warner shook her head, wiry grey hair escaping from her mop cap. "If Audrey goes with you? Goes with you where?"

Alette looked at Audrey's mother directly. "I have made a decision. I plan to travel to Essendor to claim what is rightfully mine. But I would be stronger with my twin sister by my side. Audrey needs to speak to you. To ask any questions that she has. Then it is up to her to decide what to do."

MOTHER
Audrey

Audrey had always known that the parents she had grown up with were not hers by birth. She had been told that her adoptive mother had been nanny to a rich family in the city. There had been a change in their fortune and they had become destitute. It was a difficult birth and her real mother had lain dying. Her real mother had put Audrey's care in the hands of her faithful nanny. Her father had himself been taken shortly afterwards, so it was just Audrey and the nanny.

But now she knew that the story was not completely true. The only mother that Audrey had ever known sat across the table from her upstairs at the mill and told her the full story, from its royal beginnings, through to what happened after she had left the woods.

"We travelled to the east just as your mother – Queen Bia – had instructed. It was not easy. I hid myself as much as I could. I hitched a lift on a vegetable cart for part of the journey and walked the rest. When I came to Lullgrove, the soles of my boots were worn right through. It felt like a haven here; like it was somewhere I was meant to be. I was still a relatively young woman then, still of childbearing age. No one questioned that you were my very own. I told them I was a poor widow – that my husband was a guard who died in the invasion."

Audrey nodded. Apart from the royal connections, this was the same story that she had heard from birth; the truth she had always accepted.

"Then I came here. I met your father on the very first day I walked into the village. He was a widower and his poor wife was taken in childbirth along with the baby. It seemed like fate. Ours was a short courtship and he accepted you as his child without question."

Audrey felt tears prick at her eyes. Her dear, gentle father, who had only been gone a year.

"People in the village soon forgot that you weren't his child. People only remember what it suits them to and we were a well-liked family, I suppose. A family that folk could rely on. Your father never knew the whole truth about you. I suspect he guessed that there was more to the story but he didn't ask. That was his way."

Audrey felt glad then that her father had not known. He was a simple man who hadn't liked change. He would have found this conversation very difficult.

Her mother sighed. "After a while, I even started to forget myself. I stopped thinking about it every night. Stopped worrying that the king's men would come for you. Stopped imagining that your sister would come to track you down."

Audrey patted her mother's hand and she continued.

"As you got older, I worried about your strange imaginings and the questions you asked. Your mother had some strange ways and I wondered if she had passed some on to you. I still wonder. Tell me, what are these powers that the sorcerer speaks of?"

"I don't know," said Audrey. It was true. She did not know, even though Maneo and Alette were both convinced. Something to do with the bread? Or the unicorn dream? Both seemed important somehow. Now she felt foolish admitting to her mother that she wasn't sure.

Her mother rubbed both hands roughly over her face and then placed them on the table.

"Audrey, my dearest daughter. I want you to know that you have a choice. You do not have to go with them. If you choose this life, then we can go back to the way we were. No one need ever know your real identity. People believed you dead for thirteen years. They would not question a thing if Alette returned on her own. Alette was always the bigger one; she can fight this battle on her own."

Audrey shook her head slowly, the tears streaming silently down her cheeks. She took her mother's hands across the table. "Dearest mother. You do not understand. I have found my twin. The part of me that was always missing. She tells me that she needs me. And if she needs me then I go with her, whether that means to the other side of the kingdom, or into the next world."

And Audrey's mother put her head on the table and wept deeply for the loss that she had always known would come.

HARVEST MOON
Alette

Alette and the sorcerer agreed that they would wait for Audrey for two more days – until after the Harvest Dance. This gave

Audrey and her mother some time to organize how Madam Warner would cope in Audrey's absence. She wasn't getting any younger and couldn't manage the mill and the bakery on her own, so her nephew on Mr Warner's side was sent for – a spotty-faced boy of fifteen. He could do any heavy lifting and work the mill. Nobody was to know the truth about Audrey's journey. The agreed story was that Alette was a distant cousin and Audrey had been given the chance to train with her and her uncle in the magical arts. The villagers would believe that – Audrey had always seemed a bit different to the rest of them.

Alette kept her distance from Audrey while she made preparations. The twins would have plenty of time to catch up on the lost years once they were travelling together.

But Audrey was keen for Alette to attend the Harvest Dance.

"Please come, sister. It is my chance to say goodbye to everyone here and I would love you to see the village looking its best."

Maneo did not think much of the idea. "You don't really want to go to the Harvest Dance, do you, Alette? Why not stay here at the inn with me? We'll leave the villagers to their celebrations and leave feeling fresh in the morning."

Alette did not particularly want to go to the Harvest Dance

but she wanted to follow Maneo's instructions even less. She was quite keen on the idea of an evening away from his company. So she agreed to go with Audrey while Maneo stayed at the inn to plan their route.

Audrey suggested that Alette call for her at the mill so that they could walk there together. When Alette saw Audrey waiting outside in her finery – a bottle green dress, which hung off her thin body – she realized she had no fine clothes to wear. Audrey offered to lend her something – her best dress if she wanted it – but anything of Audrey's would have been much too small for Alette. So Alette wore what she always wore: soft leather riding leggings and a loose white shirt. These clothes had served her well on every other occasion she had encountered.

The walk down to the dance was pleasant. The evening was dry and warm, the smell of evening primrose hung in the air and a deep orange Harvest moon lit the way. Audrey chattered excitedly all the way. She seemed to want to show everything to Alette; to give her an idea of what her life was like. Alette listened intently. It was all so different to the life that she had known.

"The dance itself takes place in Farmer Donnelly's barn. His twin girls will have decorated it for the occasion. But because the weather's warm, the villagers will spill out on to the green. They'll have the hay bales out."

It was as Audrey had described. The place was full of chatting, smiling, jostling folk. Alette had not known there were so many people in this sleepy village.

"They're not all from here. Families bring their carts and come from villages from a dozen miles away. We're known for our Harvest Dance," Audrey said proudly.

As they pushed through the crowds, Alette realized how out of place she looked. The other girls of their age, who assembled in giggling groups on the green, wore frothy, pale dresses, and gypsophilia flowers in their hair. She tugged at her shirt, checking for stains, and ran her fingers through her unbrushed locks.

Alette was grateful when Audrey took her to the barn first. It had been cleared of animals and hay, and a thin layer of sawdust was sprinkled on the floor. The barn had been "starrified" with garlands of white and yellow autumn flowers. The close air inside smelled faintly of cow dung but that didn't seem to be of concern to anyone. The enthusiastic band – two fiddle players and an accordionist – had already begun to play, although no one had yet taken to the dance floor.

Audrey slipped an arm through Alette's and led her to where the village's seasonal bounty was arranged on checked cloth-covered harvest tables. It made Alette's mouth water. Potatoes, wheat, ripe cherries and green-sheathed husks of corn. Fat orange pumpkins, whole seed-stuffed sunflower heads and dark-green cabbages. Alette had never even tasted most of these foods before. Over in the wilds of the west, food had never been much of a priority. Maneo would buy their food in bulk and try to store as much as he could. Mostly it was dried or preserved in vinegar or salt.

In the middle of the table was some beautifully crafted bread, depicting a city on a hill and two unicorns, nose to nose. Alette glanced over at Audrey. This must be her work. She wondered when she had created it. Did anyone think it strange?

Audrey smiled at her. "Makes you hungry, doesn't it? Don't worry, they'll serve the hog roast later. And Madam Woodcroft is handing out barley twists to all the children. Look – she's over there – outside."

Alette followed her sister to claim their sweet treat, and they sat awkwardly together on a hay bale, sucking the twists. Alette didn't know what to say to her sister. They were so different from one another. But Audrey kept talking. She pointed to a group of three girls in matching blue gingham. "Those girls go to school with me."

"I thought you worked in the bakery."

"I do, but mornings are spent in the schoolroom. Unless we have a busy time."

The girls walked straight past them without greeting Audrey. Alette looked at the charming trio, wondering if their matching frocks were planned. If she had grown up here, instead of in isolation by the coast, would she too have a pretty frock and flowers in her hair? It struck her that even Audrey seemed somehow apart from the other girls in the village, with her big dreamy eyes and strange shorn haircut. Maybe some people didn't quite fit, wherever you put them. Alette had always felt more at home with horses. She could never have a closer friend than Storm. Perhaps even her own twin sister would not match up.

The music stopped for a moment as the band moved from the barn on to the green in a bid to get folk dancing.

"Do you have these dances very often?" Alette asked.

"Oh no. This is a big event in the village. People look forward to it for months. We gather together around the maypole for our spring celebration, and sometimes for midsummer, but the biggest festivities are saved for the Harvest. We have this barn dance at the start of the Harvest and then Apple Day at the end. What about in your village?"

Her twin really did not know her at all yet. "I do not come from a village or town. I live in a remote location with just the sorcerer. We rarely see people."

"Oh," said Audrey.

The music started up again: a popular jig that tempted a few dancers on to the green. Alette and Audrey sat in silence for a little while longer, Audrey tapping her foot to the music and Alette bolt upright and motionless.

Soon, the group of girls from Audrey's school had gathered around them. They seemed particularly interested in Alette. One girl, with starchy white bows tied to the end of her plaits, whispered in Audrey's ear, loud enough for Alette to hear, "Who is your friend, who dresses like a boy?"

This was the first time either of them had needed to use their cover story. Audrey looked uncomfortable. "She is my… cousin."

"I thought your cousins were the Smiths who lived in Oxleigh Green?" The girl was not easily duped.

Audrey's cheeks flooded with colour. "This is my mother's … estranged sister's daughter."

"Oh."

The girls sat with them for a while but soon drifted away when neither of them said anything of interest.

Next, it was the boys' turn to approach. Again, they came in a small pack and loitered near to them. Then a tall boy with dark hair and reddish cheeks broke away from the group and approached Alette. He twiddled a half-eaten barley twist with both hands.

"Do you want to dance?" He spoke with the same musical lilt as Audrey and the rest of them. It was a nice sound.

Alette stared at him and then at the group of people dancing on the green. A caller was shouting out instructions and they were whirling and jigging in time to the music. "No, I don't think so," she said.

The boy flushed further and retreated to his pack.

Audrey's eyes widened. "You just said no to Rowan Fisher. All the girls want to dance with Rowan Fisher."

"Do they?" Alette watched him approach a beautiful blonde girl in a lilac dress who followed him happily to the green. "Do *you* want to dance with him?"

Audrey gave a small nod. "Yes, I think so."

"So why didn't you tell him that just now?"

"He didn't ask me." Audrey paused. "It's not him. I'd just like someone to ask me."

Alette shook her head. She didn't understand these peculiar

.

courtship rituals. She had never met any boys or heard any music before tonight. Alette looked at her sister. "Would you like to dance now?"

Audrey giggled. "I'm not sure what everyone would think."

"I care not what they think. Nor should you. You will be leaving this place tomorrow. You can teach me."

Alette took her twin by the hand and they skipped to the village green.

"This is an easy one. We should be fine," said Audrey.

Audrey was right, the steps were easy to learn. Three steps forwards, three steps back, turn and twirl your partner. Alette took the role of the boy, being taller, but Audrey showed her what to do.

Then suddenly everyone was holding hands in a big circle. They circled to the left, walked into the middle, circled to the right, and then crossed hands to swing their partner. They swapped to a new partner.

Alette realized she was good at dancing. She was quick and fit and remembered the steps easily. She danced with four or five different partners in the circle dance and then it was back to original couples again.

Audrey was also a good dancer. She kept time and seemed

to know which way her sister would turn. This was not the first time they had danced together, of course. Just two nights ago, they had circled nose to tail in the fields not far from here. Alette wondered why Audrey hadn't mentioned their shared power since. Maybe she felt, as Alette did, that there was not much more to say. This evening, they twirled and waltzed under the starry sky in perfect unison.

"Are you having fun?" asked Audrey, as she swung a little girl in a pink dress around. Alette nodded.

When they were red-faced and breathless, they decided it was time to sit out the next dance and retreated to the hay bales.

Audrey picked up some of the corn husks which had been scattered around for the little ones to play with. "I can show you how to make a corn dolly if you like?" She reached inside the pocket of her dress and took out a strange, intricately woven harvest knot which she handed to her sister. Alette stared at it and turned it over in her hands.

"I made it myself," said Audrey. She took three stems of wheat and began to deftly plait them together. Alette watched. It seemed an odd thing to do and did not look at all enjoyable.

"Here," said Audrey, handing her three stems of wheat of her own. Alette took them without enthusiasm.

Audrey seemed to misread her lack of interest as apprehension at the task. "We can start with an easy one," she said.

Alette watched her for a minute more without attempting the task herself.

"Why?" she asked.

The pink spots came back to Audrey's cheeks and she lowered the barely started craft into the full skirt of her dress. "No reason," she mumbled.

They went back to their previous silence.

Perhaps conversation wasn't their strength. Perhaps they were better at dancing.

GOODBYE

Audrey

Audrey was to take the family horse, Cassie. She was a good-natured bay – mostly used if they needed to take the wagon into town. Her cousin had brought his horse with him, who would be able to do the job just as well.

"Anyway, you and Cassie will no doubt be home before we know it," said her mother, patting the horse's neck and looking abruptly the other way. Audrey wondered if she should agree, or say something reassuring, but she didn't know quite what.

"Are you wearing that for the journey?" asked Alette.

Audrey looked down at her serge frock and white apron. "I don't have anything else."

"What about your shoes? Won't they slip in the stirrups? Will they even last the journey?"

"I hope so." Audrey wore a simple pair of leather slippers. They did not look half as sturdy as Alette's riding boots, but again, they were all she had. She did not own any travelling clothes. She had never travelled anywhere.

As they loaded up the saddlebags, Audrey wondered if she was doing the right thing. She was about to embark on a long journey with a cold sorcerer and her strange, brittle sister. A journey which, one way or another, would have life-changing consequences for all of them. There had still been very little talk about what would happen when they reached Essendor. They would claim their right to the throne, Alette had said. But what would that entail? She guessed Zelos would not be too keen to give up his throne. He had killed their parents long ago and wanted them dead too, Maneo said. So presumably he still wanted them dead. How would they –

two young girls and a studious sorcerer – defeat a powerful king? Was this where they would use the mysterious powers that Maneo spoke of?

Audrey pulled herself together. They didn't know each other, but they would get to know each other. They might even learn to love each other. Everything would be all right.

Her mother had baked them some hard rye loaves, which, though not as tasty as the usual bread, should last them for the journey. She helped Audrey pack the bread and other provisions, including hard-boiled eggs, walnuts and fruit.

Maneo was sitting on the back steps, studying his map. He ran a finger along it, tutting, then stood up abruptly. "Right, I think we are ready to depart."

"May I see the route?" asked Madam Warner.

Maneo shook his head and folded the map in sharp creases. "I think it best that we keep our route a secret, for everyone's safety, don't you agree?"

She sighed and nodded, then bid a polite farewell to Alette and Maneo. She held Audrey in a tight embrace and pressed kisses into her hair. "Keep well, daughter," was all she said.

Audrey stood back and met her mother's gaze. "I hope all remains well at the mill. I am already making plans for a decorative bread for wintertide. An oblong, with a central robin and a border of mistletoe…"

Her mother hugged her tight again, then Audrey mounted Cassie and adjusted herself in the saddle. Madam Warner didn't stay to wave them off but retreated rapidly back into the mill, a handkerchief pressed to her face.

WHAT IF?
Alette

Alette watched Audrey say goodbye to her mother, fascinated by their tight, warm embraces and the love between them. She wondered how, thirteen years ago, Audrey's fate and her own had been decided: who chose which twin should go with which adoptive parent. The nanny had said Alette was always the bigger one. Had the sorcerer picked her, knowing that she would grow up hardy and healthy? Or had the nanny felt sorry for Audrey? The weaker one of the litter, picked out for hand-rearing?

Perhaps it was entirely random and fate had chosen which path they would each lead. She tried to imagine the soft baker's wife as her own mother. Would she, Alette, have worn a mop cap and apron, and baked decorative breads for the village fair? She could not imagine such a life. Surely the wilderness would have called to her. She would have run away to where she knew she belonged.

And what if Audrey had grown up with her sorcerer father? Would she be stronger, tougher? Or maybe Audrey would have softened him. Once again, Alette tried to imagine a jug of wildflowers on the kitchen table back home, but she could not. Right now she could not even bring to mind the kitchen. It had only been five days, but that part of her life now felt as though it belonged in the past. She would never return to that house.

CHAPTER SEVEN

THE JOURNEY BEGINS
Audrey

It was just over two hundred miles to Essendor. As they left Lullgrove, they discussed their plans, their horses walking three abreast.

"We should complete the journey in ten days or so," said Maneo.

"Surely we can cover two hundred miles more quickly that that?" said Alette. She seemed to contradict most things he said.

Maneo shook his head. "We will not travel by the main roads. It would only draw attention to us. We will travel cross country, through the fields and forest."

Audrey shuddered. "But is it safe? I have heard that out in the wild there is a risk of dark magic and strange creatures."

Alette snorted and Maneo gave her a sharp look. "Do not mock. Some of these village tales may indeed be true. But we must remember that as a sorcerer I have some power against dark magic. And you girls have your own powers, which will protect you if used wisely."

The powers again. Audrey was still not entirely sure what Maneo was talking about.

"But we must keep these powers hidden," he continued, "and only use them at such times we deem necessary for training. Agreed?"

Both girls nodded. Audrey felt too silly now to speak out and say that she had no special gift.

"Also, it is of utmost importance that we reveal to no one that you are twins. Now that the two of you are together, we are more vulnerable. Danger is everywhere. Zelos knows that you are growing up somewhere in the kingdom. Until he has proof that you are dead, he will continue searching for you."

Alette stared at Maneo. "How do you know all this?"

"What do you mean?"

"How do you know what Zelos thinks or if he is still searching? We have not seen any of his men. For all we know, he could have given up the hunt years ago."

"I have made certain assumptions based on Zelos's character. He does not sound like the sort of man who would easily give up on a mission."

"You taught me never to make assumptions. It is unscientific."

Maneo sighed. "That may be, but I maintain that it may be dangerous if your identity as twins is known. For the purposes of this journey I suggest that we refer to you, Alette, as my elder daughter and Audrey as my younger daughter."

"How old are we pretending to be?"

"I suggest that Alette has just turned fifteen and Audrey is twelve. Agreed?"

"Agreed," said Alette. "Anyone would assume I was the older sister."

"Agreed," said Audrey quietly.

"I still think we could complete the journey in under ten days," said Alette.

Maneo shook his head once more. "The terrain is not smooth and the horses will be walking most of the time. We need to allow time to stop and rest them. Remember that we are in no particular hurry to reach Essendor. No one is expecting us and at the moment, the element of surprise is to our advantage. If we want to stop and rest for a day or two, then that is what we shall do."

Audrey was grateful for the slower pace. Cassie was not old but she was certainly not as fit as Alette's horse, Storm, who was used to long gallops in the rocky terrain of the west.

Audrey had imagined companionable trots with her sister, chatting as they travelled side by side and catching up on the lost years. But the reality was different. They tried to stick to worn tracks, so spent most of the day single file, with Audrey at the back and Alette at the front. Despite what Maneo had said about not rushing, Alette seemed to be constantly driving her horse on.

Audrey tried to keep at a relaxed pace without worrying that Alette was pushing on ahead. She gazed at the farmland all around them. Already, towards the end of the first day, they had travelled further than Audrey ever had before. The scenery at least was familiar to her. Most farms and villages had held their harvests and the golden wheatfields had the shorn and spiky appearances of upturned scrubbing brushes. There were some furrowed fields and some green, all marked out by hedgerows.

But they were approaching a forest and beyond this, on the horizon, were hills and mountains. She had never been to the mountains before. Would they go over them, or around them? Perhaps even through them – there might be a tunnel hewn into the rocks. She could ask Maneo or Alette, but they didn't do much talking and she did not like to ask.

The deep blue sky was dotted with clouds and these had been gradually changing colour from pure white to streaked with orange and grey. It was getting late, and Audrey wondered where they would stop for the night.

As if answering her question, Maneo pointed into the distance.

"There seems to be an old hay barn, there on the edge of the forest. We will aim for that and stop for the night there."

"Already?" said Alette, but when Maneo nodded, she did not protest further.

The barn was currently being used for storing hay bales. It was missing part of one side and was overgrown with trees and ivy, but it seemed structurally sound and would keep out the worst of the elements. The girls fed and watered the horses and set to work building a fire outside the barn.

Audrey yawned. She wasn't used to long days in the saddle and felt sore. She was ready for food and rest and not much else.

RUNNING TOGETHER
Alette

Madam Warner had packed a delicious stew, which they heated up in a pan over the open fire. Once again, Alette marvelled at the new flavours that she had gone her whole life without tasting. She wiped her bread around the tin bowl to mop up every last trace of sauce. Audrey used a spoon to eat hers, taking tiny, delicate mouthfuls. It was no wonder she was thin.

When Audrey finally finished her meal, the sorcerer sat up. He rubbed his hands together for warmth but also maybe out of enthusiasm. "We are a safe distance from any villages or towns. Now would be a good time to see you change together. You will be more powerful as a pair. We need to see what magic you can create together."

A rush of excitement flooded through Alette's fingertips and toes. She felt ready to change again. To run with her sister out in this wilderness. Maybe then she would feel that connection with her twin once again – that bond that was missing now. Alette took a couple of deep breaths and nodded at Audrey. "Together? Now?"

But Audrey didn't stand up. She bit her lower lip.

Alette stood at her side and put her hand on her sister's shoulder. Maybe she was shy. Maybe they should try this further away from Maneo's watchful gaze. "Shall we head to that open field over there?"

Audrey turned her gaze to Alette. "I do not know how."

"What do you mean? You do. You ran with me that first night."

"But that was just a dream!" Audrey's voice rose to a high pitch.

"If it was a dream, why can I remember it too?"

"I don't know. Maybe it wasn't a dream."

"There must have been other times before that when you changed?"

"No," said Audrey. "That was the only time. The first time I thought of unicorns was when I made the decorative bread."

"Bread?" Alette ran her fingers through her hair. What was her sister talking about? This was important and she seemed to think they were still in the bakery. Alette took a deep breath. "It was real, the other night. Not a dream. Remember how you felt then. Maybe you could recall the feeling?"

"All I know is that I was running. Running to find you. And then I was galloping. We were galloping together."

Alette grabbed hold of Audrey's hand and pulled her to her feet. "Running? Running, you say? Then let us run!"

The two girls ran together, out of the woodland and into the clearing. At first they ran side by side but Alette was soon way ahead. She turned and saw that Audrey was red in the face and clutching her side.

"Come on," called Alette. She whipped her head around, black hair flying in the wind. Then her hair was a mane and her legs had thickened. She transformed, first rearing back on her hind legs and then falling forwards on to her forelegs. She galloped around the field as they had done the other night, but this time, her sister didn't join her. Audrey remained in human form. For a short while, Alette saw her watching. Then Audrey closed her eyes, trying, perhaps, to transform. But she stayed as she was. Eventually, Audrey turned and walked back into the woods.

Alette galloped round and round until the frustration about her sister had gone. Then she returned to her human form and walked, tired and sweaty, back to the camp where Audrey and Maneo were waiting.

Alette stood in front of her sister, hands on hips. Audrey's cheeks were streaky, with dirt and perhaps tears. Her eyes were a little red. Was she crying because she couldn't do something? As if that would help!

"What happened?" asked Alette.

Audrey's voice was quiet. "I don't know. Like I said, I don't know how to change. I am not like you."

The frustration came flooding back. "But you are like me! You are my twin! You should be *exactly* like me! And we know that you have the power, I've seen it with my own eyes."

"Maybe it was a one-off."

Alette sat down abruptly. "Well, this is marvellous!" she said sarcastically. "We are on this journey to claim our right to the throne. The twin princesses. More powerful together. But it looks as though it will be one powerful princess and one . . . one baker's apprentice!"

Audrey looked down at her apron and folded the corner into a square. She said nothing, and Alette felt a small stab of guilt.

The sorcerer sighed and rubbed the bridge of his nose. "Alette, Alette. You must be patient. Your sister has not had the same instruction as you. This is all new to her."

"So what can we do about it?"

"Have patience! All we need is time. Remember that we are not in any hurry. For now, let us eat."

BIRDS IN THE RAFTERS
Audrey

Audrey was glad when they retreated into the barn for the night. She was relieved to be away from Alette's scornful looks and Maneo's scrutinizing stare.

They each found a spot in the hay and buried in with their blankets. It was warm and sweet-smelling at least, and not as scratchy as Audrey had feared. But still, she couldn't sleep.

She had never spent the night anywhere other than home. Her little room with its washstand and window now felt like the height of luxury. Here there were holes in the roof and birds flapping and fluttering in the rafters. Bits of detritus fell around her and made her start. There must be mice and rats in here as well – would they run over her in the night? She shuddered and tried to think of something else.

Alette was disappointed in her. She seemed so sure that they shared this incredible power, but it was something that Audrey was only just beginning to understand. In some ways, it made sense. All those strange thoughts and dreams she had experienced. Her imaginary friend who had always felt so real. Yet the ability to transform into a unicorn? It seemed impossible. She had known deep down that the other night had been more than a dream. But it was a big step from knowing this and accepting it, to being able to make it happen at will.

Audrey felt so alone. She missed Shadow – the voice that had been with her since childhood – which was strange because she knew that Alette and Shadow were one and the same. Audrey longed to go to her twin now and curl up near her as they must have done as tiny babies. She knew that if her sister was beside her she would feel safe and sleep soundly.

Of course, this was something she would dare not try, for Alette would undoubtedly push her away.

RAGE AND NETTLES
Alette

They travelled for two more days. One night they managed to find another barn and then an abandoned wagon.

Every night after they had eaten, Maneo would talk to Audrey about her powers, but Audrey seemed unable to accept that she really had them.

"Alette, perhaps you can help Audrey," he said on the second night.

Alette was scraping their plates clean from an earlier meal and rinsing them in water she'd gathered from a stream. "I doubt it," she replied. Alette had already tried to help Audrey. She had run with her, hadn't she? But she couldn't make it happen. Maneo was the sorcerer, not her.

"Perhaps you can help Audrey understand the process that you go through when you enter your transformed state."

"I don't have a process. It's just something that I do. I have always done it."

Maneo rubbed the back of his neck. "That is not strictly true, Alette. You have only been managing your own transformations for a couple of years. Before that they only happened occasionally.

Please, try to tell us what it is like for you. Is there something you say to yourself?"

Alette shrugged. "I do not say anything. I just try to feel the way that I feel when I transform."

"And how do you feel?"

Alette sighed. This felt so personal to her, as if she were giving Maneo and Audrey access to her most private thoughts. But then she did want her twin to be able to transform with her. She would try to oblige and give them the information they needed.

"When I feel . . . anger . . . I transform. I feel a hot rage that I do not know what to do with. It starts deep within my chest and has to come out somewhere: through my fingertips and toes. I send the rage to those parts of me and then they become unicorn. It is only when I transform that the anger leaves me. When I am a unicorn, I can run and stamp and rear up in a way that is impossible for me when I am a girl."

"Anger," said Maneo thoughtfully.

"Yes, and if I do not feel angry about something, then I make myself angry."

"Audrey, do you think you could try that?"

Audrey's eyes seemed to widen in her pixie-like face. "Anger. I could try, I suppose—"

Alette sighed forcefully. Her twin had clearly never had an angry thought in her life. "Go on, Audrey – imagine that you've burnt the bread or that Madam Woodcroft has run out of barley twists or that Rowan Fisher has asked another girl to dance—"

"That's enough, Alette," said Maneo sharply.

Audrey's eyes were pink and the tears were coming again. Why did she have to burst into tears every time they mentioned magic or unicorns? If crying triggered her transformation then everything would be fine.

Alette sighed again and stomped off. Audrey knew nothing about magic or about travelling or even about horses. All she knew was how to bake bread and darn socks. But as much as Alette was annoyed with her twin, she was also annoyed with Maneo. He was supposed to be a great sorcerer, wasn't he? He had taught her how to harness her own power, hadn't he? So why couldn't he do something about her twin? If Audrey carried on at this rate then they *would* be eighteen before they were ready to confront their uncle in Essendor. And Maneo didn't seem to be in any sort of a rush. He hmmed and harred and cleared his throat and did absolutely nothing.

It was easy to transform. As easy to Alette as swimming, running or climbing trees. She could feel anger any time she chose. And she chose now. Her solo walk soon became a solo canter and then a gallop. She galloped the anger away, through the fields, wondering how it could be that one twin inherited all the rage.

After a couple of days of travelling across empty fields, they reached the edge of the woods. Half a mile away was a small hamlet, which Maneo saw as a good opportunity to top up food supplies and take care of the horses.

"I shall take all three horses over to that farmstead. I should be able to find hay and a blacksmith to check their shoes. It is best that you stay here so as not to draw attention."

Alette sighed. "Can't we come with you? I'm hungry."

"No. We are nearer to Essendor now and each step closer brings danger for you. I will buy bread and milk at the farm if I can. You girls sit and rest in that clearing. Have a drink of water and a stretch but don't stray too far. I shall return as soon as possible."

Maneo left and the two girls sat on treestumps in the clearing. Alette picked up a stick and poked at a stone that was stuck in the sole of her boot. "How long do you think he will be?"

"I do not know, sister. But I do know that if we stay here and ask ourselves that question it will feel longer – like waiting for bread to rise! I suggest we take a little stroll around this clearing. Near enough that we hear Maneo when he returns."

Sometimes Audrey's positive attitude baffled Alette. "A stroll! We have been travelling for days! Don't we want to stay in one place for a while?"

"Perhaps. But we might find a little brook where we can bathe our feet or some blackberry bushes. Imagine how good some fresh berries would taste with the bread and milk that Maneo brings back."

At the thought of food, Alette jumped to her feet. "Lead the way!" she said. She followed Audrey through a gap in the trees on the opposite side of the clearing. There didn't seem to be any blackberry bushes.

"There is a fresh crop of young nettles here," said Audrey. "I can make a nice nettle soup over the fire later."

Audrey picked a few nettles with her bare hands and stuffed them into the pocket of her apron.

"Don't they sting you?"

"No, the young nettles do not sting. You can even eat them raw. Try some." Audrey rolled a few of the leaves into a tight ball. "This flattens the prickles and stops them from stinging."

Alette took the unappetizing-looking green ball. "Are you sure?"

Audrey nodded and Alette popped it in her mouth and chewed experimentally. The nettles tasted earthy and green and actually quite pleasant. Maybe Audrey knew a bit more than just baking after all.

"I was thinking of blackberries or bilberries or even some edible mushrooms but if nettles are all we can find then they will have to do," said Audrey. "It's a shame it's not spring. We won't find many young ones at this time of year and the older nettles are too coarse."

"Whatever you say! Shall we turn left or right here?" said Alette.

"I think probably left. We shouldn't go too far though – remember what Maneo said."

Alette snorted. "Maneo! We won't see him for a while. He's probably tucking into fresh bread and soup in the farmhouse kitchen by now. He only told us to stay behind so that there would be more for him."

They pushed through the trees on their left.

"I'm sure Maneo would have taken us with him if he wasn't worried it was too much of a risk—" Audrey stopped. "Oh, look!"

There before them was a well-kept whitewashed fence, containing lush green grass and rows of trees. Alette peered up at the branches and saw apples – they had found an orchard! Alette grinned. She could not think of a better place to rejuvenate before the next leg of the journey.

CHAPTER EIGHT

THE ORCHARD

Audrey

Alette unlatched the gate to the orchard and strode right in. There were rows and rows of healthy apple trees, all laden with red fruit. A walkway cut through the middle of the trees, leading to a cluster of busy beehives. Audrey followed cautiously behind Alette. The bees buzzed, a pair of blue tits called noisily to each other in a chirpy whistle and an orange-tipped butterfly fluttered past.

In front of the walkway, yards from the gate, was a waist-height wooden sign. It was positioned so that it couldn't be missed, although Alette stepped to the left and bypassed it. She looked up into the first tree and reached up to choose an apple.

"Wait!" said Audrey. "We may not be allowed to help ourselves. I think this sign is important." She read aloud:

"Pluck an apple from my tree,
One or two are yours for free,
Three or four are twice as nice,
But after that you pay the price."

"Wonderful! One or two for free." Alette twisted an apple from the branch and bit into it appreciatively. "I have to say, this really is the sweetest apple I've ever eaten. It must be the soil around these parts or something. You have to taste one."

A bee buzzed past Alette's left ear and she batted it away absent-mindedly. Audrey continued studying the sign.

"Don't be too hasty, sister. I am still trying to assess exactly what this notice means. Do you think when it says three or four are twice as nice that you have to pay for those? Or only when you reach five? And is it one or two per person or per party?"

"Per person will be acceptable," a high voice replied. Audrey jumped. "Take what you need to satisfy your hunger pangs."

Audrey looked around for the source of the voice, but there was no one. Even Alette seemed to have wandered off.

"My mistress is happy to share her harvest and help weary travellers. She is only angered by those who take more than they need. Eat, rest a while and move on with your journey."

This time, Audrey located the voice above her head. She looked up and saw two legs in green stockings dangling from the branches. An apple fell from the tree, closely missing her head.

The person in the tree giggled. "Oops, sorry! I just meant for you to try one. You haven't yet touched an apple."

Audrey bent down and picked up the fallen fruit. She rubbed it on her apron. "It doesn't look bruised," she said.

The person in the tree dropped down to the ground. He was almost exactly the same height as the sign in the orchard, which reached to Audrey's elbow. His skin was a yellowish green and covered in red freckles. These markings started on his cheeks and spread down to his chin. He wore a flat brown cap and his ears, which were the shape of sugared almonds, stuck out from underneath.

"Go on, try it," he urged.

Audrey took a small bite. "Mmmm, delicious." She looked around for Alette, but couldn't spot her.

"They are good, aren't they?" asked the little green man.

Audrey nodded. "Excuse me, but who are you?"

"My name is Ribston Russet, chief gardenarian of the apples," he said.

"And, if you don't mind me asking . . . what are you? I mean, to what tribe or . . . race . . . do you belong?"

"I am an orch."

"An *orc*?"

"No! They are nasty goblin-like creatures. I am an orch. An orchard elf. I was grown here in this very orchard and I am now chief gardenarian," he repeated proudly.

"Do you mean guardian?"

"No – gardenarian. It's like a cross between a gardener and a guardian."

"Well, you obviously do a good job. One of the first things I noticed when we walked in here was that it is so tidy. There are no apples on the ground."

The orch puffed out his chest. "Thank you. It is a full-time job."

Audrey carried on eating her apple. "This really is lovely."

"Do stick to the rules though, won't you? My mistress doesn't like it when travellers take too much for free. Ah, here she is now. The orchardess."

A woman appeared behind Ribston, which was strange, because Audrey hadn't seen anyone open the gate. She was taller than Audrey but shorter than Alette and she leaned on a longish staff that was whittled from applewood. Her wrinkled skin was mottled and she wore a flowing white dress that skimmed the ground. Her hair was braided into two long grey plaits, which reached past her waist.

Alette was clearly interested in the arrival of the orch and orchardess. She wandered back into the clearing, crunching on a fresh apple. Audrey was nibbling the juicy flesh of her own apple right down to the core. The orchardess eyed her sharply. "I see you have helped yourself to my apples. And I am sure you read the sign here. May I ask how many have you taken?"

"Just one or two each. That's right, isn't it, Alette?"

Alette nodded.

The old woman turned to the orch. "It's funny, but I find that once people have tasted my delicious apples, they often lose count. Are the girls' calculations correct, Ribston?"

"I'm afraid I couldn't be certain. I was talking to this delightful young lady," said Ribston, pointing to Audrey.

Alette shrugged. "Never mind, you'll just have to take us at our word."

The old woman smiled. "It sounds as though we should ask the other gardenarians. Could you call them, Ribston?"

Ribston obliged. "Gardenarians, assemble!"

Audrey looked up into the trees. Were there other orches hidden away up there? Alette was doing the same – she seemed a little jumpy. But she hadn't eaten more than her fair share. Had she?

Ribston called out again and there was a loud buzzing sound from the direction of the hives. A swarm of bees emerged and flew in a great dark cloud towards them. They buzzed around Ribston's and the orchardess's heads, the noise growing louder. Audrey didn't mind bees but it was still a disquieting sight. Neither Ribston nor the orchardess were wearing a net. Weren't they worried about getting stung?

And then it struck her. The bees were the other gardenarians. They were reporting back.

The orchardess spoke softly to the bees. "Thank you. Please check for me."

The bees flew off to where Alette was standing. They swarmed around her, settling on her travel bag. Alette recoiled and dropped the bag. It tumbled to the ground; the flap fell open and a dozen apples rolled out on to the neat grass.

The old woman continued smiling but shook her head slowly from side to side. "It looks as if someone has been a little greedy."

Alette had perhaps been planning her excuse. "I wanted to take some for our horses. They have not eaten either and have to travel all the way to Essendor. It seemed so unfair to—"

But the orchardess was not interested in excuses. She tapped the sign with her stick. "The warning was very clear. And now, you will have to pay the price."

THE PRICE OF APPLES
Alette

Alette took her money pouch from her belt. She knew that there were not very many coins in the pouch, but how expensive could a few apples be?

"How much are they, exactly?"

The orchardess stared at her with a pinched mouth. "These apples were not for sale. You took over and above what was offered to you. For each additional apple that you have stolen, you must work for me for a full year."

Alette's eyes widened. "What? That would be seven years!"

"Yes, my dear. You did take a great many apples without my permission. You have tasted them and you know how good they are. The price is high."

She nodded to Audrey. "You, on the other hand, are free to leave."

Audrey shook her head. "I stay with Alette," she said.

Alette was baffled at this. Did Audrey have a plan? Why didn't she just leave and find Maneo?

"As you wish," said the old woman. "A nice gesture of sibling loyalty. You are siblings, I take it?"

"Yes," said Audrey, smiling at Alette.

"And who is the elder sister?"

Audrey smiled again. "Actually, we're—"

"I am!" said Alette, throwing Audrey a quick look. Audrey nodded.

"I see," said the orchardess, raising her eyebrows.

Alette was starting to get exasperated with this woman. She was tempted to transform and use her magic but she remembered Maneo's warnings about transforming in front of others.

For now, she squared up to the woman. "What is to stop me walking out of this gate right now with all these apples and however many more I fancy? I have horses waiting. You would never catch me!"

The orchardess laughed and gestured to the gardenarians. It was a subtle crook of the finger but it sent the bees swarming angrily to the gate. She tapped her staff at the base of two apple trees and they grew rapidly, branches and leaves creeping towards each other. In seconds, they had grown thickly over the gate and intertwined with each other's branches. Alette span around. Twisted branches surrounded the whole perimeter of the orchard. There wasn't a single gap.

Alette ran to the gate, braving the bees, and tried to prise two of the branches apart with her hands. They were completely inflexible, as if made of stone.

The orchardess laughed. "Oh, my girl, you will never get out that way! Nor this way!"

She thrust her staff upwards towards the sky and a thatch of thorns appeared, criss-crossing their way above the trees. The light levels dropped and it felt to Alette as though she had been dropped into a wicker picnic basket. Little slivers of light adorned the orchard floor.

"Your horses will be waiting a long time," said the orchardess. "But you are safe here with me. I offer you a bargain. There is one way to avoid paying for my apples, and that is to do some special work for me. Right now, it is harvest time. I need to pick these apples and get them to the cider press. If, working together, you can pick every single apple in the orchard by sunset, then I will free you from your seven-year task."

Alette felt herself losing control. This was only meant to be a little diversion before they carried on with the journey. She looked up into the tree above her. There must be hundreds of apples in its branches, and there were dozens of trees.

"Every single apple? But that is impossible!"

"Nothing is impossible. And mind you put them all in the baskets," said the orchardess, walking steadily towards the gate. She bent two of the trees apart, as Alette had tried to do earlier. This time the trees swung apart easily, as if the orchardess were stepping through a pair of velvet curtains. Alette dashed to follow her but, of course, the wall of trees was once again impenetrable. She shouted and swore as the bees started swarming around her.

"When my father hears about this he will be furious!" she yelled. She tried again to prise the trees apart – this time leaning right back to use her full bodyweight. Audrey stood and watched.

"Can't you help me?"

"I'll try, but I suspect an enchantment holds those trees fast," said Audrey, stating the obvious.

She came and grabbed Alette around the waist. Audrey's pull was surprisingly strong but she was right; there was no way they were going to move any of the enchanted trees.

Alette crumpled into a heap on the ground. "Now what are we going to do?"

APPLE PICKING
Audrey

A large black bird flapped down from a tree and pecked at one of the apples that had rolled out of Alette's bag. He was a raven, with a white mark at his throat. Ribston tried to shoo him away but he was persistent, puncturing the skin with his hooked beak.

"This might sound strange, but I think I know this bird," said Audrey.

The bird lifted his head and stared directly at her.

"Doesn't one black bird look very much like another? Those ravens are so common – I see them everywhere." Alette looked briefly at the bird and he flapped away. But Audrey had not seen many ravens before. Perhaps they were more common in the west of the kingdom.

She looked at Alette, still slumped on the ground. The news of their task had been too much for her and she had given up on it already.

Audrey, however, remained undaunted. It was certainly an enormous job, but as the orchardess said, nothing was impossible. And here was her chance to show Alette that she was not weak and useless.

"Where there's a will there's a way," she said softly. Audrey looked up. Through the gaps in the thorny canopy it was still possible to get a sense of the position of the sun in the sky.

"So – it is early afternoon now. What time is sundown?"

Alette looked up. She seemed surprised that Audrey was taking control.

"I don't know. Around six?"

"That means we have four hours to pick all the apples. An hour to spend on each quarter of the orchard. It seems very, very difficult, but not impossible. We must concentrate all our efforts and not waste a single moment."

She stared at Alette, who surprised her by promptly standing up.

"Let's work together," Audrey continued. "One of us will

pick the apples and pass them to the other, who will place them in the basket. We will take turns."

"Good idea," said Alette, who seemed back to her normal self. "I shall pick first."

Alette climbed the nearest ladder and pulled at an apple. It pinged off and she dropped it on the ground below.

"Not like that!" said Audrey. "Have you never picked apples before?"

She climbed up the same ladder as Alette and showed her how to twist the apple upwards and roll it from the branch. She deftly picked three, which she carried back down the ladder in her apron.

Once Alette knew the technique, she worked quickly. They were a good team and intuitively knew when to reach out or pass to each other.

"Back in the village, we have an Apple Day," said Audrey. "As autumn comes to a close, all the villagers work together to pick the apples and then we have a party, with apple juice, cider and—"

"Apple cake?" guessed Alette.

"How did you know?" said Audrey. She laughed. "It's funny. I was looking forward to this year's celebration – I was hoping to be crowned the Apple Princess. That was before you told me I was a real princess."

"Shhh!" said Alette. Since the bees had caught her with the apples, she was acutely aware that they might be listening in on their every word. Or that strange elf – their leader – who seemed to have disappeared when the work began.

Audrey continued collecting the apples in silence and Alette felt a little sorry. She enjoyed these tales of normal life. A life she might have led if things had been different. Maybe one day she would attend an Apple Day celebration, drink some fresh cider and dance with a boy. What other normalities had she missed out on? School, and toys, perhaps, when she was younger? Sharing secrets with a best friend?

Now she knew Audrey, perhaps she would be closer to that normal life. Audrey smiled and caught her gaze. She looked quickly back at the apples. If only she knew how to return such warmth. But Alette felt hard, brittle. If you hit her with a toffee hammer she would shatter into a hundred tiny pieces.

As the sun moved in its slow arc across the orchard, the girls' fingertips grew sore from plucking apples and their necks ached from looking up into the trees. But they didn't slow down. They had only managed to strip four trees of their apples and there were dozens more to go. It became very obvious that if they carried on at this rate they would be a long way off completing the task by sundown.

Alette began to get frustrated, climbing back down the ladder and sighing heavily.

"There must be a quicker way!" she cried. She ran to one of the younger trees, reached into the mass of branches and shook the trunk hard. Apples bounced out of the tree on to the green grass below.

"Careful! You'll bruise them!" The orch, who had been raking the grass a few yards away, ran to rescue his precious fruit from the ground.He hadn't disappeared altogether, then.

"The old witch didn't say anything about protecting them from bruises," said Alette, still shaking the tree. "If they're all going in the cider press anyway then what do a few bruises matter?" But she could see that even the shaking method was not going to dislodge all the apples in time.

She sat down and cried tears of frustration. "I'm hungry, I'm tired and I'm sick of looking at apple trees. I can't stay here for another seven years!"

Audrey came and sat next to her, putting her arm around her. "I would rather be in here with you for seven years than out there without you."

Alette wiped her tear-stained face with her sleeve. "I could transform," she whispered. "I would be stronger then and I could barge each of these trees in turn!"

Audrey shook her head. "It would be too risky. We mustn't reveal our true identity."

"Well, I am sick of picking apples. I say we give up on this impossible task. Maneo will come for us – he will get us out of here. His magic will be enough of a match for hers."

Audrey wished she could be so sure. Maneo didn't even know which direction they had wandered off in. Would he really think to look for them in this tangled mass of trees?

The orch had been watching the girls intently, and now he stepped out from behind an apple trunk.

"There might be another way."

TALKING TO TREES
Alette

The orch sidled closer.

"You mustn't tell anyone. My mistress would be livid. I don't know what she'd do to me if she knew."

Audrey nodded and gave him an encouraging smile. "We promise not to tell."

The orch looked in Alette's direction, checking that she would also keep silent on the matter. But Alette didn't know what to think. Why should they trust this strange little green man? If he was that keen to help them he could have asked his tiny stripy spies to lie about the number of apples she'd taken.

But Audrey nudged her. "I will not tell either," she said gruffly.

This seemed enough for Ribston and he began to talk to the girls, checking all around him as he did so. "You must remember that trees have feelings too."

He approached the tree that Alette had been shaking, patting its trunk as if he were calming a startled pony.

"This poor old girl. She's not made for kicking or shaking. If you hurt her, she will hang on to her apples all the tighter. She needs to relax, to know that she is giving her fruit to friends. For a good reason."

Alette tried to catch Audrey's eye. This elf had clearly spent too many years alone with his apple trees and had lost sight of reality. But Audrey was captivated by the orch, hanging off his every word.

He circled his arms around the trunk and rested his cheek against the bark in a tender embrace.

"Join me!" he said to the girls.

Audrey went to the tree and hugged it from the other side. Alette hung back, not fully trusting these enchanted trees.

Ribston began to sing in a squeaky high voice. If there was a tune then Alette couldn't follow it.

"Sweet apple tree
Pray, hear my plea
Apples be free
Bestow upon me!"

There was a pause.

He stayed close to the trunk and whispered, "Please, for me."

Ribston took a few paces back and indicated Audrey should do the same. Then, like someone shaking their hands dry, the tree shook her branches. One, two, three abrupt little shakes. After a few seconds, the apples began to roll along the branches, plopping gently on to the ground. The rest followed in a great thunder of apples.

Alette and Audrey gazed up into the bare branches. Not a

single apple left. They whooped and shrieked, running around to collect all the fallen fruit and put it in the empty baskets.

Alette couldn't believe it. The strange little man had been absolutely right.

"Thank you, tree!" they called.

Ribston and Audrey moved on to the next tree and the next, embracing each and whispering kindnesses until each tree happily gave up her produce. Alette soon joined in. Now that she had seen the results, she was happy to hug them. Soon all that was left to do was scoop up the apples and pour them into the willow baskets.

Afterwards, the girls lay on their backs under the bare branches. They were exhausted. Patches of pink sky showed through the thorns above them – it was still not quite sundown. The orchardess would have to release them.

Ribston shuffled off to chat to the bees. They could hear what he was saying. "Now, there's no need to mention this to the mistress. We were just helping this nice young girl and her sister." The bees buzzed in what sounded like agreement and Alette felt grateful to Ribston, but a little guilty as well. She hoped he wouldn't get into any trouble for helping. Even if he clearly preferred her sister.

The pink patches of sky soon turned grey and dark blue and the girls knew that night had fallen. As she had promised, the orchardess reappeared in the orchard. Alette and Audrey stood by the full baskets of apples to meet her, chins jutting proudly. The orchardess examined the tree closest to them.

"No apples. Very good," she said with a wry smile.

She did the same with the next tree, this time checking very thoroughly along each branch. If she was expecting to find an apple that they had overlooked then she would be disappointed.

The orchardess narrowed her eyes at the girls. "No apples again. Not a single one," she said suspiciously.

She threw her arm up into the air. "Gardenarians!" she called. "Check these trees for me."

The bees obediently buzzed out of their hives in a large dark cloud and split into smaller groups. They swarmed into one tree at a time, checking it thoroughly. The bees didn't find a single apple, not even a tiny, underripe one. One bee buzzed close to the orchardess's ear, reporting back. She stiffened and glared at the girls.

"You could not have done all this by yourselves!" Her voice was raised.

"It doesn't matter how we did it," said Alette assertively. "You said that if we picked all the apples and got them into the baskets then we would be free to leave."

"No!" screeched the orchardess. "This is my orchard! I decide what is fair and I make the rules. I see exactly what has happened – I have been deceived! Betrayed by my own worker. Ribston! Come here now."

But Ribston was nowhere to be seen. The orchardess looked half-heartedly behind a couple of trees and then gave up. "So be it," she shouted into the orchard. "Stay here with these girls. I shall decide what to do with the lot of you in the morning."

NIGHTFALL
Audrey

When the orchardess had gone, Alette cursed and raged against the unfairness of it all. "That old crone should keep her word! She promised us she would set us free, yet she's keeping us here. When Maneo finds out, he will be furious."

Audrey nodded, but she didn't feel so sure. If Maneo were going to help, wouldn't he be here by now? Maybe he had given up on them. Maybe he had assumed that King Zelos had found them, or that wild forest beasts had carried them off.

With the night came the cold. The girls sat together near the blocked-off gate, Audrey's cloak wrapped around them for warmth.

Alette crunched on an apple. "I shall eat as many of these as I want now. Hear that, you old witch? You can keep me here for fifteen years now!"

Audrey wished that her sister wouldn't be so antagonistic. Her attitude certainly wasn't going to help them out of their plight.

"Where are we going to sleep?" said Audrey, trying to change the subject.

"How about here?" said Ribston, gesturing to the patch of green grass near the outer perimeter.

"On what?" said Alette.

Ribston looked confused. "Why, on this soft, springy grass. What else is there?"

Audrey smiled at Alette. "At home, we have beds, with coverlets made of cotton or linen and mattresses stuffed with straw or feathers."

"Beds," repeated Ribston, with a wistful look in his eyes. He rushed off and returned with a couple of burlap sacks and some straw for each of the girls so that they could make themselves as comfortable as possible.

He picked a tree a few yards away, climbed up with no noticeable effort and settled down in the V of the trunk. He closed his eyes.

Audrey thought how content he looked. "Do you always sleep in this way, Ribston?" He had no covering whatsoever.

Ribston kept his eyes closed. "When the night is as balmy as this one, then yes."

The girls exchanged a glance – neither would describe the chill of the autumn night as balmy.

"When there is snow on the ground I might fashion myself a hole in the ground."

"Like a burrow?" asked Alette.

"Like a burrow – yes."

Audrey imagined what it might be like to spend the night in the ground. She thought of her own room at the mill, which was now home to her cousin, and her mother. Was Mother missing her? Of course she was; Audrey knew that. She tried to imagine what her mother would say if Maneo returned to the village without her. Would he tell her that he had lost her in the woods? But Audrey found this difficult to imagine. She still had faith that they would get out of this orchard.

Alette's rhythmic breathing and Ribston's gentle snorts told Audrey that they had both fallen asleep. It was strange to Audrey that Alette should so easily fall asleep when she was full of anger. Audrey herself would not have been able to drift off in a temper. But then if she had discovered anything so far about her twin, it was that they were very different.

Audrey gazed up at the thorns criss-crossing above her. If they had not formed her prison, then she might have thought them beautiful. The blackness of the thorns contrasted with the royal blue of the night sky. Audrey thought she might be able to see little stars through some of the gaps. She squinted and concentrated so hard that she forgot about all her worries and she too fell asleep.

Hours later, Audrey awoke suddenly. Something had woken her. For a couple of seconds, her brain tried to catch up. It wasn't morning yet. What had disturbed her sleep? She blinked and her eyes adjusted. Someone was leaning over her. The orchardess!

Their eyes met in the darkness. The old woman's were pale, milky, cold. She raised her hands to Audrey's throat. Audrey gasped. Did she mean to murder her in her sleep? But the orchardess was studying her necklace. She took the silver pendant between her thumb and forefinger, breathed on it, rubbed it. Audrey instinctively reached up and grabbed it back but the orchardess had already seen what she wanted to see. Audrey sat upright as the old woman stood and went to Alette's side. She gently examined her necklace in the same way. Alette did not wake.

The orchardess returned to Audrey and smiled. She spoke in a low murmur.

"I have seen these pendants before. I knew the people to whom they belonged. Long ago, a pair of siblings used to come here at night-time. A girl and a boy. It began when they were around ten years old. They came each month when the moon was full. They would play hide and seek among the trees. They crunched apples in the moonlight."

"My mother...?" breathed Audrey.

"Yes, your mother and your uncle. The twins, Bia and Zelos."

"I didn't know they were twins! I thought Zelos was her younger brother."

"He was younger. By five whole minutes. Bia born just before midnight and Zelos just after. They were so different and yet so close. I saw them hold their pendants together – two halves of a whole."

Audrey closed her fist protectively over her pendant. Had this half belonged to her mother, or her uncle?

"They loved it here but they were far from their home – the palace," continued the orchardess. "I was often curious about how they got here – such a long way for children to travel on their own in the night, even with the moonlight as a guide. I always knew which night they would arrive, so one night I climbed the tallest tree and waited, clinging to the branches. It was cold up there and uncomfortable, but I had an excellent view. I could see the hills and valleys laid out like patchwork. I could see the path that they would take, lit so brightly by the moon."

"And what did you see?"

"I saw your uncle, riding a magnificent beast. At first, I thought it was a black pony but then its horn caught the moonlight and glowed a bright white. It was a unicorn."

Audrey listened intently. Another unicorn? She remembered her mother's words at the bakery about dreaming of unicorns and betrayal.

"I watched him dismount the beast. He was riding bareback so he slid easily to the ground. Then the unicorn rose up on its hind legs. Its legs became a girl's legs; its forelegs became arms. There was Bia. And the pair of them ran together to my orchard. They never knew that I saw her transform. Never knew that I knew their secret. But you knew it, didn't you?"

Audrey didn't respond. Had she known it? Maybe. Her real mother had been able to transform into a unicorn. She had passed her power on to Alette. And possibly to Audrey herself. Her mother had been the Midnight Unicorn of Essendor. Audrey probably had known this, although she hadn't admitted it, even to herself.

"They only came and played in my orchard a few more times after that. The visits grew less and less frequent. Then one night, when they were just a little older than you are now, they argued. The boy, you see, was jealous of his twin sister. He did not have the ability to transform as she did. And he was the younger twin, which meant that he was second in line to the throne. He wanted to rule instead of her. She was the one with the gift, he said. Why couldn't she let him be the one with the power? She said, when the time came, they could rule together as the rules of the kingdom allowed, but he would not accept that.

"Jealousy does terrible things to a person. He ripped the pendant from his neck and threw it down here, by this tree. I picked it up after he'd run off. It was not damaged, just a link broken in the chain. It was set with opals that flashed white like the horn on the unicorn's head. I would not forget that design. I gave the pendant to Bia and she thanked me. Said she would be so sad to lose it."

Audrey felt a rush of gratitude towards the orchardess. Like her mother, she was glad that neither pendant had been lost. But before she could say anything, the orchardess's expression darkened.

"They never came to see me again. Neither of them. They never thanked me for their time here or said goodbye. People are all so selfish. That was when I decided to stop giving the apples away for free. We have to pay for what we take in this world, do we not? Even those of royal blood should pay."

The orchardess's voice grew louder. Alette stirred but did not wake. Ribston kept snoring.

"Now I have a new secret. The twin princesses. Not murdered in their cradles after all, but all grown up and heading in the direction of Essendor. Why would that be, I wonder? King Zelos will be most interested to hear about it. And I have them both safely caged in a hidden spot." She smiled coldly at Audrey. "Why would I want seven years' labour from you when I can command a high price from the king? He has been searching the kingdom for you for the past thirteen years. Think how pleased he will be when I can deliver you both to him. He will pay me in gold and I will never have to work again."

Audrey looked the orchardess squarely in the eyes. "You must do what you think is right, of course."

The orchardess didn't waver. "As I grow older I stop thinking about what is right for the world and concentrate on what is right for me. Who will look after me when I am older and frailer? Not the bees. Not this useless orch." She pointed to the sleeping form of Ribston. "I am on my own and I have to look after myself. I feel sorry for you, child, if not your impertinent sister, but you will soon fade from my memory as I live out my days in comfort."

The orchardess swooped off to the other end of the orchard, her white dress billowing out behind her. She left through the gap in the trees as she had done before.

Audrey watched her leave and wondered if she would go directly to the king, or wait until the morning to betray them.

ESCAPE
Alette

Someone was shaking Alette's shoulder. Someone wanted to wrench her from her deep and pleasant sleep. Alette opened her eyes, trying to make sense of her surroundings. Then she focused on the baskets of apples and the events of the day before came back to her in a rush. Audrey was wide-awake already and at her side, doing the shaking.

"We must escape," she said urgently.

Alette stared at her. Had she only just realized that? "I know," she said. "We are waiting for Maneo to help us."

Audrey looked agitated. "You don't understand. Time is now of the essence. The orchardess knows everything. She knows the secret of our birth and our escape. She even knew our mother. Our mother was the Midnight Unicorn of Essendor! Now the orchardess is talking about selling us to the king."

Alette sat bolt upright. She had already guessed her mother's secret after piecing together the reflection in the water and Maneo's tale of her birth. But it was true. Did Maneo know? This would have to be a conversation for another time. Right now they had to focus on getting out of this orchard. The last thing they needed was the king's men turning up. "You're right. We have to get out of here."

Overhearing, the orch jumped down from his tree. "I'll help. I feel responsible for you getting trapped here, and my mistress is not the forgiving type. She will show no mercy to me or you."

Alette looked up into the trees and above. "Can we climb out?"

Audrey shook her head "I think the thorns stretch all the way across."

"Still, I'm going up to check," said Alette.

Alette had been climbing trees all her childhood. She knew exactly which tree to pick – one with a thick branch low enough for her to grasp.

"Be gentle with her," called Ribston. It took Alette a while to realize that he was referring to the tree and she rolled her eyes. Still, she remembered how generous the trees had been yesterday when giving up their fruit and tried not to kick her feet too hard. She held on tightly then jumped and swung her feet up to the branch so that she clung on like a monkey. From there, she was able to shuffle around into an upright position so that she was sitting comfortably on the branch.

"Orch, do you have a saw or any cutting tool on that belt of yours?" she asked.

Ribston passed her a small, wooden-handled handsaw.

She called to Audrey. "Are you going to join me?"

Audrey shook her head. "I have not climbed a tree since I was seven and even then, I wasn't very good at it."

Alette was not surprised. She shrugged and began her ascent

to the top. Down below, Audrey put her hands over her eyes. "You're making me giddy. Please be careful!" she called.

Alette grinned. "Don't concern yourself with my safety. I've been climbing trees for many years with no one to catch me when I fall."

It was true that Alette was a natural. She stretched out her long limbs to reach for increasingly higher branches. Then she was lost in the leaves for a moment before she popped out at the very top of the tree. She could no longer see her sister or the orch at ground level although she could hear their voices.

"How does it look up there?" called Audrey.

Alette assessed the situation. "There are thorns everywhere. They stretch all the way over the tops of the trees and down to the other side. We are in a cage."

"Can you break through?"

Alette tried Ribston's tiny handsaw on the woody thorns but, as she suspected, it was completely ineffective. "No. These aren't normal thorns – I might as well try sawing through a steel post."

The orchardess was not going to make it easy for them to get out of here. Audrey shouted up to Alette again. "Are there any gaps in the thorns?"

"None big enough for a person."

"What about for an orch?" called Ribston.

"Not even for the smallest orchard elf," replied Alette. "Just big enough for birds or tiny creatures, although I can't think why they would want to find their way into this dark orchard."

Alette's attention was suddenly drawn by a flutter to her left and a black head and beak poking through one of the larger gaps. "It seems that a creature *is* trying to get in. A big black bird again. Like the one you thought you knew, Audrey."

"The raven?"

"Yes! Crow, rook, raven, whatever he is. He is most eager. He is squeezing through a tiny gap. . . . he's through!"

The raven flew down past Alette, his giant wings nearly brushing her cheek. Alette followed, climbing swiftly down from branch to branch and then jumping lightly from the tree to where Audrey and Ribston stood.

The bird flew in wide circles around them then landed on the ground between them. The feathers under his large beak fluttered in the breeze. Audrey stared at him.

"This is the same bird. I feel certain I know him. And he knows us."

The raven leaned forward and cawed at her, moving his wings in a short motion, like a shrug.

"A memory from long ago is coming back to me. You will think me foolish but I seem to think it was when we were in our cradle."

Alette did think her quite foolish. Surely no one could actually remember being a baby? "I do not remember that," she said.

The raven cawed loudly. *Cor-vus.*

Audrey looked delighted. "Yes! It's Corvus, isn't it? I remember you!"

Alette shook her head slowly, raising her eyebrows at Ribston, who either didn't see or pretended not to notice.

The bird walked forwards, hopped a little and chattered away in some unknown bird language. He dropped something at Audrey's feet.

"Look, he has a message for us." She picked it up and showed them. A black feather.

Alette recognized it straight away. "It is the feather from Maneo's hat! He knows where we are! He has sent this bird!"

The raven hopped around in a circle and cawed again as if trying to get their attention. This time he dropped something by Alette. A little gold oval – smaller than a button. Alette placed it in the palm of her hand. It weighed nothing. It caught a sliver of morning sunlight and reflected colourful rays.

"If I know Maneo, then this is our key to escape. But what is it and what do we do with it?"

Ribston shot forward and grabbed it out of Alette's hand. "I know exactly what it is!"

"Careful!" said Alette. "We don't want to lose it in the grass."

"Yes we do," said Ribston. "That is exactly what we want to do."

Ribston tucked the oval into the pocket of his shirt and ran to the centre of the orchard. He pulled up a couple of handfuls of grass, unhooked a small fork from his belt and began loosening the earth.

"What are you doing?" said Alette.

Audrey's face broke into a wide smile. "He's planting it! Of course! It's a seed."

Alette smiled too. "A magic seed from Maneo."

Ribston made a hole a couple of inches deep. He plopped the seed in, covered it with loose earth and patted it down. Audrey filled up a watering can from the trough and sprinkled water on the site.

The three of them stared at the small bare patch of earth, holding their breath. Nothing happened. And then . . . something. The earth jiggled and a small, golden shoot pushed its way through.

"An apple seedling," said Ribston, proudly.

The raven cawed and flapped away, above the trees, no doubt reporting back to Maneo.

"Thank you, Corvus," cried Audrey. "Tell Maneo it's growing!"

"But how will an apple seedling get us out of here?" said Alette.

The shoot divided into two round-edged leaves and then started growing upwards. It opened up and more leaves emerged from the centre of the plant.

"It's growing quickly!" said Alette.

Soon the seedling looked like a branch stuck into the earth. It still had a golden shimmer.

"If it carries on like this it will be fully grown in minutes," said Ribston.

"I wonder if it will bear golden apples," said Audrey.

"But what are we supposed to do with those? Golden apples are no use to us while we're stuck in here," said Alette.

The tree grew larger, developing a proper trunk and widening branches. It grew taller than Ribston, then Audrey, then Alette, but it showed no signs of stopping.

"Mark my words, this tree is going to grow taller than all the others," said Ribston, impressed.

Alette stared up at the thorny canopy above them. "Of course! It is going to break through!" she said. "Let's start climbing before the lowest branches are out of reach."

Ribston went first. Despite his diminutive size, he had no problems tackling the tree and seemed to scamper up like a cat or a squirrel, clinging on to the bark.

The girls quickly gathered their bags and strapped them securely to their backs. Alette swung herself into the golden tree the way she had done before and started climbing.

After a while she paused and looked down. Audrey had tucked her dress into her drawers and climbed all the way up the apple-picking ladder and then on to a branch. Now she looked terrified. "You can do it!" she said, reaching out a hand to help her. Somehow, Audrey managed to inch her way up. The tree continued growing at speed even as they climbed.

Suddenly, Ribston shouted, "Don't climb any higher! I think we are about to break through."

Alette looked up. Ribston was right. Either the tree would burst through soon, or it would hit the enchanted thorns and break apart.

Ribston adopted a crouching position to protect his face and hands from the thorns. The girls now did the same, Audrey struggling a little to keep her balance in the branches.

There was a hideous cracking as the fight between tree and thorns began. Branches, twigs and barbed tangles rained down on the girls and they desperately clung on, hoping that their golden tree would not be sent crashing to the ground. But the tree triumphed. Like a spring bulb breaking through the surface of the earth, the tree sought light and air. It creaked and splintered its way through the thorny mass, then spread its branches wide.

When the girls realized they were on the other side of their cage, they opened their eyes and laughed at the sight of the bright blue sky. They waved up at Ribston, who was now climbing down the tree. "We don't want to keep going!" he shouted. "Who knows where we might end up."

He came to meet them on their branch and they held on for a few more moments until the giddying growing came to an end. It seemed that the tree had finally reached its full height.

Down on the ground, someone in a yellow floppy hat came running around the corner and waved up at them. Maneo. Alette realized that she had been wondering if she would ever see him again. Maneo gesticulated but they were too far away to see what he was trying to tell them.

"Thank you for the magic seed!" called Audrey. "We're out!"

Alette lifted a hand in a token greeting, but she had other

things on her mind. "It does feel good to be out of the orchard, but how are we going to get down?"

MANEO'S STORY
Audrey

Audrey, Alette and Ribston edged along one of the longer, lighter branches. Their combined weight made the branch droop over the top of the orchard. Maneo moved closer to them so that they could see and hear him properly. "No one jump off before I've got it secured, otherwise the others might be catapulted back over the orchard!" he shouted.

The plan worked well and the branch gradually bent closer and closer to the ground. When the branch was four or five feet away, Maneo stretched out and grabbed it. Ribston jumped off first, landing nimbly on both feet with a little bounce. Then Audrey slid off into a much less graceful heap, and finally Alette, who refused everyone's outstretched hands and pounced off on to all fours like a cat.

Audrey expected to see a moving father and daughter reunion between Maneo and Alette but there was nothing, not even a quick hug or peck on the cheek. Audrey couldn't understand their lack of emotion. She pictured how her mother would be if they were reunited, and the thought made tears prick at her eyes.

Once everyone was safely on the ground, Maneo released the branch. It sprang straight back into position with alarming speed, and a golden apple from the end of the branch was projected into the distance. None of the party saw where it fell.

They turned and looked back at the tree – at the great height of it. Audrey could hardly believe that she had been all the way up there moments before. She would not want to climb it again in a hurry. A cloud of bees emerged through the hole in the thorns, buzzing loudly around the golden trunk. Perhaps they had decided not to stay in the empty orchard by themselves.

Everyone dusted themselves down. Audrey untucked her dress, Alette removed thorns from her untidy hair and Ribston stared at the sorcerer whom he had heard so much about. Audrey thought Maneo looked more tired than usual, with a pale complexion and dark circles under his eyes.

He cast a brief, puzzled look at Ribston and then focused back on the girls. "Could someone explain to me what has transpired beyond these trees?" he asked sharply.

Alette sighed. "After you went to the farm, we went for a short walk and found an orchard." She pointed to the mass of trees and thorns. "Behind there. It was a glorious place and the apples were delicious but then an evil old crone tried to trap us there for seven years for eating her fruit."

Audrey and Ribston both glanced quickly at Alette. Was she going to confess that she had been responsible for ignoring the sign and stealing the fruit? Alette lifted her chin defiantly. No, it did not look as though a confession was imminent. But Audrey would not reveal the truth unless Alette wanted to.

Maneo probably knew that there was more to the story but he didn't probe further.

"I was longer than expected because the farmer and his wife were so kind and hospitable. They provided food for our party – although they think we are a band of travelling minstrels – and for the animals. Their farrier offered to re-shoe all three horses so I left them there and came back to tell you. When I found you both gone, I suspected some foul play and began my search."

"We were worried you wouldn't find us," said Audrey.

"I soon sensed the magic nearby and followed it here. I saw the mass of trees and thorns and guessed that you were trapped by some spell," he said.

Alette looked incredulous. "Then why didn't you magic us out of there?"

"I attempted to reverse the magic but I could not identify the charm that had been used."

"This is the problem with magic spells," said Alette. "They are good for lifting items off the ground for a few moments, or creating a pretty explosion, but are they ever of any real use?"

Maneo did not rise to the provocation. "It must have been a strong sorcerer to cast such a spell."

"A mere farmer," said Alette, with a smirk.

"An orchardess," said Audrey, more kindly.

"Sometimes these rural folk with their specialist spells can be very powerful. In the end, I decided to find you without magic. I walked around the perimeter of the trees until eventually, I heard you talking. I did not want to shout for fear that the sorcerer—"

"Orchardess," said Alette.

"Yes, the orchardess – for fear that she would hear, so I sent a sign with a raven. I hoped that you would be able to hide the seed until it was a safe time to use it."

"How do you know Corvus?" asked Audrey. "I had a strong feeling I had seen him before. He triggered a memory of my cradle."

"That is unlikely," said Maneo. "Black birds look much the same everywhere, do they not?"

Something about Maneo's expression made Audrey not want to ask more about the bird.

"Where is the enchantress—?" asked Maneo.

"Orchardess," said Alette.

"Yes – orchardess – where is she now?"

"I suspect she has gone straight to Essendor to inform King Zelos of our whereabouts. She means to hand us over to him for a hefty sum."

Maneo looked about as if expecting Zelos to appear from behind a tree at any moment. He frowned. "Well then, we must make haste."

"Can we not rest here a short time? I still need to eat and to bathe," said Alette.

The sorcerer shook his head. He reached into his travel bag and pulled out a hunk of bread and some hard cheese, which he divided between Audrey and Alette. "You may eat this on the way."

CHAPTER NINE

THE JOURNEY RESUMES

Alette

Alette tore into her food hungrily and Audrey broke hers in half to share with Ribston. They picked up their bags and prepared to leave the clearing.

"Who is this?" said Maneo, gesturing to the orch as if noticing him for the first time.

Ribston thrust his hand out towards the sorcerer. "Ribston Russet: chief gardenarian."

"He is an orch – an orchard elf," explained Audrey.

"Charmed," said the sorcerer, shaking his hand once again.

"Goodbye, orch. Thank you for whatever part you played in helping the girls."

Ribston fell down on to his knees. "I have nowhere to go. Please, sir, let me accompany you and I will be a faithful servant. I am speedy, a good climber and handy with my tools." He rattled his tool belt.

The sorcerer helped Ribston back up to his feet and rummaged in his money pouch. "I am afraid there is no place for you on this quest. Here, take these coins and find an inn for a few nights' rest while you decide what to do—"

"No," said Audrey firmly, pushing away Maneo's hand and the bag of coins. "We would have not escaped from that place without Ribston. He acted against his own mistress for us and it was he who planted the seed to free us from the orchard. He will join us. Not as a servant but as a key member of our party."

Maneo moved his head back very slightly in surprise and Alette smiled to herself. She was not sure why Audrey felt so strongly about the small green man but she enjoyed seeing her fighting spirit. Ribston looked from one face to another, looking to see who would have the final word. On this occasion, it appeared to be Audrey. Maneo said no more and began walking to the other side of the clearing. The orch trotted along beside them.

"How far to the farmstead?" asked Alette, through a mouthful of bread.

Maneo shook his head. He explained that they could not go back for the horses.

"The king's men will search for us in every cottage and farm along the way. When the farmer and his wife report that I have been there, as they surely must, then Zelos's men may wait there for our return."

Alette stopped walking. Leave their horses behind? As if they were extra luggage to be dispensed with? "What will Storm think? I have always cared for Storm. He will not understand."

"The horses will be safe where they are. The farmers are kindly folk who will look after them well. One day, in the future, if all goes to plan, we can repay them for their kindness."

Alette put her face in her hands and Audrey put an arm around her. "I feel for you, Alette. I too am sad at the thought of being parted from my own sweet mare."

Alette shrugged her off. Audrey didn't understand – her horse was an old family nag. They didn't have the same connection. Storm had been Alette's best and only friend for the past few years.

Maneo urged them on. "You do understand that this journey

has changed? We can no longer take our time. Zelos's men will be on our tails. They know where we are heading and they will find us before we get there if they can. All our lives are at risk."

"So how will we travel to Essendor?" asked Audrey.

"We will have to continue the rest of the journey on foot," said Maneo.

Alette looked at him, incredulous. "But isn't it miles away?"

"About another sixty miles. But it will be easier that way. We do not have to stick to the main routes on foot and it will be easier to hide if necessary."

Alette pointed back to the orchard. "What are we going to do with the golden tree?"

Maneo raised an eyebrow. "*D*o with it? Absolutely nothing, I'd have thought."

"But it's a golden tree! A magic tree! Who knows where it leads. There could be a whole new world up there past the clouds."

"That will be an adventure for the next traveller then. Perhaps the king's men will be distracted by a spot of giant slaying or a golden goose. We have other things we need to do. Like overthrow an evil king."

"What about the apples, then? *Golden* apples," said Alette.

Maneo shrugged. "Feel free to take one if you want to carry

it, but I for one would not want one weighing down my knapsack for three score miles. Whatever you do, we must make haste."

Maneo headed off down a path which the girls had not yet explored.

Alette tested the weight of her bag, which was heavy with regular apples. "I suppose we could always come back for them one day."

Ribston giggled and whispered to Audrey, "But you are princesses. When you take the throne back, you will have golden crowns, golden dresses and golden carriages. You won't need golden apples!"

"I suppose so," said Audrey.

"Are you really princesses?" asked Ribston gleefully.

"Yes, but we need to keep quiet about it," called Alette. The orch was going to give them away before they had travelled a mile.

Maneo led the way out of the woods. In his search for the girls he had got to know the area very well. The paths were narrow and twisting so they had to walk in single file. Alette and Audrey followed, with Ribston running along behind. He had to take three steps for every one of theirs.

After a few hundred feet, Maneo turned abruptly.

"What is that *irritating* noise?"

There was a distinct buzzing sound that seemed to be following them through the woods. They turned to see Ribston wearing a slightly guilty expression and surrounded by a noisy swarm.

Maneo peered at them. "Are they *bees?*"

Ribston nodded.

"They cannot come with us. This is ridiculous. We are attempting to avoid attention from the king and his spies and you encourage a swarm of *bees* to follow us!"

"I did not encourage them," muttered Ribston. "They come of their own free will."

The sorcerer turned back and continued walking, shaking his head. "Well perhaps you *could* do some encouraging. I would be grateful if you could encourage them to buzz far away from here."

Ribston nodded, then addressed the swarm.

"Gardenarians. You have worked hard and always done as I have bid you but now I tell you this is the end of our journey together. You cannot come on this new adventure with us. You may return to the orchard and await your mistress, or investigate the golden tree, or fly free and find a new orchard, a new hive. You decide."

The bees buzzed around Ribston's head for a moment,

perhaps saying their goodbyes. Then they swarmed off in a black cloud, back in the direction of the orchard.

Ribston wiped a tear from his speckled cheek and carried on behind the girls.

The four trudged silently along, looking down to avoid stumbling on uneven ground or tree roots. After a few miles, they stopped for a short rest. Maneo, Alette and Audrey found places to sit and stretched out their legs, circling their feet to ease the aches.

Ribston didn't seem to need to rest like the others. He was fascinated by the trees. He put his hands on them and drew his face close.

"I would have thought that you'd have had your fill of trees," said Maneo.

"But in the orchard there was only one type. Just the apple tree. Not that they were all alike, you understand. They all had their own personalities. But they did look and smell similar. These ones are all different – look at the trunks. Here, the bark has thin grooves and here it is deep fissures. This one is nearly smooth."

"If you like trees so much, did you never think to venture beyond the gate to see what was out there?" said Alette.

"Oh no." The orch shook his head seriously. "The orchard

was my world, you understand. And there was always so much work to do."

He went back to the trees, inhaling deeply.

"What is this one with the smooth bark? It smells glorious. I could stand here all day and breathe in its scent."

Audrey smiled, looking at the slender trunk and green needles. "I think it is a young white pine tree."

"Come and smell it! It is something else – so sweet and refreshing." Audrey ran to join him. They circled their arms around the tree and sniffed together.

"The smell of the pine is produced by chemicals. A mixture of hydrogen and carbon," said Maneo.

"Mmmm, it's like mountaintops and winter festivals," said Audrey.

"As if you've ever been to a mountaintop." Alette couldn't believe that half their party was sniffing trees. Yet a little bit of her wanted to join them. To giggle and be free.

"Shhh," said Audrey suddenly. There was a rustle in the bushes. They all looked in the direction of the sound and saw the distinctive black-and-white coat of a badger. Soon he ran off in the other direction.

"Unusual to see a badger at this time," commented Maneo.

"They are normally nocturnal. Anyway, we had better continue on our way before we get too comfortable here. We could do with covering another few miles before nightfall."

The journey became dispiriting, because one part of the forest looked much the same as any other. It created the impression of walking for hours but not actually travelling anywhere. At one point a young muntjac deer stood across their path. It stopped and looked at them with big eyes, as if caught doing something wrong.

"Don't worry – we won't hurt you," said Audrey, reaching out a hand. The deer stayed where it was for a second, before bolting into the trees.

Alette laughed and shook her head. "I have never seen so many woodland creatures. They seem drawn to you, Audrey. What do you do – charm them from the woods?"

Maneo appeared to consider this. "It is a skill. Power over nature. Your mother had the same traits, of course."

Alette said nothing. This was a rare mention of her mother. She longed to hear more but Maneo offered nothing further and she did not want to ask, so they carried on walking in silence.

Some hours passed in this fashion, with minimal conversation and little change in the scenery. Just trees, ferns, very little light and a slow, uphill trudge.

Then, up ahead of them was an opening in the trees, with sunlight flooding through and an expanse of blue sky.

They picked up speed to see where the opening led, and the view made them all catch their breath. They were high up, looking down into a deep valley with a wide river at the bottom.

On the other side of the river was a stretch of green grass and then a sharp rise to rocky cliffs and some wooded hills. Beyond the hills were green fields and more hills. And beyond those – who knew?

They were so high up that they could look down on the buzzards swooping beneath them. The cold, peaty smell of the forest had disappeared, replaced with the ripe green aroma of fresh air.

They stood there for a moment, breathing it in.

"I did not know that the world was so big," said Ribston.

"Nor I," said Audrey. "Until this journey, the furthest I'd travelled was to the ironmonger's in the town if Father needed something."

Maneo shielded his eyes from the sun. "If I am correct, then Essendor is in a straight line in that direction – over the hills to the northwest."

Alette stared, as if she might see the castle of Essendor through the impenetrable grey clouds that circled the mountaintops. But she saw nothing. Her legs ached, her feet were blistered and her joints were stiff from sleeping under the stars last night. This journey was beginning to feel impossible.

Audrey seemed to be feeling the same. "If Essendor is in a straight line *that* way, then how will we cross the valley?"

Maneo took off his hat and fanned himself. The day was hot and they had been walking at a brisk pace. He looked down to the river – one way and then the other. There didn't seem to be any narrowing in either direction. "I suggest that the best way for us to travel is down. If we make our way to the riverbank then we may find a ferryman or someone willing to rent us a boat. If not, we could always build a raft or swim across."

Audrey looked at her shoes. "I am unable to swim," she muttered.

Alette threw up her hands in exasperation. "Of course! Why should a baker's daughter have ever learned to swim?" She sat on the ground with a thump and drew her knees up to her chest. "Anyway, once we get down there, we have to get up the other side again. That could add another whole day to our journey time."

"Better than carrying along in this direction – we may never find a way across," said Maneo.

Ribston was exploring a little way down the hillside. Now he stopped and shouted up to the others, "Oh look – there's a bridge."

THE TOLL TROLL
Audrey

They scrambled down the dusty bank and looked at the bridge Ribston was pointing to.

It stretched from one side of the valley to the other across its narrowest part – a distance of thirty yards or more. It was constructed of wooden planks and rope handrails. Despite swaying gently in the wind, it looked reasonably sturdy and in good repair.

Maneo smiled an unusually broad smile. "Well, this is good news. We can be across this valley and over the peak of that hill by sunset."

Alette clapped her hands together and Ribston puffed out his chest, pleased to have been the one to make the discovery. Audrey put on a brave smile. She was not keen on heights and looking at the bridge made her stomach lurch, but she didn't want to share this with her sister – Alette already thought her weak and foolish. Audrey prepared for the crossing in her mind. If she held on to the ropes on either side and didn't look down, she would survive the experience. She had recently scaled an enormous tree, after all!

They drew closer. Sitting near the end of the bridge was a large green creature, as tall and wide as two large-sized men. He wore a tattered sleeveless shirt that displayed his wide shoulders and tree-trunk arms, and he was holding a huge, glistening, olive-coloured fish that flapped its tail occasionally.

"What is that creature?" asked Audrey.

Maneo peered in the direction of the bridge. "I'm no expert but I'm pretty sure from the colour that it's a tench. It's similar in shape to a carp but carp are always brown or bronze, I think—"

"No, not the fish! The big ugly creature holding the fish!" said Alette.

"Oh, him. He's just a toll troll. Zelos has posted them on just about every bridge in the kingdom. They always get a bit overexcited about their job, you know the type. A little bit of responsibility goes to their heads."

The troll bent his head down and bit off the fish's head with one giant bite. Blood ran down his chin and he wiped it off with the back of his hand.

He looked up as they approached. "Here they come, I see them now! Thinking they are going to TRIP-TRAP over my bridge. Save themselves a journey! Yes, my bridge is good for that. You will save about two days walking if you cross over here. But it doesn't come for free. No, ho, ho! NOTHING comes for free!" The troll crunched on the remainder of the fish: scales, bones, tail and all.

"See what I mean?" said Maneo. "Maybe I should try out my new crushing spell."

Audrey shuddered. "Crushing? That sounds rather cruel."

"A freezing spell then."

"Can't we just pay the toll?" said Alette. "I know we have a finite number of coins, but doesn't this count as a necessary outgoing?"

Maneo sighed. "If only it was easy as that. But the toll is never as straightforward as a couple of silver coins. There is always some riddle or task. You'll see, it's a real bore."

"I think it sounds fun," said Audrey.

As they grew nearer, they could smell the troll – a smell of week-old fish. When he spoke, the tench stench was even worse. "Halt, travellers! Do not put a foot on the Bridge of Bartholomew."

Alette laughed. "Bridge of Bartholomew? Isn't it a rather small bridge to have such a grand name?"

The troll crossed his arms over his chest and raised his voice. "It is a BRIDGE, as you see, and BARTHOLOMEW is my name. It is MY bridge. We can call it the Bridge of Not Yours if you prefer. Because it is NOT YOUR bridge. You may only cross if it is acceptable to ME. And it isn't."

Alette opened her mouth to say something but Audrey put her hand on her arm. She had already learned that although her sister was brave and strong, she – Audrey – was the more diplomatic. "I think that the Bridge of Bartholomew is a lovely name, don't you, Ribston?" Ribston nodded his agreement. "In fact, we would love to cross your bridge . . . sir . . . if you would be so kind as to let us."

The troll puffed out his chest at Audrey's use of the word "sir". "Perhaps we could come to some arrangement."

Audrey nodded and smiled. The troll also nodded and smiled. "You choose. Do you want to PAY or PLAY?"

"See?" muttered Maneo. "It is never straightforward."

But Audrey was listening intently. "Pay or play?"

"You may PAY the toll or PLAY my game! Come on now, tell me – are you going to PAY or PLAY?"

Audrey smiled again. "That sounds rather fun. I suppose we'll play!"

The sorcerer sighed. "Bad choice."

The troll rubbed his hands together. "The game involves three riddles. Get them right and you earn the right to cross my bridge."

Maneo sat on a rock and rested his chin on his hand. "I told you! Three riddles! We may well be here all afternoon."

"Oh. We can pay, then, if you prefer?" said Audrey, consulting the rest of the party.

The troll shook his head and stood up straight. "No, the girl already decided. Play, she said. PLAY it is. Now pay attention: I will say each riddle just once! No repeats! Are you ready?"

"Hang on," said Alette. "If we get them right, we cross the bridge. What about if we get them wrong?"

"Then you have to go round the long way. Or I throw you in the river." He bent down, picked up a rock and hurled it into the valley to illustrate his point. Audrey heard the distant plop as the rock met the water.

"Which is it?" squeaked Ribston nervously. "Throw us in or let us go round the long way?"

The troll waved his hand dismissively. "We'll see how I feel. Now LISTEN very carefully to the first riddle…"

The troll adopted a new, formal voice, to read the riddle aloud.

My first is in green but not in red,
My second's in grow but never in bed,
My third is in lawn but not in mow,
My fourth is in seed and also in sow,
My fifth is in shower and also in hose,
Find me in the meadow (look under your toes).

"Grass!" said Ribston. "So easy! You are asking a gardenarian a question about something that grows!"

The troll narrowed his eyes. "You are correct. I always start with the easiest riddle. More fun that way."

Ribston looked around for approval.

"Yes, well done, Ribston," said Audrey, "but next time try not to blurt out the answer. We should all agree together first."

The troll looked stern. "Now for the next one. Listening, everyone? Here we go.

Each one appears from the ground with a pop!
And they nibble away on the lush hilltop.
One hears a bang and he thumps. They all stop.
Then his friends all depart with a
Hop, hop, hop.
Who am I?

Ribston giggled. "Who are you? Who are you? You may as well have said what has a bobtail and lives in a burrow! The answer is—"

Audrey clapped her hand over Ribston's mouth. "We need to discuss each question, remember? What does everyone else think?"

"I think rabbit," said Alette in a monotone.

"I wasn't listening but I agree with Alette," said the sorcerer from his rock.

"I am also in agreement," said Audrey. "Ribston?"

Ribston nodded.

Audrey smiled. "Then it's unanimous. Toll troll, is the answer to your question . . . rabbit?"

The troll pursed his lips. "Yes, it is."

Ribston clutched his stomach and rolled around laughing on the grassy bank. "Such easy riddles! So, so easy!"

The troll stood over Ribston, shaking his head. "So my riddles are too easy for you, are they? Want a harder one, do you? Well then, hear this: your party may cross the bridge, but only in the correct order! Get it right, and you can carry on your way without paying a penny. Get it wrong, and the bridge will move away beneath your feet and you will be swept away! Hahahaha!"

The troll rubbed his hands together, laughing nastily.

Alette looked unimpressed. "It is quite a small bridge over quite a small river. I very much doubt that we would be washed away anywhere. We would probably just get damp feet." Audrey wondered if Alette felt as brave as she looked, because this didn't have the ring of truth about it. To Audrey, it looked like quite a long bridge, which was very high up over a very cold-looking river, and if they fell in they would quite possibly die.

The troll turned his back to them. "So be it! Then you are free to risk it!"

Audrey put a hand on Alette's upper arm. "Come on, let's try to figure it out." To the troll she said, "How will we know the correct order?"

"Ahaha! Yes! That is a very good question. How will you know? How indeed? You must listen closely to me.

First the smallest,

Then the greenest.

Third the tallest,

Then the keenest.

"Hahaha! What do you think? Easy, isn't it! I give you two minutes to discuss it between yourselves."

Alette yawned. "This one does sound easy, too. Ribston is clearly the greenest."

The orch looked affronted. "Green? I am not green! Not like that horrible troll. I would say I was a light shade of sage with red undertones."

"Yes, but you are still the green-*est*," said Alette. "Unless you want to send the troll over the bridge with us."

"No thanks," said the orch.

"But it can't be Ribston," said Audrey. "He is definitely the smallest, so he goes first. No doubt about that. But how can he be the greenest and the smallest?"

The troll giggled maliciously. "Easy, isn't it? One minute left to decide!"

Maneo joined in now. "Remember that these sorts of riddles always require some lateral thought. What else can the word green mean, if we are not thinking about colour alone?"

"Envy?" said Audrey. "Is anyone here jealous of anyone or anything?"

"Or innocence? Naivety?" said Alette.

Maneo nodded. "So now who is the greenest in our party?"

"Ribston again?" said Audrey.

"No, you of course, Audrey! You are like a fresh green shoot that has just pushed its way out into the world," said Alette. Audrey looked faintly surprised as Alette pushed them into place. "Ribston first, then Audrey. But who is taller out of you and I?" Alette looked Maneo right in the eyes. They appeared to be exactly the same height.

Ribston looked from one to the other. "You should take off your hat, Maneo, and Alette, flatten down your hair. Now stand back to back."

They did as they were told but there still didn't appear to be any difference.

"I suppose we'll just have to decide who is the keenest. But keenest at what?" said Alette.

"Keenest vision? Or perhaps keenest to achieve our goal? For both of those it would be you, wouldn't it, Alette?" said Audrey, panicking now as they were surely running out of time.

"Time up!" shrieked the troll. He laughed. "Easy, was it? The easiest riddle yet? Is this the order in which you plan to cross the bridge?"

They stood lined up – Ribston, Audrey, Maneo and then Alette.

"Yes. Is it correct?" asked Audrey, her stomach churning.

"We will have to see, won't we?"

"How do you even know the answer yourself?" asked Alette. "You can't possibly know which of us is keenest."

"You're right, lady! An old troll like me doesn't know the answers to these questions. But I don't have to know! There is magic all around us here. The questions and the answers come from the bridge itself. The bridge never lies!"

Alette threw her hands up. "The bridge never lies? What's it going to do – collapse and send us plummeting into the river? You'd have to build a new bridge then, which I'm sure you wouldn't want to do. No, I think we're going to survive this crossing. Come on, people; in the order we agreed."

They all took a few more steps towards the bridge. The talk of collapse and plummeting was making Audrey feel a lot less confident, but she didn't want to share this feeling with the others. They already thought she was "green" and inexperienced in the world. One glance at Ribston told her he was feeling the same way. She smiled at him. "It will a perfectly safe crossing," she told him. "Keep your chin up and your eyes on the path ahead. Whatever you do, don't look down."

Ribston nodded, gulped and stepped gingerly on to the first wooden slat. He looked back briefly and Audrey gave him a reassuring look. She wished that she could heed her own advice – she kept sneaking peeks at the valley below.

When the time came to step on to the bridge, Audrey tried to ignore the voice in her head telling her to stay on firm land. She urged herself on, telling herself just to put one foot, and then the other, on to the wobbly crossing. Her head swam as her feet found themselves on such an unreliable walkway. She looked to the solid ground at the other end of the bridge. How many wooden slats lay between her and the other side? Perhaps a hundred. She counted them off as she walked, avoiding the gaps. Four ... five ... six...

The troll laughed to himself. "First the smallest, then the greenest. Keep walking, oh green one! Who can be next? Ho ho ho!"

Maneo stepped calmly on to the bridge and then Alette leapt on behind him, making the bridge sway violently from side to side. Ribston lost his balance and cried out. Audrey gripped the rough rope handrails so tightly that the skin on her hands burned.

"Ho ho ho!" laughed the troll again. "That one at the back is keen. The girl with the mark on her face. But is she keen enough?"

There was a *clang*. Audrey turned to see the troll shut a heavy gate across the entrance to the bridge and lock it with a large iron key. Her heart beat quicker. Why had he locked them in? And why was he laughing so much? She looked ahead. Ribston had recovered from his shaky moment and was nearly at the other side. She had perhaps twenty more slats to go. Then, there was a rattling noise and a low rumble. The wooden slats of the bridge suddenly began to rattle alarmingly, as if they were not properly attached.

At the far side of the bridge, a slat fell open like a trapdoor, creating a gap which led straight to the valley below.

Ribston was in the process of stepping on to that plank. His foot shot through into nothingness and he shrieked. Audrey forgot all about treading cautiously and rushed to help him. Ribston lay on his front, his hands scrabbling at the ground at the end of the bridge, one leg dangling over the river.

Audrey grabbed him under the armpits and lifted him up and

out of his predicament. He was lighter than the little girl that she had swung around at the Harvest Dance.

"Careful, I bruise easily!" he said, but he looked relieved to be safe.

As the troll's laughter echoed across the valley, they stepped together over the gap and on to the firm ground on the other side of the bridge.

"How did that happen? What's going on?" said Audrey. She peered across to see what the troll was doing. There was a handle to one side of the gate, which the troll was turning slowly towards him as if he were putting clothes through a mangle.

"Wrong order! You were right about the smallest and right about the greenest but wrong about the tallest and wrong about the keenest!"

As he turned the handle, more slats on the bridge flapped down in a seemingly random order. Alette and Maneo were not even a third of the way across.

"The bridge says that Alette is one sixteenth of an inch taller than the sorcerer. And Maneo, why, I have never seen a man keener to complete a mission. Can the rest of you not see it in his eyes?" The troll laughed again. "Of course, it is of no consequence now, because you are all going to DIE!"

THE WRONG ORDER
Alette

Maneo lifted his wand and pointed towards the troll. "Stop it! Stop this at once you despicable troll, or I shall—"

A gap opened up below Maneo and he fell through as Ribston had done, with one leg dangling and the other twisted awkwardly behind him. He had to hold on to the slats either side to stop himself slipping further.

"Do finish your sentence, sorcerer. You shall ... what exactly? Cast a spell on me? Doesn't look like your wand arm is free!"

But the troll was so busy mocking Maneo that he forgot to watch Alette. She managed to turn around and lay on her stomach, stretching out her arm as far as it possible. It just reached Maneo's wand. He wiggled his fingers gently, edging it towards her. For a second, neither of them were touching the wand and Alette briefly pictured the wand rolling off the bridge and down into the emptiness below. But she managed to grasp it and point it at the troll, muttering one of the only incantations she knew by heart. A lifting spell. She had practised this charm over and over again, sitting at the kitchen table with Maneo.

Lifting and dropping apples, books, cutlery, but never trolls. Until now.

The troll was still closely watching the sorcerer. As he began to rise up towards the sky, Alette couldn't help but laugh at the look of bafflement on his face. He looked rapidly left and right and then up and down, waggling his arms and legs in an effort to stay on the ground.

"Heeeelp!" he cried. From his heightened position, he saw that Alette was in control. "Put me down!" he cried. "Stop this spell and I will set you all free. You can have my gold."

But Alette lifted him right over the iron gate so that he was hanging over the valley. She released him. He tumbled down, like a giant apple falling from a tree, then splashed into the river.

It was too far away to tell if the troll sank or swam, but they didn't spend too long trying to figure it out – they were in a tricky situation themselves. Alette and Maneo were stuck on the bridge with the gate locked behind them and huge gaps in front of them that were impossible to cross. And Maneo was still dangling. Alette tried to pull him up but she twisted her arm in the process.

"Try another lifting spell," said Maneo, but Alette shook her head. She was not confident enough in her lifting spells to be able to control exactly where she put people, and she didn't want to send Maneo hurtling in the direction of the river too.

She caught Audrey's eye. Would she be able to help? She had clearly been nervous crossing the bridge, so Alette could hardly expect her now to tightrope-walk to her rescue.

But as Alette watched Audrey's face, she saw something different in her expression. The nervousness seemed to melt away, replaced by a look of determination. Audrey fixed her gaze on Alette and pressed her lips together. She was focusing. Planning something.

Alette hadn't seen that look on Audrey's face before and it took her a little while to figure out what was happening. Alette wasn't sure if it was a trick of the light, but Audrey's skin seemed to be growing darker and her hair lighter. It was only when she fell to her hands and knees and a shimmering horn began to grow from her head that Alette realized what was happening. Audrey was becoming a unicorn. Despite having this power herself, Alette had never witnessed a transformation and had no idea what it looked like.

"She's transforming," gasped Maneo.

Alette couldn't take her eyes off her twin. She had never seen her look so beautiful. Colourful light radiated from her horn like the colours of the opal in her pendant. She lowered her muzzle, snorted softly and turned away from Alette and the bridge, trotting towards the trees.

"Where is she going?" said Maneo.

"She is taking a run-up," said Alette.

When she was a few feet away, Audrey galloped back towards the bridge, head nodding and muscles straining. Her hooves clattered on the first part of the bridge. Then her forelegs rose up and she leaped into the air, her white mane blowing around her and her tail and hindlegs rising up behind her. She easily cleared the gap, which must have been around fifteen feet. She landed next to Alette, who swung herself up on to her sister's back. Maneo was able to grasp her above her fetlocks and pull himself up. Then Maneo too climbed on to Audrey's back and she made the jump once again in the opposite direction, carrying the three of them to safety.

Maneo collapsed on to the ground, rubbing his leg where it had been caught. Ribston looked on open-mouthed, unable to speak. Alette stood in front of Audrey, one hand on top of her muzzle and one below her chin. She leaned in and inhaled the sweet, horsey scent of her fur. Audrey was breathing deeply, recovering from the exertion of the leaps.

"Thank you, sister," said Alette. They were safe.

CHAPTER TEN

THE OTHER SIDE OF THE BRIDGE
Audrey

It took a few minutes for Audrey to turn back into her human form. When she did, she was tired. She didn't know if it was the jump, the excitement, or the transformation itself, but she felt she could curl up and sleep. Maneo handed her a flask of water and she drank gratefully.

Ribston stared at Audrey, as if viewing her in a completely new light. "You were astounding. That jump. The rescue. In all my years in the orchard, I never saw a thing like it."

He looked from Audrey to Alette and back again. "Can you both change into unicorns?"

Alette nodded. "But we have to keep very quiet about our powers," she said. "Nobody knew that our mother was the Midnight Unicorn and I believe she kept it that way for a reason. The more people that know about our powers, the greater the threat to us. There are always those out there who are distrustful of magic."

"Of course, Princess Unicorn," said Ribston. "I mean, Princess Alette. I mean ... Mistress Alette."

Alette rolled her eyes and handed Maneo's wand back to him. "Thank you," he said, placing it inside his cloak. "That was an excellent use of sorcery, Alette. Are you sure I cannot convince you to carry a wand of your own?"

Alette shook her head. "I do not want to be a sorcerer. I only used that spell because it was one I knew and because we were in desperate need."

"No matter. Your own powers are great enough. Speaking of which, why did you not transform yourself? You could have made that leap yourself easily as a unicorn."

"I did not have the strength. My arm hurt, and the spell I used on the troll took the last of my energy."

Maneo put the tips of his fingers together. "Interesting. And you, Audrey? You surprised us all. You managed a transformation with seeming ease despite all you failed efforts in the past. Can you explain this?"

Audrey shook her head. "No. I mean… Yes… I wanted to help my sister and it just . . . happened."

Maneo cleared his throat. "It just happened. I see. Audrey, you need to work on harnessing that power. And Alette, you must make sure you rest and rejuvenate both mentally and physically before we reach the castle."

Audrey looked down into the river. It was difficult to tell from this height how deep it was, and if there was much of a current. "Will the troll survive?" she asked.

"Probably," said Maneo. "They are hardy beasts with skins as thick as any elephant's. Also, they are good swimmers. This beast will probably catch himself a fish supper and then come climbing back up the mountainside."

Alette laughed. "He won't be pleased with us. Do you think he will follow us to get his revenge?"

"I doubt it. Trolls are very lazy creatures and do not have enough brain power to bear grudges for long."

"What about his gold?" said Alette.

"It's on the other side of the bridge."

"We could get it. If Audrey transformed again." Alette stared at her, waiting for an answer, but Audrey didn't say anything for now. She wasn't sure that she would know how to transform again, or if she had the strength to do so.

Luckily, Maneo didn't seem interested in the troll's gold. "It's not worth it. Remember that if this mission is successful, none of us will have to worry about money again."

For a moment, Audrey thought that Alette was going to insist. She was so drawn to adventure, even if it was risky or inadvisable. But then she seemed to change her mind.

"Yes, let us leave it there. It would be tainted. The next weary traveller will be only too pleased to discover it when they reach this place."

"Unless Zelos's men discover it first," said Ribston.

"If Zelos's men are on our tail then at least this broken bridge might slow them down," said Audrey.

Maneo nodded. "But still, we don't want to be seen. Let's get ourselves away from the bridge and into the cover of the trees once more. Are you ready, girls?"

Audrey nodded, in spite of her exhaustion. She wished she had a horse to ride, at least, rather than the endless drag of putting one foot in front of the other. She wouldn't say anything, though. Alette seemed to be pleased with her since the transformation on the bridge, and she didn't want to ruin that. Audrey herself was amazed that she had managed to walk across the bridge, not to mention change into a unicorn. As a unicorn, she hadn't worried about the height of the bridge or the danger of the leap. She hadn't felt like herself. Or, rather, she had felt like a more powerful version of herself. And she still had no idea how she had managed the change.

She hoped that Alette wouldn't ask her any more questions about it, but right now, her sister seemed intent on quizzing Maneo. She walked along beside him, matching his stride.

"Why were you the keenest?"

"What do you mean?"

"Well, we got the order wrong. I was slightly taller and you were keener. But I doubt you are keener than I to confront the murderer of my parents."

"I doubt I am either. It is meaningless. Toll trolls tend to favour games that involve misfortune for their opponent."

"But the troll said that the bridge never lied," chimed in Ribston.

"The troll said a lot of things and most of them were utter

rubbish," replied Maneo. "I think he was the keenest himself. The keenest to see us fall to our deaths."

They soon reached the woods, which looked very similar to those on the other side of the bridge.

"Trees are all very well but I do tire of them after a while," grumbled Alette. "I feel that I never properly see the sun under all this shade. I would prefer to be in an open space where I could run for miles and not encounter a single obstacle."

"I love to be near trees," said Ribston.

The only noise was the occasional animal or bird and Alette crunching on her apple supply from the orchard. Every time she finished an apple, she threw the core into the bushes.

"Just think how many trees there will be if each one of those pips finds fertile ground," said Ribston.

"This is the last one," said Alette eventually, holding up a red, shiny apple. "I have eaten more than my fair share. Would anyone like it?"

They all shook their heads. "As long as I live, I never want to eat another apple," said Audrey.

"Funnily enough, the orchard experience didn't put me off. In fact, I wish I'd taken more for the journey," said Alette, eating the apple herself and throwing the core into the bushes.

From somewhere in the direction that it landed, there came a squeak. Quite a loud, strangled-sounding squeak.

BRAMBLE
Alette

Audrey widened her eyes. "What was that?"

Maneo continued stalking ahead. "There is no time to investigate such trivialities. We need to find another safe and sheltered spot by nightfall. Make haste!"

But Audrey was already stepping into the undergrowth, treading slowly to avoid the stinging nettles. "It sounded like a creature in pain. I couldn't continue on our journey not knowing, could you?"

"Yes, I could," said Maneo.

"I could live my whole life without knowing," said Alette, leaning on a tree.

"I could not," said Ribston loyally. "May I be of assistance?"

"You could help me look. I think it came from over here— Oh!" Audrey bent down and reached into the brambles. She pulled out a white, furry creature the size of a cat but with long floppy ears. A rabbit. It looked stunned. She nestled it gently in the crook of her arms and it didn't move.

"It's a rabbit!" said Ribston. "We sometimes had such creatures visit us in the orchard. But they were browner. And smaller."

Maneo raised an eyebrow. "Small, brown rabbits are quite common. One doesn't normally find large white beasts roaming free. This rabbit, however, was not the creature that made the noise."

"How can you know that?" said Audrey, stroking the animal and placing him back on the forest floor.

"Because rabbits do not squeak."

"What sound do they make?" asked Ribston.

"Rabbits do not make a sound. Apart from the occasional thump of their back feet if a predator is close."

Alette laughed. "How are you an authority on rabbits? Have you been busy pulling them out of hats?"

"I am merely stating a commonly known fact," said Maneo.

Audrey watched the rabbit carefully. "I am sure it is the rabbit that squeaked. I think he is injured."

Alette rolled her eyes as Audrey examined the rabbit more closely.

"The poor thing seems to be dragging one foot. It is at a strange angle. Oh, look, there is a gash in his back leg." She plucked a handful of yellowish green moss from a nearby fallen tree and pressed it against the wound.

"This should staunch the flow of blood," she said.

"How do you know all of these old remedies? Moss for wounds, eating stinging nettles?" said Alette "One would think you had grown up with outlaws in the forest, not at a flour mill."

"Oh, they are things that everyone knows," said Audrey. She took off her apron, folded it in half and, with a few deft knots, fashioned it into a sling, in which she placed the rabbit. "When we settle down for the night I shall tend to his injury."

Maneo looked on incredulously. "The creature is huge. Tell me you do not mean to take it with us?"

"I do," said Audrey.

"Good idea. We can put it in the cooking pot," said Alette. "I love rabbit stew."

Audrey spun around, her eyes flashing with anger. "If you put this animal within three feet of a pot, I shall return to Lullgrove and leave you to complete this quest alone. That is a promise."

Alette laughed at Audrey's spirited response. She had been half-joking about the pot, although she really was fond of rabbit stew. She couldn't help feeling that eating a white rabbit was somehow different.

Maneo sighed. "Such fanciful notions! This is, I suppose, the price of undertaking a quest with two young girls. First an elf and then a pet rabbit! Are you planning to acquire anything else along the way? A fairy in a toadstool house, perhaps?"

Ribston flinched. "I am not just any old elf. I am an orch."

"And I am not the one with fanciful notions. *I* have not been the one acquiring pets. Or anything else for that matter," said Alette.

"No, you just weigh yourself down with a few pounds of apples at any given opportunity."

Alette glared at Maneo. She was annoyed with him for considering her in the same light as her sister, who was scared of the dark and climbing trees and would have her head turned by any endearing animal. Couldn't he see how different they were? She was also slightly annoyed with herself for temporarily feeling sympathetic towards the animal. Of course white rabbits and brown rabbits would taste the same in a stew.

But Maneo seemed to be particularly cantankerous today. For once, she wasn't going to start an argument. But she wasn't going to talk to him either.

Ribston was also quiet. Perhaps he felt usurped in Audrey's affections. She danced ahead, the ten pound woodland animal strapped to her front. She petted him, stroking his back and whispering reassuring words in his long ears as they went.

"I think I will call him Bramble, seeing as I found him in the brambles," said Audrey.

Ribston raced to her side. "A fine name, Princess Audrey."

"Could you please stop calling her Princess Audrey?" said Maneo with a loud sigh.

Audrey wasn't even listening. Her entire attention now seemed to be focused on the rabbit. "He seems to like it when I scratch him here, just between the ears. The fur is extra soft there."

Ribston stroked the rabbit and confirmed that yes, it was very soft fur indeed. Alette and Maneo both declined to find out for themselves. Alette could not understand Audrey's instant devotion. She loved Storm and missed him so much that it ached, but Storm was a horse: a majestic, intelligent horse. Storm had a purpose. He could carry her, or carry her belongings. And he could sense her mood; knew when she was in the mood to gallop fast or go slow; knew when she needed a friend. He would come and drape his heavy head over her left shoulder and let her stroke his nose. What could a rabbit do? At the moment, not even hop.

Yet Audrey was making a ridiculous fuss over a dumb beast. She continued to lavish attention on him for the rest of the day. "We'll get you to a safe place and have you all better before you know it," she crooned. Audrey seemed to draw people (or at least orches and woodland animals) towards her. Was it because she was gentle? Alette didn't seem to have that same quality – at least, she didn't think she did. She hadn't really spent enough time around other people to know.

That evening they made their camp in the woods. They found a spot near a stream that was not too exposed. Alette was not sure what they would do if this quest continued into late autumn and the nights grew cooler.

Alette went to the stream to fill the cooking pot and Audrey came too but she brought her own bowl to fill. She needed water to treat her fluffy patient. She took the basin back to the clearing, unwrapped Bramble from the apron and lay him on the ground. She ripped one half of the apron into rags, which she dipped in water. She removed the bloodied moss from the wound and used the wet rags to clean it.

"It still looks bad. What can I do with a broken leg?"

Maneo was consulting his map, running a finger along it. "The best thing would be to put the creature out of its misery," he said without looking up.

"That can't be true," said Audrey. "What would you say if Alette or I had broken a leg?"

Maneo sighed. "I suppose I would fashion some kind of splint."

"Would you not cast a healing spell?" asked Audrey.

Alette laughed. "His wand cannot heal. It can transform or shift or restore but not heal."

"That is untrue," said Maneo. "Healing magic is a possibility but it requires a certain type of energy that renders the sorcerer weak. Essentially it requires the energy of the spell-giver to transfer to the spell-receiver. In most cases, there is little to gain from that. Instead, I would bind up the leg with some sort of support in the hope that the bone fused together."

"Then that is what I shall do." Audrey stalked off into the trees to find something suitable to use as a splint. "Nobody touch the rabbit," she ordered.

Alette stirred the pot. Supplies were getting low but she still had some dried beans and bacon that would make a flavoursome soup. After a few moments, the trees rustled near where Audrey had gone seeking her splint. She glanced up. At first, when she saw the sleek black fur on the creature's legs she thought it was Storm. He had come to find her. Then she saw the white mane and horn, and dropped her spoon in the cooking pot. It was Audrey, in her unicorn form.

Audrey whinnied and gently blew air through her nostrils, then nodded in Alette's direction. Alette nodded back. She preferred her sister when she was a unicorn. She didn't feel anger or annoyance as she did sometimes when they were in their human state. Her feelings were uncomplicated, like they were with Storm. Now, when Alette looked at her, she had the urge to run – to run through the fields together. That seemed to be how they communicated best.

But Audrey didn't look as though she wanted to run anywhere. She walked slowly out from the trees, tail swishing, and made her way over to where Bramble lay. She bent her head, and for a second she thought that Audrey was going to use her nose to nuzzle Bramble, in the way that Storm sometimes did with her. But Audrey lowered her head further and Alette realized she was dipping her horn into the water bowl. A gentle light shone from the bowl as if it were reflecting back a strong shaft of sunlight. Then Audrey raised her head, turned, and walked back towards the trees, tail still swinging rhythmically.

Alette used a second spoon to lift the first from the stew but splashed her arm with the hot liquid. "Ouch!" she cried. It burned. She walked over to the water bowl that Audrey had touched. Maneo, too, folded his map and came to investigate.

Alette dipped a finger into the water, which was still gently glowing, and rubbed the water on to her scalded arm. The three red marks faded to pink and disappeared, along with the pain. She showed her arm to Maneo.

"I think Audrey has made a healing potion," said Ribston.

Maneo nodded and Audrey walked out from the trees in human form. "Does it work?" she asked, in the voice of a concerned parent.

"I think so," said Alette.

Audrey knelt by Bramble. She dipped a rag in the potion and wiped it across the damaged area. The blood cleared magically from the matted white fur, and the wound shrank. She took a fresh rag, dipping it and winding it tightly around Bramble's leg. "A broken bone might take longer to heal," she said.

Finally, she tucked a blanket around Bramble as if he were a baby. "There."

Alette stared at Audrey. "What happened in the trees?"

"I don't know," said Audrey. "I found a small piece of tree

bark that seemed the right size and shape for Bramble's back leg." She stopped.

"Go on," said Maneo.

"I'm not sure if I can properly explain. It was almost as if I thought, or knew, that there was a better way. And then I felt tingling in my legs and they began to lengthen. This time I knew what was happening – that I was changing – and I knew that I could heal Bramble."

"Most interesting," said Maneo. "That is the second time you successfully managed to transform. And yet it seems it is still not a conscious decision on your part. Are you beginning to understand your power? Is it something that you might be able to harness, so that you can change at will?"

"I think I am understanding it a little better." Audrey lowered her eyes.

"And...?"

"Well, it seems to be linked to what I am feeling. That is, more than what I am trying to think. I can tell myself to change over and over again, but I have to feel it to make it happen."

"That is exactly what I told you," said Alette. "I change when I am feeling anger. So when I need to transform, I have to make myself feel angry."

"Yes, it is just as you said. I am working on it."

Maneo leaned forward and cleared his throat. "So something about this ... furry creature enabled you to change into your unicorn form?"

"Yes, I wanted to help Bramble. It was the same on the bridge. When I saw Alette over the other side, so helpless—"

"Helpless? I don't think I was quite helpless—"

"Well, in danger then. When I saw my sister in danger, I wanted to make her safe. I suppose it was a kind of rage, as Alette described, but not like one I'd ever felt before."

Alette was not sure what she thought of this news. She had desperately wanted Audrey to take control of her power, so that they could be stronger together, but now that she seemed to be doing just that, Alette didn't feel happy. Her sister seemed to have different powers to her own – Alette had never healed anyone. And Maneo seemed so impressed and excited by Audrey. He never questioned Alette about her time as a unicorn.

She pointed to Bramble, who was hopping very slowly in a circle in a circle around Audrey. "The healing seems to have done the trick."

"Oh, his leg is better! He's not dragging it any more," said Audrey happily.

As if in response, Bramble hopped faster. This was the first time they had seen him move at speed and they all laughed at how quickly he ran. His fluffy tail bobbed up and down comically and he zigzagged his way into the undergrowth. Then he was gone.

Alette raised her eyebrows. "Well, that's the last we'll see of your rabbit, I'm afraid, Audrey. All that attention you gave him and not even a nose-twitch of thanks. Are you glad you carried him for nine miles now?"

Audrey looked at the place in the bushes where he had dived in. Her voice was low. "I suppose if he's happy then I don't mind where he goes. Maybe he will find some others of his kind. Oh, he's back!"

Bramble shot out of the undergrowth once again and sprang into the air, twisting his back legs behind him.

"He is dancing a jig," cried Ribston.

Maneo shook his head. "No, this is quite usual rabbit behaviour. They do it when they are relaxed and content."

Alette raised her eyebrows. "More interesting rabbit facts."

Bramble hopped back over to Audrey and she stroked him between the ears, just as he liked. "You can stay with us for as long as you like, Bramble."

THE VIEW FROM THE HILL
Audrey

After a good night's sleep, they set off again.

There was a low mist this morning. It hung around them and muted the autumn colours of the leaves. Unlike Alette, Audrey loved trees, but even she found this unending woodland suffocating. At least it had been colourful before. Now everything had a blue-grey tinge and the long tree trunks were black and foreboding. Even the smells of the woods seemed deadened by the cold mist that filled her nostrils. Her feet hurt and her legs ached and they had only been walking for an hour. She trudged along, dragging her feet and wishing there was some way of magicking herself to a more interesting location. She would ask Maneo but she could already guess what his answer would be.

Bramble hopped along beside her, sometimes venturing ahead or lolloping into the brambles for a snack, but always returning. The faithful Ribston walked on her other side.

"I feel as though we have been travelling constantly uphill! My legs are burning. Maybe we could have a break?" said Alette.

Nobody replied. There was more silence. More uphill trudging.

Then, after a few minutes, Ribston cried out.

"A ship! I see a ship!"

"A ship? I doubt it, we're about four score miles from the nearest coastline," said Alette.

"But there is a mast and a sail, like those on a ship."

"I don't think so, my dear Ribston," said Audrey, squinting into the distance. She could see white mist and little else.

But the orch must have had keener eyes than the rest of the party, for after they had travelled a few more feet, the others began to make out the same shapes on a distant horizon. Two tall trees leaned together to form an arched frame for their view. Audrey could see why Ribston would think it might be a galleon, especially as the mist gave the impression of things floating. But the mist was gradually lifting and she could tell the view was of a large building on a hill.

Maneo stopped and swung his travelling bag down on to the leafy ground. "That, my friends, is the city of Essendor."

So the city on the hill was real. It had seemed as if they would never reach this place. Now it was a few miles away, emerging before them like a forgotten dream. The mist in the woods lifted higher, swirling around the treetops, and clear shapes revealed themselves: houses, walls, the castle.

Maneo narrowed his eyes, and Audrey wondered what he

was thinking. When did he last look upon Essendor? Was it thirteen years ago, when he left with baby Alette, or had he been back since?

"I thought the journey would take at least another day," said Alette.

"It will," said Maneo. "The city is still miles away. And remember we cannot use the main routes. Now, more than ever, we must be stealthy and avoid detection by Zelos's men. Today, we will descend the hill. Tonight, we will sleep by the river. Tomorrow, we will cross the river to the castle."

Alette sighed in response. Audrey couldn't tell if the sight of the city excited Alette or made her nervous. To Audrey, Essendor looked exactly as she knew it would: just as she had modelled it on the bread. No wonder her mother had fainted. The pointed turrets of the castle, the twisting stone steps. It felt like looking at a picture of home, which was strange, as she had never set eyes on the place before. At least, not since she was a baby.

But something was not quite right.

"There are no flags flying on the turrets."

Maneo looked at her quizzically. "You are correct. There were always red flags flying when your parents were on the throne."

Alette seemed agitated. "I do not recognize anything about it. I may have seen it in a painting or printed picture before but it stirs nothing in me – no sense of recognition."

"That is hardly surprising," said Maneo. "You left this place when you were but two weeks old and have not returned since. That is far too young for any memories to form."

Maybe, thought Audrey, but her memories were rushing in all at once.

Yellow roses. A raven calling. Danger.

Even Bramble seemed moved by the sight. He hopped close to Audrey and put his paws on her legs, above her knees, almost as if he were seeking reassurance. Was he scared? She picked him up and stroked him.

Ribston shook his head slowly. "Never have I seen such a beautiful place. You are telling me that there is a person living in each one of those pretty little buildings?"

"Not just a person but whole families. Families sitting around fires on this chilly morning. Families telling stories. Families enjoying time together," said Audrey.

"And even in the big building itself?"

"The castle, yes."

"Well. What a place," declared Ribston. "I see now how

wrong it is for a bad soul to rule this city. This city's ruler should have integrity and honour. I feel it in my core."

They began climbing down the other side of the hill, and the castle disappeared from sight once again. Audrey had the feeling that it had all been a dream, brought about by some magic in the mist. If they could not see Essendor, then she could not really be sure it existed.

The hill was steep. In some parts they could walk steadily downhill; in others they were practically sliding down. Audrey's knees hurt and her leather slippers were ruined. They stuck closely to trees and bushes in an effort to stay hidden and there was not much conversation. It was a long day.

That night, at the bottom of the hill, they made their camp some distance from the river. They were close enough to access water but far enough to remain under the protection of the trees.

They ate a basic meal, then settled down in shelters constructed from sticks and blankets. Maneo explained that they would discuss the last part of the plan in the morning. There was no need to worry; he had it all organized. Maneo had his own shelter on one side of the fire and the girls shared a shelter on the other side. Ribston slept as he always did, up in the comfort of the trees.

Audrey and Alette lay down comfortably with less than an arm's width between them. As Audrey drifted off to sleep she remembered how she felt that first night in the barn. How strange it had felt then to be making a bed out in the open. But now it was starting to feel almost normal. The noises of the night didn't bother her – not the owls or even the distant wolves. She knew that she would sleep soundly all night if it weren't for their proximity to Essendor, which made her feel nervous. She hoped Zelos's men were not lurking in the bushes waiting for a quiet moment to attack.

As a result, she didn't fully relax, but still managed to get a couple of hours sleep before she was disturbed. Alette woke her, jiggling her shoulder and whispering in her ear. "What's that sound?"

Audrey listened. The sound came quickly. A regular thumping,

Thump, thump, thump.

And again,

Thump, thump, thump.

Whatever was making the sound was very close indeed.

The girls listened for a couple of minutes and then, as Audrey fully awoke, she realized where it was coming from.

"It's Bramble! He is thumping his big back feet on the ground."

Alette lay back on her bed. "Is that all? That rabbit is a

pest! Can you not quieten him? Stroke him or whatever it is that you do?"

"You don't understand. Rabbits thump if they are scared of something or someone. Maneo told us, don't you remember?"

"I can't say that I do."

"Well, there must be a predator on the prowl. Bramble is trying to warn us. What shall we do?"

"I'll go out to see what's bothering him. It's probably a fox." Alette stepped out into the night, her blanket around her shoulders. Audrey thought she should probably go with her, but the thought of something lurking yards away made her shudder. She may have been happy with the sound of distant wolves, but she did not want to encounter one up close. Still, she leaned half out of the shelter and watched Alette. If her sister needed her then she would be at her side in seconds.

Alette broke a long stick off the shelter and lit it using the smouldering embers of the fire. Audrey couldn't be sure if this was so that she could see better, or to fend off wild beasts that might be lurking. Wolves, perhaps, or trolls. For some reason, a clear image appeared in her mind: the toll troll biting the head off that fish yesterday. The blood dripping down his chin. She shuddered.

Then Alette laughed. Audrey jumped at the unexpected sound and looked to see the source of her sister's laughter. Not wolves or trolls at all. It was a squirrel and a tiny grey mouse. They were both pictures of perfect innocence with eyes that looked too big for their tiny heads. Both animals seemed stunned by the unexpected light of Alette's torch. They looked around in a panic, then glanced at each other and scuttled in opposite directions.

Audrey ventured fully out of the shelter, as Alette continued laughing. "I can't believe it. The woodland creatures follow you even when you are asleep, Audrey! They probably dance around outside the window of the bakery to ensure you have sweet dreams!"

Audrey smiled in the firelight. This was actually quite a comforting thought.

Alette raised her voice and called into the undergrowth. "As for you, Bramble, next time you decide to warn us of predators, please make sure they are larger than you!"

A thump came in response. The girls had no way of telling if it was an annoyed thump, an apologetic thump, or if he was still concerned about the predators. As the girls made their way back to their makeshift beds, something cracked. A stick or twig, a few yards away in the darkness. They looked up, alert once again. Was it another innocent animal? It had sounded like the sort of sound made by a large creature. Before they had a chance to investigate, a half shout, half scream, like a war cry, broke the air. Bushes rustled, sticks cracked and someone burst into the clearing.

A man. He ran to the fireside. Like Alette, he was carrying a flaming torch, which he brandished wildly.

"Spies! Cowardly spies! Be gone!"

Audrey didn't know whether to run or fight. She looked to Alette, who instantly adopted a defensive pose, the torch held before her like a sword. "Get back or you will be sorry!"

The man stepped back, raising his hands in a position of surrender, but surprisingly he didn't seem particularly interested in them. He was looking around for something – or someone – else.

Audrey assessed him. He wore simple peasant's clothes – a loose tunic and trousers. And a leather thong around his neck that was hung with different items: feathers, seed pods and a whistle. He had kind eyes and a full beard. He didn't look like someone who meant to kill them in their beds.

Alette ignored his kind eyes and thrust her torch close to his chin. Audrey hoped she wouldn't set his beard on fire. "We are not spies, stranger! But what of you? Who are you to attack a camp of innocent travellers?"

Alette's voice rang out in the silence of the night. How could she be sure that there were not ten more men hiding in the darkness?

The man was still looking around. "You don't understand—" he started to say in a low voice, but he was interrupted. Something fell on to him from above. In the dim firelight it was hard to see what was happening but the man's face was partly obscured. He shouted, "Get off! Get off!" as flames burst up around his feet. He must have dropped his torch in the dry leaves.

Audrey saw then that it was Ribston who clung to the man's back and shoulders, hands around his neck. He must have jumped down from his tree on to the man.

Alette took the blanket from around her shoulders and beat it on the ground, attacking the fire. Then Maneo was at her side, muttering magic words and pointing his wand at the dying flames, which fizzled away instantly.

Alette swung around to face him. "Where have you been? I thought you were going to leave us to fight alone."

Maneo sighed. "I was watching and waiting, Alette. As I have explained before, patience and planning are often the only tools you need to win the battle. Now, orch, leave that man alone." Ribston slid from his back and the man glanced down at his three-foot tall attacker. Strangely, a little bird flew to the man's shoulder and settled there, cocking its head this way and that.

Maneo eyed the man suspiciously and kept his wand trained directly on him. "Why do you call us spies, stranger? We are merely travellers on our way to Essendor. We are down on our luck and hope to find work in the city."

The man rubbed his hands over his face and sighed. Audrey could see that he was actually quite a young man, although his beard made him look older.

"I was not accusing you of being spies. I was tracking two others – who have been lurking in these woods for some time – but they will be far away by now."

"We did not see anyone," said Alette, looking around her.

"You did. You stared right at them and scared them away."

Alette shook her head. "You are mistaken."

The man shrugged. "Have it your way."

"No – explain further. Who are you and what did you mean by this?" asked Maneo.

"I do not need to tell you anything," said the man. "You lie about your own identity. Why should I reveal mine?"

Maneo narrowed his eyes. "What makes you think we are lying?"

"Because I know who you are. We met before, not far from here. I was young, but I never forget a face. Or a hat. It is a raven's feather, I believe?" He glanced over at Alette and Audrey. "And I can guess who you are."

The man reached into a leather pouch hung from his belt and pulled out an old coin, which he handed to Maneo. Maneo took the coin and turned it over. It was a thick, hand-struck coin with a unicorn's head on one side and a square punch mark on the other. He nodded slowly and scrutinized the man. "One of Queen Bia's coins. I gave one to a child, I remember. You must be the boy... the Boy River?"

"The very same."

CHAPTER ELEVEN

THE BOY RIVER

Alette

Audrey, Alette and Ribston all looked at one another and shrugged. Who an earth was the Boy River?

Maneo passed the coin through his fingers, turning it over and over. "You did not spend this. Why?"

"I was a poor child. I thought that people would wonder how I had come by it. They would think it stolen, probably. So I kept it. For a time, I hid it in a magpie's nest. She enjoyed looking after it. Then I kept it on my person. Under the reign of Zelos, times grew difficult. My family were hit hard by Zelos's harsh taxes. My mother did her best but we were still hungry. I lost a sister to tuberculosis. Still, I didn't see how I could spend a coin like this without drawing attention to myself. I would be accused, I knew it. And the gold would probably end up in Zelos's pocket. He is like a magnet for gold."

River gently took the coin back from Maneo, polished it on his tunic. "This coin felt like my only link with the past. My childhood, when things were happy and carefree."

He put the coin back in the pouch.

Maneo lowered his wand. "Then we are friends."

"I have no friends apart from those animals that choose to join me in the forest." The little bird on his shoulder chittered in response.

"But perhaps we share an enemy."

"Perhaps."

Maneo used his wand to strike up new flames on the smouldering embers. They all stared at one another in the firelight. Alette wondered why the stranger was known as "the Boy River" when he was nearer a man than a boy. She wondered about the strange assortment of things he had strung around his neck and about the wild bird that seemed to belong to him.

Ribston was also staring at the Boy River. He bowed low.

"My apologies for assaulting you. When you ran into our camp I could only think that you meant the princesses harm."

Alette gave Ribston a sharp look. She had told him before about discussing their royal identity. But River didn't seem surprised. He had obviously correctly guessed who they were. He shrugged. "No harm done."

Maneo beckoned him over to the fireside. "Please, sit with us for a few moments. You can probably guess our mission. We mean to challenge King Zelos, so any information you can give will help us to defeat him and to restore peace to our kingdom."

"It is not my kingdom. I have no kingdom. I answer to nobody but myself."

"But you count King Zelos among your enemies?"

"That man is no king. That man is responsible for the poverty of my family and the death of my sister."

"So please, sit with us. Talk a while. That is all we ask of you."

Audrey stepped forward, unwrapping a cloth bundle. "We have bread."

At that, the Boy River's interest was piqued. He sat down immediately and reached out a hand for a hunk of hard rye bread. From the way he ate, Alette guessed he had not seen bread for a long while. What did he live on out here?

"Who are the spies of whom you speak?" asked Maneo.

River spoke through a large mouthful of bread. "They were here at the camp." He pointed to Alette. "She looked straight at them."

Alette, who was also munching her way through a piece of bread, shook her head. "We thought we heard someone but when we came out of our shelter, we saw only some woodland animals."

"Those were the spies."

"What?"

"There is much you do not know. Zelos is an evil man. And a greedy one." The Boy River turned to Alette. "You look like him. Your uncle."

"Thanks," she said sarcastically. She was fed up of people telling her she looked like her uncle. Did they think she was the bad twin?

River shrugged and continued. "Under his rule, poverty and starvation are rife. Many have turned to crime. Yet the prisons are empty. Instead, he uses his magic to enchant people. His debtors are all around – poor enchanted beasts who will do anything to gain his favour. They will report on enemies, strangers, even friends."

"The squirrel and mouse," gasped Audrey.

River nodded. "Spies. They have been following me for weeks, reporting back to Zelos with my every move. I have no idea what he hopes to learn from my whereabouts. He probably thinks I am planning an attack, whereas I actually have no interest in his city, his kingdom. Now they seem to be transferring their interest to you."

Maneo looked thoughtful. "How do you know this?"

"I know animals. I can tell when they are behaving as they should and when they are not. And Zelos knows this about me."

"Are all his spies disguised as squirrels and mice?"

"No. Many different creatures – a rat, a faun, an otter. One poor soul was even transformed into a spider. I'm not sure he will survive. I feel sorry for them but still, they are not to be trusted and you must be on your guard."

Alette turned to Audrey. It was all coming together. "The badger in the woods. And the muntjac deer, do you remember? We laughed about them but they weren't drawn to you at all! They were spies!"

The Boy River laughed. "I'm afraid that in all likelihood you have not been attracting wildlife out of the woods. It sounds as if Zelos has had a number of men after you. You may be certain that he knows exactly where you are right now and that you are on the path to Essendor. Just as the pike waits in the weeds for its prey to swim closer through the muddy waters, Zelos will be waiting for you. When you reach him, he will attack."

Maneo was silent with his thoughts, stroking his tiny beard. But the girls listened to River's every word. "So what can we do? How can we defeat him if he is prepared for us?" asked Alette.

"You can also be prepared. You can avoid his spies wherever possible, remembering that they could be the size of a gnat on the underside of a leaf. So try to say as little as possible out loud."

"How can we do that?"

"Make one plan now. Agree what you are going to do and then don't discuss it any further. Trick them. Start upon one route and then use another. Lose them however you can. And never forget that Zelos is waiting for you."

"But we do not know the back routes. We rely on maps. Will you take us?" asked Alette enthusiastically. River would be the perfect guide.

He shook his head. "When that man . . . that imposter . . . sat on the throne, I vowed that I would never again set foot inside the city walls of Essendor. It is stolen land, cursed land, and I want no part of it. I stay here, in the woods, where I am free."

Maneo stared hard at him. "The girls are trying to reclaim

what is rightfully theirs. Perhaps you would help us get closer? Do you remember where we last saw each other, thirteen years ago? Do you think you could help us reach that point?"

The Boy River sighed, then nodded slowly. He stretched out on the dry earth. "I will be your guide. The people will be pleased to see you return to Essendor. After the murder of the king and queen, the kingdom was plunged into mourning. For now, go back to your beds. I shall lie here by the fire and alert you if there is any further danger."

Ribston climbed his tree and shouted out goodnights to all. The girls shuffled back towards their shelter, and Maneo nodded his thanks and retired in the opposite direction.

Just as the girls were about to crawl into their shelter, the Boy River called to them. "What we really need . . . what Essendor needs . . . is for the Midnight Unicorn to return."

A glance passed between Audrey and Alette, which the Boy River misread. "The unicorn was real, you know. She saved me from drowning when I was a small one. I would not be sat here in front of you if it were not for that beast. And I remember her too. She had eyes like opals."

Alette nodded. "I believe . . . we believe . . . that if we can free Essendor from Zelos, then the Midnight Unicorn will return."

The Boy River nodded. He stared at them for such a long time that Alette began to wonder quite how much he knew. "If the Midnight Unicorn returns," he said, "then I will come back to Essendor. I will call it my city once again. But only then."

BREAKFAST
Audrey

In the morning, they were all up with the sun. The Boy River picked up a pan and a spear. "I will go and catch us some breakfast. There is nothing like fresh grilled fish to start the day."

"Can I watch?" asked Alette.

"If you like."

Alette raced after him through the trees to the river, and Audrey, Ribston and Bramble followed a little way behind.

At the shoreline, River rolled up both trouser legs. The girls, the orch and the rabbit stood in a row, watching. He turned to them, amused. "I don't normally have an audience. You will have to be quiet."

He waded into the water and stood with the tip of his spear hovering below the waterline. He didn't move. Audrey held her breath. He still didn't move. Not a flicker. He stood for so long that she started to wonder if he was going to do anything at all. Then, he drew the pole very slightly back over his shoulder and thrust it forcefully into the water. It was such a sudden motion that Audrey jumped and grabbed hold of Alette's arm. They all laughed and River withdrew his spear to show them the point. No fish. He adopted the position again and, this time, Audrey was prepared when he jabbed it into the riverbed. And again, and again. On the fifth attempt, when Audrey was beginning to think that this method would never work, River held up his spear triumphantly. A large, silver fish wriggled on the end. Breakfast.

Maneo emerged from the bushes behind them, clapping his hands together slowly. "Now that, people, is how it's done. Such patience."

Audrey wondered exactly what Maneo knew about it. She had never seen the sorcerer exhibit such hunting skill.

The Boy River gutted the fish at the river's edge, the innards slipping out into the water. He put it in the empty pot and they walked back to the fireside together. They all sat in a huddle, quietly discussing their plan for the day, while River scaled the fish with his hunting knife – silver flakes flying all around him – before laying it on two sticks over the smoking embers of the fire. Audrey tried not to think about how the fish had been swimming around in the water minutes earlier. She tried also to get the image of the troll biting into the fish out of her mind. But when she smelled River's catch roasting on the fire, she couldn't help but look forward to the taste. And it did taste good. They sucked the cooked white flesh from the skeleton and Alette threw her fishbones over her shoulder.

"Don't throw them away!" said River. He was collecting his on a maple leaf at his side, Audrey noticed. "I'll grind them up to add to soup another day."

The wren that was once again perched on his shoulder twittered its agreement and everyone laughed. This Boy River was curious in so many ways. "You love animals, don't you?" asked Audrey.

River nodded.

"So how are you able to hunt and kill?"

"I think because…" River chewed thoughtfully. "This fish stood a chance."

Audrey didn't comment any further but she thought she understood and that maybe she felt the same way.

With the fish, they ate more bread. The supply was very nearly at an end but Audrey didn't like to mention this, as she didn't want the Boy River to withdraw his offer of help. Instead, she let him devour as much as he wanted, and share crumbs with the little wren. It was a pet, she supposed, or at least a very tame bird. She would like to know but she didn't like to ask the Boy River too many questions. He seemed like the sort of person who was used to spending time on his own and didn't want to talk for the sake of talking. Like Alette, she supposed. And Maneo. Maybe even like herself, although she would always make pleasant conversation if she thought that those in her company sought it.

The only person who really wanted to talk was Ribston. Right now, he was off in the woods, gathering fresh dandelion leaves and flowers. She would boil them up in the cooking pot and they could wash down the last of their breakfast with hot dandelion tea. She went to check to see if the water was boiling.

Bramble hopped over and stretched out by her side. Audrey passed him the odd dandelion leaf as she stirred the pot.

Ribston huffed at this as he came over with more leaves. "With all due respect, Miss Audrey, I am not collecting leaves to feed to that long-eared layabout. They are supposed to be for our morning brew."

"Oh, Ribston, I'm only feeding him one or two. They're his

favourite. Look, he loves them!" Bramble ate the leaf, pulling it away from Audrey's hand and munching urgently.

The Boy River looked up at their conversation, noticing Bramble for the first time. "Where did that rabbit come from? He doesn't look like the usual type that we get around here."

Audrey laughed. "Don't worry – he is travelling with us. He had an injured leg and I helped heal it. He has been with us ever since."

The Boy River still looked suspicious and now Ribston folded his arms as he assessed Bramble. "I think the Boy River is right. We should keep a close eye on him. You can never be too careful."

Audrey laughed again. Surely they didn't suspect Bramble of being a spy? She stroked him. "All he wants from us is our dandelion leaves."

River helped the group clear away all evidence of their camp, kicking earth on to the fire and scattering the sticks from the shelters. "Zelos may know that we're on our way but we don't want to make it too easy for him and his spies to track us," he explained.

Then they were on their way, following the Boy River. His movements were not easy to predict. Every time it looked as if he would surely turn one way, or use a pre-trodden path, he would turn ninety degrees and stride off in a different direction. They crossed the river at a narrow point on a couple of fallen tree trucks that were hidden by low willows. Then, they were climbing up hill again, approaching the castle from behind.

Audrey couldn't decide if the Boy River knew these woods better than anyone and was taking them on the most amazing off-road route, or if this was all a trick and he was going to lead them straight into the clutches of King Zelos. It surprised her that Alette and Maneo were following him so blindly. It was unlike Maneo to place his trust in anyone, let alone someone he barely knew. His experience of this man was based on one short encounter back when the Boy River had been an actual boy. Yet Maneo followed him as closely as the others. Audrey and Ribston were right behind them, with Bramble hopping somewhere close by.

"Prin— Miss Audrey, one thing I still don't understand is why was Bramble thumping last night?" asked Ribston.

"He must have heard River approaching."

"But he started thumping long before River appeared. Do you think he knew that the squirrel and mouse were spies?"

"How could he have done?"

"I don't know, but maybe it is worth keeping a close eye on him?"

"Don't be ridiculous, Ribston. He is just a rabbit."

Ribston quietened again and Audrey felt bad. He was clearly a little jealous of Bramble.

She listened to the conversation that was taking place between Alette and River. Alette was being uncharacteristically chatty and telling River about her thirst for adventure.

River sounded amused. "You sound like my youngest brother, Colby. He is desperate to save the world. He wants to come with me out here. Wants adventure. But I make him stay with our mother. My older siblings have all flown the nest and have families of their own. She needs one of us at home. He will have his time."

Audrey could not believe that just a week ago, it had been she who had been carrying out the normal routine at home and thinking that adventure would never knock on her door. Back then, she would not have thought herself capable of going on a journey like this.

As the sun rose higher in the sky, they reached a large woodland clearing, scattered with crispy fallen leaves. There was a large oak with leaves the colour of flames and a pair of silver birches, their pale yellow leaves in bright contrast. A fallen moss-covered tree stretched across the middle of the clearing. Ribston instantly jumped on to it and began to walk along as if it were a highwire in a circus. "This is a lovely straight trunk. It must have lain here for ten years but it still seems so alive!"

Behind the trees was a high wall built from pale grey stone, with spikes on the top. Behind that was another wall, the wall of a building. It took Audrey a short while to realize that this was Essendor castle. They were so close, she could have thrown a chestnut seed and hit it from here.

River tapped his staff decisively on the ground. "This is where I leave you. It is the correct place, I believe, Sorcerer?"

Maneo looked around at the trees, particularly studying the fallen tree trunk. "Yes – this is as I remember," he said, a flicker of excitement twitching his features.

River began instantly to retreat back into the trees, followed by the little wren.

"Will you not stay and see us safely into the castle?" asked Alette.

"No – I will not set foot within those walls while that man is on the throne. I already feel too close for my own comfort. I wish you all good fortune in your undertaking. Should you need me in the future, then tell a small bird: a robin, a finch or a wren. All the local ones know where to find me or will know another who does."

And the Boy River was gone, vanished into the trees where he was happiest. They called their thanks but he did not respond. Again, Audrey hoped that he had not gone to turn them in. He himself had warned them against trusting anyone.

But Maneo seemed quite calm and confident. He walked around the clearing with long strides.

"How are we going to get into the castle?" asked Alette.

The sorcerer turned his mouth up gently at the edges, as close as he got to a smile. "We are going to get in exactly the same way we got out, thirteen years ago."

RESTORATION
Alette

"A long time ago, when you were babies, I cast a spell to cover my tracks. Now I must cast a new spell to uncover what is hidden and return things to their natural state. I shall need complete silence if I am to recite it correctly. It is not a difficult spell but it has many verses."

Alette coughed loudly, then laughed. "Sorry."

Maneo peered down his nose at her. "I would treat this seriously if I were you. One slip of the tongue when I cast this spell and you could end up hopping your way over to that forest swamp."

A joke from Maneo! Alette was pleased. Whatever happened, when this journey was over, maybe they could get back to being father and daughter again, or whatever they called themselves now.

Maneo drew himself upright in preparation and pointed his wand at the fallen tree trunk. It was covered in bindweed, fungus and was probably home to any number of woodland creatures. Maneo muttered a string of unintelligible words and the tree trunk began to shudder.

Ribston hopped from foot to foot. "The tree isn't dead, is she? She's alive! I knew it!"

Alette shushed him. Twigs snapped and wood dust rose off the ground, making Ribston sneeze. The tree moved in short sideways movements for a few seconds. A tiny creature – a vole or shrew – ran out in confusion. Then, very gradually, the end of the tree furthest from Maneo raised a few inches off the floor.

It was not, after all, a tree trunk with one end lost in the bushes. It was a whole sweet chestnut tree, not dead but hibernating. Its leaves were the pale green and ochre colours of autumn.

Creaking and groaning, the tree slowly shifted from horizontal to vertical. Forest detritus that had covered the trunk dropped away, revealing smooth grey-purple bark with deep, spiralling fissures. Dozens of prickly husks bounced to the ground.

Eventually the tree stood, roots firmly in the ground. It was as it had been thirteen years previously – perhaps a few inches taller.

"What a beauty," whispered Ribston, gazing up at the autumn colours.

Alette had watched the whole procedure open-mouthed. Now she turned to Maneo, impressed. "Wow. That is the most striking spell I have ever seen you cast."

"You have seen me produce a golden seed and grow a golden tree. You have seen me start fires from nothing and fight our foes. Yet I lift a tree from the forest floor with a basic restoration spell and now you are impressed?"

Alette smiled. "This spell had impact. It was less like a magic trick than some of the others." She was enjoying this banter between them.

A voice came from behind them. Audrey. But sounding very shaky indeed.

"I promise you, Maneo, that this was certainly one of your most interesting spells."

Alette and Maneo turned to see Audrey pointing into the bushes.

A man was curled up on the ground. He was pale, shivering and clearly confused. He was also completely naked.

Alette started when she saw him. "Who on earth is that?"

Audrey took a few moments to reply and when she did, she was barely able to get the words out. "He— It's— I think— I mean to say— It's Bramble!"

BRAMBLE
Audrey

When the tree spell had started to work, Audrey's first thought was for Bramble. After nursing him back to health, the last thing she wanted was for him to be flattened by a rolling tree trunk. But he seemed happy enough, hopping about in his namesake plant on the forest floor. It amazed Audrey how he chomped his way through the thorny sticks, unbothered by the sharp prickles.

When the tree started to lift behind her, Audrey was momentarily distracted by the creaking noise until a new sound drew her attention right back to the rabbit. Bramble squeaked. Just like he had done that first day.

She watched him keenly. What was he trying to tell her? She heard a rustle in the bushes a few yards away. Bramble froze in position: nose in the air, left paw raised slightly above the right. His ears pricked up. All that moved was his twitching nose.

And then Bramble began to change. His ears waggled furiously and changed shape, shortening as if they were retracting into his head. He was changing colour too – darkening from bright white to dusky beige. His legs lengthened and his face flattened. He was turning into a human. A man. Their eyes met. The man was staring at her in exactly the same way that Bramble had done when she found him on the forest floor. He was scared. For a moment, Audrey wanted to reassure him: feed him a dandelion leaf. But she knew she had to tell the others.

Now she pointed towards the naked man.

"He— It's— I think— I mean to say— It's Bramble!"

"Bramble?" repeated Alette. "Bramble the rabbit?"

Audrey nodded dumbly. The information still hadn't quite reached her brain.

Maneo acted quickly. "Of course! I should have realized that the beast was enchanted. Its odd appearance. And that squeak. No normal rabbit would make a sound like that. The spell I cast to return things to their natural state has worked on everything in this area, including the rabbit. Here – give him this cloak to protect his modesty."

Audrey passed the cloak to the shivering man.

Maneo turned to Ribston. "You, Orch – do you have any rope?"

Ribston nodded. He unclipped a looped rope from his toolbelt.

"Bind his hands behind his back. And his ankles."

"No!" cried Audrey.

Ribston followed Maneo's orders and Maneo turned to her. "This is no longer your pet rabbit. This is a man who has been following us for the past three days. He has heard all our plans and knows all our secrets. We have no idea whom he has told. And now we are going to obtain some answers."

Maneo rose above the seated man and pointed the wand straight down at his head like an arrow. "I will ask you some questions. Speak the truth, or you will regret it. What is your name?"

"Berwick Tilbury," replied the man rapidly, his voice cracking.

"Did you cast the spell to disguise yourself?"

"No, sire – I am not a man of magic. I am a simple peasant."

Maneo looked him up and down. "I believe you. So who cast this spell of transformation?"

"Zelos." The man's voice trembled.

"As I thought. And why?"

"I owed him a great debt. I stole from him. My family were starving. He threatened me with death. But then he said I could work for him. To repay the debt."

Maneo narrowed his eyes. "Working in what capacity?"

The man hung his head.

"As a spy?"

Berwick nodded miserably.

"Just as the Boy River suspected. You were following us?"

"Yes. Zelos wanted to know your movements. If I reported back to him with information then he said the debt would be paid. He would undo the spell – free me from the enchantment. But then when you helped me . . . I could no longer betray you."

"You are free now, Bramble— I mean Berwick," said Audrey with a kind smile.

Berwick did not look happy at this news. He looked rapidly

from right to left. "Zelos will be angry. Angry that I am talking to you. They will tell him. He will know."

"Who will tell him?" asked Alette, looking about her in the same way Berwick was doing.

"The others."

"The squirrel and the mouse?"

"Yes. They are two brothers called Harding. They have reported on countless civilians. They were the ones who informed on me when I stole. Now they will tell Zelos I have turned against him. He will be after me as well as you."

Audrey tried and failed to imagine the two sweet little woodland creatures as hardened criminals.

"They will have reached Zelos by now," said Berwick. "He will know that you were here."

"I did hear a rustle in the bushes while Maneo was casting his spell," said Audrey.

Maneo was still pointing his wand at Berwick. He kept it trained on him and sat on the woodland floor. "Tell us everything you know and we will decide what is to be done."

Berwick took a deep juddering breath and his words tumbled out.

"Zelos has spies everywhere. Here in Essendor, in the

castle and out in the forest. He is always tracking his enemies' movements; always looking for crimes against him. The Harding brothers have reported on a lot of people – they must be near to gaining their freedom. That's what makes them so callous.

"Anyway, Zelos received news of two people he was hunting and we were all told that they were now the 'most wanted'. We were given descriptions and told to report back on them, and them alone. We prepared ourselves to leave Essendor and travel to the east of the kingdom."

"You were looking for Alette and me?"

"Yes. I didn't know at the time that you were the princesses – all I knew was that you were enemies. We all wanted to be the ones to turn you in. And then we heard that you were being held by an old woman in an orchard."

"The orchardess."

"Yes. Zelos knew her from a long time ago. She came to see him, and then together they travelled back to the orchard on horseback. He told many of us to follow – a secret army in case we were needed. When we got there you had left. We could see that someone had helped you and you had broken free."

Audrey shuddered. They had been so close to capture.

She wondered how long it had been between their escape and Zelos's arrival.

"Zelos was so angry. He cursed the old woman and she laughed at him – said he would never be half as powerful as his sister had been. That made it worse, of course. They battled each other and Zelos won."

"What happened to the orchardess?"

"He turned her into a bee."

Ribston gasped. Even after the way she had treated him, the orchardess was still his mistress. He found it hard to imagine her reduced to the size of a bee. "I wonder what will become of her. Maybe she will find the other gardenarians."

"Or maybe she will be lost in the vastness of the woods," said Maneo.

"Zelos must be a powerful sorcerer indeed to defeat the orchardess," said Alette.

"Yes. And he is merciless. Sometimes he seems to be almost ... kind. You will think that he is on your side. But he has a bad, bad heart."

"So when we found you, you were tracking us?"

"Yes. It was like a competition between all the spies. We each thought that if we found you, Zelos would be sure to give us our freedom. I was doing so well! Listening to your conversations. Predicting which way you would travel. Always staying one step ahead. I crossed the toll bridge ahead of you when the troll was telling you the riddles. But then I hurt my leg. I'd heard something overhead – a buzzard or something, chasing after me – so I was hopping as quickly as I could. I was going to hide under a bush but I caught my foot on a tree root and twisted it badly. I tried to carry on but it hurt so much. I gave up and thought that I would die there on the forest floor. Better there than at the hands of Zelos, I thought, although my family would never have known what had happened to me… Anyway, I heard you come past and I used all the power I had left to attract your attention. Thankfully, Princess Audrey heard me. Took care of me. Healed me. And now – now I would never turn you in. I am your faithful servant!"

Maneo pointed his wand sharply at Berwick's ties and the rope unravelled.

"Audrey, you seem to be adept at collecting faithful servants. What do you suppose we do with him?"

"Surely let the poor man return to his family?"

"No! If you release me then the others will tell Zelos and he will find me. He will hurt my family. You must let me come with you – I will fight for you, spy for you, whatever you require."

"We are not yet sure what we shall require, but stay with us and we will see." Maneo looked around. "We must go back to the matter at hand. Before this man's transformation, we were looking for something. I plan to get us back into the castle in the same way we got out thirteen years ago. We will know it when we see it. All of you, clear the leaves from under the tree."

As the tree trunk had lifted, the deep carpet of dried leaves had filled the space that it left. Now Berwick, Ribston, Alette and Audrey all worked hard sweeping the leaves out of the way with their hands and feet. The mulchy smell of rotten leaves rose up from the ground as they worked.

Then Ribston found something. "A trapdoor!"

They all rushed to look.

THE TRAPDOOR
Alette

Alette instantly pulled on the circular iron ring but the damp wooden door was locked. Maneo stood back and smoothed down the front of his shirt. "This is precisely what we were looking for. The door by which we left thirteen years ago and locked by my own spell."

Maneo waved his wand over the trapdoor a few times, chanting the unlocking spell. Now when Alette tugged on the iron pull, the door lifted easily. She peered in and a dank, cold smell arose from the dark passageway. It was impossible to see where it led, though she assumed it went under the moat.

"If the Harding brothers have gone to Zelos, then it is only a matter of time before he knows we are here," said Maneo. "We must act quickly and enter the castle straight away. Orch – here is a good chance for you to be of assistance."

"Anything you need!" cried Ribston.

"Hold the trapdoor open to allow the daylight to light our passage through the tunnel. When we reach the other end we will let you know with a birdcall. You can then close the tunnel. If you spot anything strange at your end, or if any foes approach, then you must let us know."

Ribston seemed to be having second thoughts. "But I want to fight at your side."

"That may be, but you will be of the greatest use here by the trapdoor. Stay at your post unless one of us tells you otherwise."

Ribston nodded and Maneo addressed Berwick.

"You – head to the gates at the south of the city. Hide yourself there. Be alert to any danger."

Berwick turned his head slightly to one side, listening in a Bramble-like fashion.

"If we fail and need to escape quickly then we know we have support. Go now to your post and do not leave unless you have received the order directly from one of us."

Berwick ran off and Alette felt a ripple of excitement – or fear – run through her. This was the first time Maneo had mentioned failing. What if they did fail? What then?

But Maneo still seemed calm. "From what Berwick has told us, it seems unlikely that we will have the advantage of surprise. Zelos is waiting for us. But let him wait. He knows that he was no match for your mother's magic, and he knows that when you combine forces against him, he will be no match for you, either. Agreed?"

The girls nodded. Audrey took Alette's hand and squeezed it gently. Alette was surprised by the sudden touch and did not respond in any way, although it felt good to know that her sister was there.

"It would be foolish, however, to walk into the castle entirely exposed. I suggest that we use the protection of an invisibility charm. I will cast this spell on all three of us. We will still be able to see our own selves, otherwise it is surprisingly difficult to walk and move as normal. But we will not be able to see one another. I suggest we place our hands on the shoulders of the person ahead in a chain formation so that we do not lose anyone. Agreed?"

The girls nodded again, and after a few more instructions, they were ready. Maneo cast his spell. Alette watched Audrey and Maneo disappear from view like a rainbow from the sky. She supposed she had disappeared too, although she could still see her own arms and legs.

They said an invisible farewell to Ribston and stepped through the square hole in the ground. Maneo went first, then Alette and finally Audrey.

On the downward slope, plenty of light shone through from the trapdoor, but when they passed the halfway point and began their ascent towards the castle kitchen, less and less light filtered through. Their eyes adjusted somewhat as they walked along but their invisibility made walking difficult. Audrey stepped on Alette's heels twice, causing her to tut loudly.

By the time they'd reached the end of the passageway, it was completely dark. Alette could hear Maneo whispering an unlocking spell. A catch clicked open and she heard a door opening. He must have found the other trapdoor, leading to the kitchen. This was confirmed by the pungent smell of cheese and smoked meats drifting into the passageway. Then came the sound of a door closing.

Maneo's whisper cut through the ensuing silence. "In the thirteen years since I was here last, someone must have moved the grain chest covering the trapdoor. That makes it easy for us to get out into the larder. It is currently all clear but if anyone comes in then make yourselves small. Hide under a shelf or press yourself into a corner. Is everyone ready?"

"Yes," replied the girls.

"Then let's go in."

INSIDE THE CASTLE
Audrey

Alette made a crow-like call loudly and clearly down the passageway so that Ribston would know to close the other trapdoor. They climbed out one at a time. First Maneo, then Alette. Audrey started to follow, but as her head and shoulders were poking out, someone walked into the larder. It was a boy, only just older than Audrey, with wiry arms and a grubby grey apron. His eyes were instantly drawn to the open trapdoor and he squeezed his brows together in confusion. Audrey knew that she was invisible but it was hard to believe when he was staring right at her. She was torn between running quickly up the steps and into the larder, or retreating back down. She went for the second option, which was a good thing, because as she ducked her head back down, the boy walked in her direction and slammed the trapdoor shut.

She was alone and invisible in a dark, cramped space. Time ticked by. She suddenly panicked that the other two would leave her there – that Maneo wouldn't care if she was left in the tunnel as long as he had Alette. What if they locked the trapdoor? She would have to walk back through the passageway, and hope that Ribston was still there to let her out.

Those thoughts soon passed and were replaced by an odd feeling that none of this was real. Maybe she was in bed at the bakery, in the middle of one of her strange dreams. It was a pleasant thought, and for a moment, she closed her eyes and leaned back against the passageway wall.

But then the trapdoor swung open again. She held her breath in case it was the kitchen boy, but it wasn't. The larder was empty of people, which meant that an invisible Maneo or Alette had opened it for her.

She climbed up the steps again, swiftly this time, carefully lowering the trapdoor behind her. Alette's hand took hers and placed it by her collarbone. She could now follow her, hand on shoulder, and know that they were together. Alette was probably doing the same with Maneo, just ahead of her.

They shuffled along in their human chain, walking at the speed of a tortoise. The kitchen was a hostile environment, devoid of cheerfulness. Three young-looking kitchen hands with thin arms and pinched cheeks stood working, heads down. There was no singing and no clattering. The place was filthy and a rat darted across the floor.

"New message from the king," called the cook. "His Majesty wants grouse for his dinner this evening."

One of the kitchen hands looked flustered. "Grouse? But the king always has partridge for his dinner."

"Well, today he wants grouse, so you'd better find some."

"Where am I going to find grouse, Miss?"

"I don't know but I'd start looking now if I were you or there'll be hell to pay. Go on, be off with you. I've got more than enough to contend with preparing His Majesty's luncheon. A full cold spread today."

Audrey caught her breath. Her mother would never allow

such foul conditions at the mill. What kind of castle was this? They were planning to claim their right to the throne but did Audrey even want to reign over a place like this? Not for the first time she thought of the village, her mother, the Harvest Dance and Apple Day. How she would love to be back there now and not creeping invisibly through a squalid kitchen in a stolen castle. But there was no hope of turning back now. One way or another she was going to face her uncle.

CHAPTER TWELVE

THE BANQUETING HALL

Alette

They made their way through the long stone corridors. Alette tried to keep her footfall as light as possible and also not to breathe, which was harder than one might imagine when one was climbing stairs. At every turn, she looked out for something that might trigger a memory from her infanthood, but there was nothing. She could not remember, or even imagine, living here, in this cold stone place where armed guards patrolled. It was not a home.

Then Maneo stopped, for they had reached the banqueting

hall. They stood outside and looked in. In contrast to the filthy kitchen, this room had a high, arched ceiling and a shiny parquet floor that was the colour of the resurrected sweet chestnut trunk. Along the left wall was oak panelling, and above this panelling were painted murals. Alette couldn't see what they pictured but she wondered if there was a portrait of her mother. She longed to see one. A great stone fireplace was alive with a blazing fire. Maneo began to move again and Alette followed him, Audrey following her. The three edged their way inside, through the open door, taking their smallest and lightest steps yet. Maneo stopped. Alette had one hand on his bony shoulder and could feel his breath coming rapidly.

Alette could see the whole room now, including the chandeliers hanging from the oak beams above. A long banqueting table dominated the room. The end furthest from the doorway had been laid formally, with a white cloth and silverware. The end nearest to them was bare. Sitting alone at the table was a dark-haired man, preparing to tuck into a fine-looking luncheon. Zelos.

All Alette could do was to stare at him. Aside from Audrey, he was the only blood relative that she had ever set eyes on. Did she look like him, as the Boy River had said? He was shorter.

Alette had her mother's height. But certainly she had the same heavy brows and determined jawline. Were they similar? Did she have the same bad blood as Zelos, like the orchardess had told them?

They shuffled closer. Alette tried not to breathe.

The king looked up. He was wearing dark red robes, gold chains and an ornate crown. Did he wear this finery every day, or only on special occasions? And if so, which occasion was this? She thought of the thin and hollow-cheeked staff in the kitchen two floors below. Did he not know that his people were starving? Did he not care? Would she care if she were queen, or would she be happy to indulge in a full spread for luncheon every day? It certainly smelled good.

In an arched cove over one of the doors stood a black bird. Alette thought it a statue at first but then it moved – bobbing its head upwards and ruffling its feathers. It had a distinctive flash of white at its neck. Did all ravens have that mark or was this the same bird that brought them the golden seed in the orchard?

Maneo stopped walking. There was silence in the room apart from the crackle of the fire and the clink of glass on glass as Zelos poured wine from a decanter. Liquid the colour of his ruby robes glugged slowly into the glass and he took a sip, looking over in their direction – seemingly straight at them. He took a handful of something from a silver bowl near him – nuts or crackers – and poured them into his mouth. He crunched loudly.

Then he stood and pushed back his chair, still carrying the wine glass and bowl. He took four steps across the shiny floor, the heels of his boots clicking smartly. Then he spoke. "You may be invisible but do you really think I cannot sense you? I am the greatest sorcerer in the kingdom. I can tell when an inferior magician has cast a spell. Show yourselves!" He did not raise his voice but still it was loud, echoing down the hall towards them.

Alette thought of what the Boy River had said about the pike in the muddy waters. If Zelos was a pike, then they were tiny fish. There may be three of them but they were sticklebacks bobbing about in the weeds. Was Zelos going to strike or would he bide his time still further?

Maneo turned and whispered in her ear. "I shall reverse the invisibility spell. We shall face him now."

Alette reached up and squeezed Audrey's hand on her shoulder. Maneo must have cast the spell because she saw him gradually rematerialize in front of her and knew that she must be doing the same.

Zelos stared at them as they appeared. Then he downed his

glass of wine and threw the crystal glass into the fire. Alette jumped at the shattering sound and was cross with herself, especially when Zelos laughed. "So you must be my nieces. You think yourselves good at hiding, I know. You have hidden for thirteen years. I sent my men across the kingdom. They were ordered to dispose of any baby twins. But they found none. You vanished. And now, when I stop looking, you come to me. Funny, isn't it?"

No one spoke. He walked towards them, silver bowl in one hand, the other hand running along the table.

"I assumed you had fled to another kingdom. But I understand that you have been here all the time. How could I have missed you?"

Alette took a few long strides towards him, so that they were standing face to face.

"Perhaps you didn't look hard enough. Perhaps you should have done the job yourself rather than sending your poor, downtrodden spies." As always, Alette was able to show a confidence she didn't feel.

Zelos held the silver bowl out towards her. "Scorpion?"

Alette glanced at the bowl and recoiled slightly. Zelos took another handful of the small, dried arachnids. He popped them into his mouth one at a time and crunched, then set the bowl on the table.

"Black forest variety. They really are delicious."

Audrey turned away from the sight but Alette wasn't going to give him the satisfaction. She kept staring at him.

Zelos raised an eyebrow. "I see Bia in her." He pointed to Audrey. "Around the eyes. Which must mean you are more like me." He stared at Alette for a few seconds. Neither of them blinked. He reached out a hand towards Alette and swiftly grabbed the necklace from around her neck, pulling it until the chain broke. "This is mine."

Alette didn't flinch. "Take it then. And we will have what is ours in return. The throne."

Zelos laughed loudly and looked at the pendant, running his thumb over the embossed pattern. "I flung it at Bia in anger when I left the orchard, all those years ago. I have not seen it since. It was not amongst her things and it was not discovered on her corpse. I have long suspected she gave both necklaces to her infants."

Alette's neck felt bare without the chain that she had been wearing every day. But she would not show Zelos that she wanted it back. She would not show him anything.

Zelos threw the necklace on to the table as if it were worthless. "I miss her. She was so beautiful. So kind. So good. Sometimes it gave me hope that I could be like her. You understand, don't you?" He smirked at Alette. Alette wondered what he saw in her. Why did he think she was like him? She was not like him. She was not cruel or self-centred. At least, she did not think she was. Was that what others saw?

"One doesn't lose a twin and not miss them, you understand. But sometimes we have to lose something we love to gain something we want. Isn't that right, Maneo?"

The sorcerer raised his eyebrows.

"You thought perhaps I didn't recognize you. Maneo. My apprentice. It has been many years and I had forgotten all about you. But now it all makes sense. I did hear news of the 'great sorcerer' who had arrived at court years ago but I didn't put two and two together."

Alette's fingers and toes fizzed. Maneo knew Zelos? Had been his apprentice? She tried to piece together what she knew. Maneo had always said that he trained with a great sorcerer. Was that really Zelos?

Maneo's voice was calm and cool. "I told you when we parted that we would meet again one day."

Zelos laughed nastily. "Yes, you did, but I didn't pay much attention to the words of a mediocre apprentice – a mere boy."

Maneo cleared his throat. "I am no longer a mere boy. You may once have been the greatest sorcerer, Zelos. But now you have competition."

"You have certainly been patient," said Zelos. "That was what drew me to you all those years ago. I had the magic. I had the power. I needed someone ready to learn. Someone who would put in the hours, learn the craft. Measure out the ingredients. Someone who would be loyal to me and support me when I needed it. I knew you as soon as I saw you."

Alette looked sharply at Maneo. She had heard his tale, more than once, of how he had met the greatest sorcerer in a tavern. Yet he had failed to tell her that the man was Zelos. She ran through the story now in her mind.

Maneo was fourteen. His mother could not support him any more. She had been sad to see him go but she knew that, out of all of them, Maneo would look after himself. He went out into the world with no skills save a few card tricks. Sleight of hand illusions. Cards up the sleeve. Simple tricks, but they took time and patience to learn. Practice, practice. He travelled from tavern to tavern, always drawing a crowd. He had a compelling manner, though he didn't speak a lot. The tavern owners were pleased. They gave him board and sometimes a hot meal. One night, things were going well. It was late and jugfuls of beer had been drunk. Maneo chose the biggest, gruffest man in the group and made his pocket watch disappear, only to discover it in under his own hat. The man thought it was hilarious. He clapped him on the back and tipped him generously. Maneo had a feeling that someone else was watching before he heard the voice.

"Call that a trick?"

The loud voice came from the next table. A dark, smiling man was scraping the remnants of some soup or broth from the bowl. The crowd turned to him.

"Call that a trick?" he repeated. The man stood, pushed back his chair. He took the napkin from around his neck and screwed it into a ball. He threw it, hard, towards the bigger man's face. But it wasn't a napkin at all. Now it was a crow. A squawking bundle of black feathers, that panicked and flapped and cawed and finally swooped towards the safety of the bar.

The crowd roared. The big man recovered from his initial surprise and laughed heartily. "More, I say!" They rushed towards this new magician and Maneo picked up his cloak. He *wouldn't be staying here tonight. But the new magician was also heading for the door. Despite the crowd's protests, he would not stay. They soon gave up and retreated away from the cold air that was swirling through the open door. Someone started singing. The magic tricks were forgotten.*

Maneo and the new magician met out in the chill air. Maneo had been outdone but he didn't mind. What he had witnessed was proper magic, he was sure. He watched the magician button his coat and wrap his scarf around his neck.

"Will you teach me?"

"I am always patient when there is something worth waiting for," said Maneo.

"You were a good apprentice but you did not know your place. You always wanted more; thought you were better than you really were."

"I am no longer an apprentice. My power has been growing over the years, and I am a sorcerer myself now. I know your limitations, your weaknesses. I spent enough time with you to know I may be a more powerful adversary than you realize."

"But remember, my power has also been growing. You know not what I am capable of now."

The two men stared at each other.

"You have my bird," said Maneo, indicating the raven.

"Ah, I always wondered where he came from," said Zelos. "I thought he was my sister's pet. I have become rather attached to him. He is mine now."

"I conjured him thirteen years ago as a guardian for the twins when they were babies, so I think you will find he is mine."

Maneo nodded to Corvus, who flew over and alighted on Maneo's shoulder. But he only stayed a moment before flapping back to the archway over the door, where he stood, statue-like once again.

Zelos laughed and removed a black wand from within the folds of his robes. "I think we have greater things to argue about than a raven, do we not?"

THE RECKONING
Audrey

Audrey listened to this exchange and as she did, she looked into the eyes of her uncle. Was something hidden there? What did he see when he looked at her and Alette, his twin sister's children? A sister whom he had once loved deeply. Audrey was sure she could see a hint of the boy who had played in the orchard long ago. Was there hope for this man yet? Perhaps there was hope for everyone.

But then Alette was walking back to stand at her side. Audrey knew she wouldn't see that softness in his steely eyes. For Alette, there were no shades of grey.

"You killed my parents." Alette's voice was husky and low.

King Zelos was also walking backwards, putting distance between them. "What makes you think that this scurrilous gossip is true? All of this happened when you were babies. How is it that you are so sure? Perhaps I am the one who was wronged and your parents were to blame. Did you ever think of that?"

Audrey thought she should speak. "We did not make up this story ourselves. We have heard the story from many different sources."

"From my old apprentice, who holds a grudge against me and a mad old nanny? I would check those sources if I were you."

"We have heard it from another too," said Audrey, thinking of the orchardess.

"Oh yes, the orchardess, with her enchanting tales of life amongst the apple trees. She wasted my time and had to pay the price. How sad that you have her demise on your conscience."

"Her demise? I thought you turned her into a bee?"

"My – that news reached you quickly! How the hive does work. Yes, she is now working hard as a bee. Maybe she lives or maybe not. We may never know."

Audrey felt bad for the orchardess, which was strange, because the old woman had tried her hardest to hand them over to their uncle. "Anyway, it is not on our conscience! You are the one responsible for your evil actions. You are responsible for all those poor enchanted souls who did no more than steal loaves of bread for their starving families."

"The naivety of youth! What will you do if you succeed in your mission to gain the throne? What is your plan for the liars and thieves and vagabonds that roam the kingdom's streets? Will you throw them all into a prison to rot? Or will you do as I do and put them to use in a more valuable line of work? Sometimes it pays to think laterally. To use your brain."

Audrey gestured at the fine food and wine on the table, and to Zelos's lavish robes and the wall hangings. "I know that I could not sit here drowning in my own wealth while my people go without food. I would put my people first. Happy and healthy people do not cheat and steal. Liars and thieves and vagabonds would not be roaming the streets if this were my kingdom."

Audrey was surprised to find herself speaking so passionately. She had not thought at all about what she would do if she were queen. She had not even managed to think as far as today's encounter, about what she and Zelos might say to one another. But now she was here, it all seemed to make perfect sense. Surprisingly, she was the one doing all the talking while Alette was quiet. But then her twin spoke again.

"You killed my parents," she repeated. "Now it is time to pay the price."

Zelos stared at her. "You are a child! You think you have the power to challenge me? How entertaining! Each of you with your own separate goals. Thinking that your real hopes and dreams are hidden away and yet so close to the surface. I can see your weaknesses as if they were marks on your body. Like this one." He pointed to Alette's birthmark with his wand.

Audrey felt Alette tense beside her and could see her tightly clenched fists. She remembered what Alette had said about the red-hot rage that flowed through her. Audrey knew what was coming next.

This time, Alette changed as she reared up, her hooves clattering down on to the wooden banqueting hall floor. It was the second time that Audrey had witnessed such a transformation, but it was still pure magic to watch. Every part of her twin changed: her hair, her eyes, her skin, her body. Yet her essence was the same. It was pure magic, but also pure Alette.

Zelos watched with a slight smile. It was difficult not to be impressed by such a sight. But then his smile disappeared.

"As I suspected. You have the power. Like Bia. You think it makes you strong."

Audrey recognized his expression. Pure jealousy. Did he wish he had Alette's power of transformation? Or was he seeing his sister right now?

"Alette *is* stronger than you. Just as my mother was stronger. The only reason you ever defeated her was because she was weakened by childbirth." Audrey could see that he was nervous – backing away from Alette and pointing his wand towards her.

"And what is it you both plan to do? Kill me?"

Alette couldn't answer in her current form and Maneo seemed to be keeping quiet, so it was left to Audrey to give an answer.

And Audrey did not know the answer. She had wondered about it. In truth, this was the question she hadn't wanted to voice, even to herself, since they had left Lullgrove a week ago. She had been too scared to ask Alette or Maneo in case they told her that she was expected to kill her uncle.

Audrey lifted her chin. "All you need to do is admit what you've done. Apologise for your mistakes and we will let you free, as long as you leave this kingdom and never return."

Alette snorted. Maybe she didn't agree.

Zelos drew himself up. "When I took the crown, I was only claiming what was rightfully mine."

"This is not true. Queen Bia, our mother, was the just heir to the throne. She was older." Audrey knew enough at least to challenge him on this.

But Zelos looked outraged. "She was not older! She was my twin. The difference was merely minutes."

Zelos was growing more and more agitated. He tapped his wand against his thigh as he paced the length of the room. Audrey felt like she used to when she watched her jack-in-the-box as a child. The lid was going to open, she knew. It was a question of when. Alette seemed also to be waiting for her moment. She stood, upright, tail not moving. Just the occasional twitch of her ears and turn of her head showed that she was alert and watching.

"Bia had everything. The looks, the intelligence and the power of transformation." He stared at Audrey. "There is always a weaker twin, is there not? How do you feel about that – to be constantly sidelined in favour of the one with all the power?"

Audrey said nothing. Zelos thought she was powerless, that, like him, she had not inherited the power of transformation. But she had! Wouldn't it be satisfying to show him, to stand there by Alette's side and support her? Zelos would truly be shocked. She tried to feel the feelings than would help her transform, but she could not.

Zelos continued his rant. "Would it have been too much to give me the throne? She knew how much I wanted it. We had talked about it when we were children. But she wanted to share it. Can you imagine? What would we have done, sat on the throne for six months at a time? A preposterous idea! It was thanks to me anyway that the chance to reign came along as quickly as it did."

Audrey gasped. Did this mean what she thought it meant? "My grandfather…?"

"Yes, my father. The old king. He would have carried on for ever; I just helped speed things along a little. To give the next generation a chance."

"You helped speed things up? Killed him? Did my mother know?"

"I suspect Bia knew but she never asked me outright. People at court assumed it was an accident. He was old and weak.

Perhaps it suited her as much as it suited me to have the old king out of the way. Maybe we all want power as much as the next person but only some of us are brave enough to admit it."

"By what means did you kill him?"

Zelos smiled proudly. "Poison. From a scorpion sting. They entered his room one night, crawled into his bed, and in the morning they were gone. One scorpion sting will not usually be fatal, but hundreds – that is a different matter – hundreds would be enough to kill a horse!" Zelos laughed hard at this. Then he stopped and pointed his wand at the silver bowl on the table.

Audrey followed the invisible line from his wand to the bowl of dried scorpions. Something moved. The scorpions were growing, coming alive. One emerged from the bowl, six legs clawing their way slowly over the rim. Audrey gazed at the hard black shell, the pincers, the curved tail. The scorpion climbed across the table, down the table leg and scuttled across the floor, heading straight for Alette. As it did so, four or five others followed, then more and more until the floor was covered with the small creatures.

"Alette!" called Audrey. The unicorn was standing still, breathing calmly through her nostrils. Her horn glowed bright white. She did not panic or try to run away. The scorpions climbed up her legs, across her back, even through her mane. Audrey could not bear to watch.

Alette shook her head suddenly and a mist began to swirl around her. Like the thick mist in the woods, only this mist was a deep pink-purple. It enveloped her until the scorpions were all hidden from view. Then she reared up, stamped back down and the mist cleared. The scorpions were gone.

Maneo laughed. "Nothing can touch her. Unicorns can neutralize any poison."

Zelos nodded. "So I see. But I notice I am facing only one twin. This is familiar to me." The sorcerer laughed and turned to Audrey. "Which one are you? Truth or Strength? I know my sister was fond of both." He pointed his wand again – this time at a bowl of harmless-looking white eggs on the table. Audrey had assumed that these were chicken eggs but now she strongly suspected that they were not. Cracks appeared in the eggs, which widened into holes. Small, flat heads with flickering tongues broke through and out came bright, peacock-blue snakes with dark orange heads and tails. Dozens of them slithered from their shells in a writhing mass, this time heading towards Audrey like a flowing river.

"Beautiful, aren't they? But once these vipers attack, you won't stand a chance."

Audrey stood watching the snakes approach her. She willed herself to change. She knew she could be a unicorn like her twin. This moment should be about the two of them, side-by-side, defeating Zelos with their combined power. Why could she not transform? Why could she not feel rage? This man killed both her parents. Now he was taunting her, threatening her. But she could feel nothing. Only emptiness and a kind of pity.

Alette was at her side. Coming to protect her. But Audrey somehow knew that, even without Alette, these deadly vipers couldn't harm her. It was as if she was wearing an invisible coat of armour. The vipers were pooling around her feet but she was protected. She may not have transformed herself, but she was still using her power.

Alette stamped her hooves loudly on the parquet floor, sending a shockwave around the room. The pictures on the walls shook. Glasses on the table toppled. The very floor seemed to shift under their feet. Again, the deep pink mist swirled around them and the snakes were gone. In her unicorn state, Alette was an omnipotent force.

Maneo smiled smugly at Zelos. "There is no spell you can cast that that will defeat Alette when she is in her transformed state."

"And how do you know that? Do not presume to know more than me about magic. I was the one who taught you – remember? And what about you, Maneo? I notice that you have been hiding back there in fear of my spells. Don't you have confidence in your own abilities? You must realize that your own apprentice magic is no match for mine."

"This is not my battle to fight, Zelos. I think you will discover that Audrey and Alette do not need me. They have more than enough power between themselves. This is their battle."

Zelos turned back to Alette.

"If you are anything like your mother was, then you won't be able to keep this up for long. Every bit of your power will take something from you."

Audrey looked at Alette and saw that it was true. Her movements were slowing and she was sweating and panting softly. She thought of how worn out Alette had been after previous transformations and how she had felt herself, that time on the troll's bridge. Just a run up and a leap, but it had sapped her energy for hours.

"And when you transform back, who will be a match for me then?" asked Zelos.

He swung around to the banqueting table and pointed his

wand at the soup tureen in the middle. He muttered a spell, his brow forced down in a frown.

The lid of the soup tureen clattered as if it were boiling. A gelatinous mass bubbled out over the sides. This was frogspawn, Audrey realized, and the frogs were hatching. They were bright scarlet frogs with uneven black markings. They hopped and jumped in random directions.

"These are the most venomous frogs known to man. They don't even need to bite or sting," said Zelos. "They just need to brush against you for the venom to kill." The shiny little frogs were everywhere.

Alette stamped again. The mist swirled, enveloping the frogs, which dissolved and floated away as if they had been just smoke. But Audrey could see that Alette had nothing left to give. She stood still, her horn shrinking and her deep colour fading. The mist was also vanishing. Alette had used the last of her power and was changing back from a unicorn to a person. A normal girl, who was now weak and pale, resting one hand on the wall as if for support.

She hadn't managed to get rid of all of the frogs. One remained, shining its bright red warning in the middle of the parquet floor. Zelos pointed his wand at the frog, directing it, and the creature took a couple of jumps towards Alette.

"What you fail to mention, Zelos, is that you too will be weakened with each spell you cast." Maneo was there, at Alette's side. He pointed his own wand straight at the frog, and it hopped back towards Zelos.

The two sorcerers kept their wands pointed at the frog. "Corvus," called Zelos, and the bird instantly flew down from his archway and landed on his shoulder. He spoke to the bird, not taking his eyes off the frog.

"Call the soldiers, now. Tell them to come here straight away." He turned back to Alette and Audrey. "I have had enough of this nonsense. I want you gone so that I can get back to my luncheon."

Maneo narrowed his eyes. "Those soldiers will have to be quick to save you."

The frog took a few more hops towards Zelos.

"Oh, they will be here in seconds."

The frog hopped back towards Maneo.

Zelos nodded at Corvus again. "What are you waiting for? Get them now!"

Corvus inclined his head towards Zelos as if he understood. Audrey expected him to fly away and leave through the window.

But Corvus wasn't nodding. He was reaching for something. Zelos's wand. In one swift motion, he flew from Zelos's left shoulder and whisked the raised wand from his right hand. With the wand in his beak, he flew right up to the rafters in the high ceiling.

Zelos took a moment to gather himself. "Bird!" he cried. "Corvus! Bring that wand back to me right now. Where is your loyalty?"

But Corvus had clearly decided to keep hold of the wand. He adopted his previous statuesque pose, but this time with three inches of wooden wand sticking out either side of his beak. Zelos gestured uselessly at the bird, who steadfastly ignored him.

Maneo laughed aloud. "There is proof for you, at last. The raven is my bird. In fact, he has been passing us messages from the castle ever since we left. It is always useful to have spies hidden around the place, is it not?"

Audrey felt the hairs on her arms prickle. This was true. Corvus had appeared many times throughout their journey and who knows how many times before that. Why had Maneo not told them about him?

Maneo nodded at Corvus now and the great bird flew down from the rafters. Maneo reached up for the wand, but Corvus flew straight past, the tips of his feathers brushing Maneo's ear. He carried on flying until he reached Alette, then dropped the wand in her lap.

Maneo laughed again. "Well done, Corvus."

With some effort, Alette snapped the wand in half and threw it into the fire. It instantly caught fire and burned away, green and red smoke spiralling from deep within the flames. "Zelos. Without this wand, you are nothing. Your magic is just smoke and mirrors. Our power comes from deep within."

A slow smile stretched across Maneo's face. "I have waited many years for this."

Zelos was looking panicked. Maneo directed the tiny frog towards him, hop by hop. Zelos grabbed an apple from the table and aimed it at the frog but it missed and rolled away. He did the same with a knife, which fell with a clatter on the wooden floor. He backed towards the tall, arched doorway at the end of the room and flung the double doors wide open. They led out on to a balcony, enclosed by a stone balustrade. Zelos attempted to shut the frog in the hall behind him but Maneo guided it expertly through and Zelos let go of the doors in terror, backing away towards the balustrade.

"Guards, guards! To the banqueting hall – now!" he

shouted, down to the courtyard below. Audrey kept her eyes on the door to the hall, expecting a whole army to burst through at any moment.

Maneo kept guiding the frog towards Zelos, who was using anything he could to try and get it away from him. He took off his jacket and whisked it around in front of him but it did not seem to have any effect.

Audrey couldn't bear to watch her uncle flailing so pathetically. Instead, she watched Maneo's expression. Maneo was entirely focused on the moment. He knew exactly what he was doing.

Zelos climbed up on to the stone railing in a further attempt to get away from the frog. It was unclear what he was planning to do – climb over and cling on to the other side, perhaps. Whatever the plan was, it failed. One foot slipped on the railing and Zelos fell backwards, arms whirling slowly, hands grabbing at nothingness.

"No!" cried Audrey, but it was too late. Zelos fell three floors to the ground below.

Maneo pointed his wand at the poisonous frog and flicked his wrist once, twice, three times. The frog vanished.

Audrey and Alette rushed to the balcony and looked over the

edge. Audrey could hear Alette breathing hard at her side. Their uncle's body lay horribly twisted on the cobbled courtyard. He was dead, Audrey knew that from one glance. A soldier stood by the body, turned it over. Soon he was joined by another. And another. From their elevated position Audrey could also see two tiny creatures standing behind the group of guards. A squirrel and mouse – the Harding brothers. They looked up, assessing where he must have fallen from. If the guards had not heard Zelos call for them the first time, then they would surely soon respond to this.

Alette said nothing. She turned from the sight of her uncle and slid slowly down to the ground, sitting with her back to the balusters. She looked pale and exhausted.

Maneo was also worn out, Audrey could tell. He put a hand on Alette's shoulder. "Thank you. I could never have done it on my own."

This seemed strange to Audrey. Shouldn't Alette have been thanking Maneo?

"Come, sit in the hall a while. You must regain your strength." He helped her up and led her through to the hall. Audrey followed.

Alette sat at one end of the table, where Zelos had been. She rested her head on her folded arms on the table. Audrey sat next to her.

Corvus flapped over and Maneo stretched out his hand for the bird to land. "That's right, Corvus, you no longer have to put up with Zelos for a master. We have returned."

Corvus ignored his hand and hovered in the air above them. He flapped so violently that a couple of sleek black feathers fluttered to the parquet floor. He cawed repeatedly until the sound began to make a word. It was familiar to Audrey. It transported her back to another time, another key moment in her life, many years ago.

"Danger!" he cawed.

"Danger!"

CHAPTER THIRTEEN

THE END
Alette

Alette raised her head up again. She felt weak and dizzy. "The danger has gone now, bird," she said. "He's dead on the ground out there."

But then she saw Audrey's face. Audrey was not so sure. She looked like an animal, alert to some threat. Her wide eyes tried to pass on a message that Alette couldn't interpret. Had the soldiers reached the room? Was there some magic in the air?

"Alette," she said, her voice almost a whisper, "I don't think the danger has passed. And I think Corvus is your bird. He has chosen you."

Maneo nodded. "This makes some sense. I did not create Corvus as a soldier, or a spy. He was a guard. And thirteen years ago I gave him orders to protect the twin princesses. This seems to be exactly what he is doing!"

Alette's mind couldn't keep up with the speed of events. If her uncle was dead, then where was the danger now? She followed Audrey's line of sight. She was looking at Maneo with fear in her eyes. But why?

Maneo was smiling now. A full smile that showed all his teeth like she had never seen before. It was unsettling.

Zelos was dead. The danger was over. Wasn't it?

"Twenty years!" Maneo laughed out loud and strode away from them, walking the length of the banqueting table. "It has taken me twenty years to reach this point. Twenty years of patient waiting. Biding my time."

Alette didn't understand. "Twenty years? How can that be? I am only thirteen."

"Of course. But I have had my eye on the throne for a lot longer than that. You know now that when I was little older than a boy I trained with Zelos. One day he would be king, he said.

When he was on the throne, he would give me such power. But he betrayed me. Turned me away. Was happy for me to slink back into the shadows, despite my gift."

Alette listened. All questions dried up in her throat. She looked sideways at Audrey as Maneo continued.

"Oh, the confusion in your eyes. Alette, the truth-seeker. Now you shall know the full truth. For there is always more to the tale…"

"After I left Zelos, I spent a short while feeling sorry for myself but then I remembered I was a survivor. I had been the one to teach myself those card tricks all those years ago. I had intelligence and patience – I could achieve anything if I set my mind to it. So I set my sights no lower than the throne. There is always a way. Haven't I always taught you that, Alette?"

Maneo was directing every word to her. He didn't even glance at Audrey.

"Getting to court was much easier – and quicker – than I expected. The illusions and parlour tricks that you deride, Alette, did me so many favours. I found that people didn't ask questions. If I told them I was the greatest sorcerer and acted like the greatest sorcerer, then they believed me and even told others. Simple transformations changed their simple world. I moved closer and closer to the throne. I had my own quarters in the castle! It helped that your mother took a liking to me. And I liked her. I was the only one who knew of her power of transformation.

"There was even a point where I thought she might care for me. At that time I was planning how I might get the old King out of the way and perhaps your Mother would turn her affections to me—"

"The old king? You mean our father?" croaked Alette.

"Yes. He was not of royal blood – he was a nobody. But Bia was devoted to him in a way I could never understand—"

"She loved him!" cried Audrey.

Maneo waved his hand as if this were of no consequence. "After she had you babies she was weakened. And then Zelos came along. This was not unexpected. I always knew he would be waiting. But what bad timing – just as I was so close! I knew that you girls were my only hope. I would have taken you both but the nanny would not hear of it."

"My mother...?" said Audrey.

"Yes, yes, your adoptive mother. That nanny. A meddling old bat. I tried to take you as well but she wouldn't let me. If you had grown up together and I had been able to train you both... But still, it was probably safer that way. It would have been difficult to keep you both hidden. And is of no consequence now."

Something suddenly occurred to Alette. "The bridge didn't lie!"

"What bridge?"

"The troll's bridge. The troll said you were the keenest. I have wondered ever since what he meant. Now I know."

Maneo thought about this. "Yes, I think that troll was probably right. I have been the keenest. And the most patient. And the most resilient. I have waited for the opportunity and I have been flexible. And now, the kingdom is mine! It has all been worth the wait!"

Maneo laughed again.

Alette stared at him. There was more, she could tell.

"I need to hear the whole truth. What happened to us after the nanny left the woods with Audrey and the Boy River, thirteen years ago?"

"So astute! Of course, you deserve to hear the truth." Maneo paused, deciding perhaps whether this next part of the story was something he should share. But he couldn't help himself. The words came pouring out.

THE WHOLE TRUTH
Maneo

"After the nanny had left, I waited. It is always best to wait, as I have told you. Never act impetuously.

"You were fast asleep. You were still at the age where I knew you would sleep for hours. I heard a rumble from the side of the castle. Wheels in motion. I wanted to know what was happening. I strapped you to my back, under my cloak, and went to investigate. It was Elden and Bia, your parents, leaving in a carriage from the back entrance. They were inside an unmarked carriage and they didn't see me. They were heading for safety and would no doubt wait for the queen's strength to return before reclaiming the throne. Then they would want you back, of course.

"It struck me then, that with Bia and Elden gone, I would be closer then than I had ever been to the throne. Their homecoming would not be in my interests. I wondered how I might prolong their absence.

"Then, as if it was meant to be, a couple of soldiers rode around the corner, carrying an unfamiliar banner. Zelos's men. I stopped them.

"'I have information regarding the whereabouts of the king and queen,' I told them.

"They were suspicious, of course. They didn't see you covered by my cloak, or they might have asked more questions. But you stayed quiet, my little conspirator. And they didn't look for you. People only see what they expect to see, remember.

"'What do you want for this information?' they asked.

"I demanded a horse. It would seem strange to them if I asked for nothing in exchange for the information. Besides, a horse was of use to me.

"The more senior soldier ordered the junior man off his horse and I took it. I led the soldier on to the westward route out of the city. It was the only road that the king and queen could have taken from the back gate. And there they were, riding ahead of us, their carriage silhouetted by the full moon. I pointed to the soldier and he rode ahead. He ambushed the driver first.

"Bia saw me. From the window of the carriage. The relief in her face. She thought I had come to protect them, of course. But I was busy protecting you, Alette.

"I looked away and rode on."

BETRAYAL

Alette

"She saw you. She knew how you had betrayed her," whispered Audrey.

"Queen Bia?"

"Our mother, yes." Alette rubbed her hand across her forehead and through her hair. "It was you. Without you, Zelos's men would not have tracked down my parents in time. I would have grown up here, with my parents."

"Perhaps. But you were a vulnerable baby. Zelos might have killed you all. I looked after you well, kept you hidden. I ensured your survival. Are you not grateful?"

Alette shook her head slowly. "I still don't understand what you will gain from this. You will never be king. The throne is ours, not yours."

"Yes, but you will not come of age until you are eighteen. They will need a regent to govern while you are still a minor. And no one is in a better position than I."

Alette spoke slowly. She was beginning to see clearly. "And then? When I come of age? Will you happily hand over rule? Or will you want me out of the way?"

"Alette, what can you mean? You have been like my own daughter. I have brought you up in my own image. We will rule together."

Alette stood at her sister's side. "What about Audrey?"

Maneo turned his attention to Audrey.

"Ah yes, poor, poor Audrey. I thought we needed your combined power as twins to defeat your uncle but as it happens, Alette could have done it all by herself. Now that deed is done, we must make a difficult sacrifice. There is no room for two queens. A clean break is needed."

Audrey stood, pushed back her chair. She was visibly shaking now.

"My own sister? You cannot mean—"

"You said yourself: she is nothing like you. She has none of your strength, your vitality, your magic. She is weak. We should have left her in the bakery with the old nanny. They are about as useful as each other."

"She is nothing like me but she is not weak. In some ways Audrey is stronger than I could ever be."

"You make excuses for her. Listen to reason. No one will know. We will say that your uncle killed her. She will be remembered kindly. You will be crowned as I had always planned and I will guide you."

Maneo raised his wand and pointed it at Audrey.

"No! What are you talking about?" Alette stepped in front of Audrey. "You won't touch her."

"Alette, I have brought you up in my image. You are like me. You may have a temper, uncontrollable emotions, but in time you will learn to conquer this side of yourself. Choose wisely now and you will be grateful for the rest of your life."

"No. I am not like you. You are not my father. You are a stranger. And I am not like Zelos. I am not like my real father or mother, either. I am like myself: Alette."

"Then you have made your choice. My heart is heavy but I have waited too long to let anything stand in my way."

Maneo cast his eyes down once more. When he looked up again, wand arm raised, the steely look was back in his eye. And this time his wand was pointing directly at Alette.

THE REAL POWER
Audrey

Maneo was going to kill her twin sister. Alette. Shadow. Her strange, bold, brave other half, whom she had spent her whole life missing until now.

He would kill her – Audrey – too. He had made that clear. But first, he was going to kill Alette, who was spent and defenceless after her transformation. He wanted to hurt the child he had raised for thirteen years, for the sake of power and greed.

It was all that Audrey needed. This is what she had been waiting for. She felt the tingle of adrenaline shooting to her fingers and toes, as Alette had described. She tried to focus on the feeling: identify it. It was not fear, nor red hot rage. This was stronger. She wanted to protect Alette. She would die for her. She would kill for her. This was love.

Audrey rested her hands on Alette's upper arms, just below her shoulders. She gently pushed her to one side and stepped forward so that their positions were reversed.

"No, Audrey, be careful," cried Alette. She thought that Audrey needed her protection but she was wrong. Audrey had more power than either of them knew. She just hadn't known how to direct it before.

"I am strong," she cried. But her voice didn't sound like her voice any more. It sounded like a roar. She was her unicorn self again now and the power was hers.

Maneo looked frightened. He hadn't believed she was

a threat to him. Audrey lowered her head and he backed towards the door.

She kept talking as she charged. "I am strong. Do not underestimate me. Stay away from my sister." The words came out as a cacophony of neighs and snorts but Maneo understood their meaning. She saw the fear in his eyes.

He pointed his wand at her and desperately mumbled his spells, but she could tell from his eyes that he knew his incantations wouldn't work. She knocked him to the floor. He sprawled there inelegantly and she stood over him. The power was hers. She bowed her head towards him. She could see the end of her horn. Pearlescent, and sharp, the tip resting against his throat. She would barely have to move her head to pierce the soft skin there. His life would ebb away. She waited. Just one word from Alette was all she needed.

MANEO

Alette

Alette spoke, but not to Audrey. She called instead to the raven. "Corvus, please could you bring me Maneo's wand?"

This time, Corvus flew off without hesitation and tugged at Maneo's wand with his beak.

Maneo said nothing as he let the wand go. He met Alette's gaze. Maneo was always plotting, always planning. He knew that Audrey would do anything her sister wanted and was waiting for her instruction. If he could influence Alette in any way, then he would. But Alette herself did not know what that instruction would be until she gave it.

"Audrey, leave him. Step away."

Audrey raised her horn from his throat and took a few steps back.

Alette felt the weight of the wand in her hands. Passed it from one hand to the other. It was familiar to her. She had trained with it often, although cast few spells.

"Maybe I should have listened to you, Father," she said. "Maybe I should have taken my own wand. If I had learned some more spells of my own, then who knows what I could have done with you. Turned you into a kinder person, perhaps. Or a proper parent. But I only know one spell." The spell she had practised daily at the kitchen table. The spell she had used at the troll bridge. It was the only one that she admitted to being able to perform confidently.

She pointed Maneo's wand at him and began to murmur.

Maneo sat up. "Do not do this, Alette. You would regret it for ever."

"All those hours spent lifting objects with no particular purpose in mind. When I asked you why, you said it would be a useful skill to have. How right you were."

Maneo was powerless to do anything as Alette lifted him from the ground. He did not panic and flail as Zelos had done but his eyes kept searching, looking around the room, at the wand in Alette's hand, at the open doors, always hoping for a way to turn events to his advantage.

"Do not do this, Alette," he repeated in a calm voice. "We can talk about this."

Audrey was at her side. Alette watched her sister return to her human form as her power ebbed away and realized Audrey had protected her, saved them both.

Maneo would have been happy for her and her sister to die. Alette made her decision. She transported Maneo through the open doors, following the same route that Zelos had taken. Maneo gripped the doorframe as he passed through, fighting against her, fighting against the magic. He was saying something, trying to influence her, but Alette didn't listen. She was completely focused on what she was trying to do.

On the troll bridge the spell had been much more slapdash. She hadn't really cared where the troll had ended up but this time, more was at stake. Precision was required.

Maneo was through the window now, hovering in mid-air. He was still speaking but his voice got lost in the breeze. She held him there.

"One, two, three, four, five," she counted slowly and quietly as she walked up to the window, Audrey at her side. Then Alette moved Maneo three feet to the right and, with a flick of her wrist, released her virtual grip and dropped him.

Now he flailed. He must have wished for wand and a flying spell. Perhaps he thought that this was it. Perhaps he wished he'd made some different decisions. He may have been shocked that Alette could do this to him.

As it turned out, Alette could not. She could not think of killing her adoptive father, even if he did treat her and her sister as pawns in his own game. Maneo did not have as far as Zelos did to fall. Alette had positioned him over a balcony the floor below, and instead of dropping fifty feet, Maneo dropped just five.

The girls looked out of the window and down upon him. He sat up and brushed himself down, then looked up at Alette in confusion. Was this the intended outcome or was she going to cast another spell to finish him off?

But Alette had known very well what she was doing and she knew that from where he was he should be able to escape the castle without too many questions.

"Go now," she called down to him. "Leave and return to our house in the west. Stay there with your potions and your magic spells. Anything of mine that is left you may throw away or burn. I will never be back. You may do as you wish but never contact me again."

He looked only at Alette. "You will regret this decision."

"I do not think so," said Alette.

Maneo stretched out his hand and for a moment Audrey thought it was a farewell gesture, but then he spoke. "My wand."

Alette drew the wand back, put it in her pocket. "No. Leave."

Maneo didn't protest. He walked along the terrace and through a door at the end.

Alette still felt tense. Would he come back to the banqueting hall, angrier than before? She didn't have the energy for another fight. She and Audrey watched the courtyard together and in a few seconds Maneo emerged from a door in the east tower. He did not turn or look towards them, but swiftly crossed the courtyard and descended the steps towards the castle gates. He was leaving.

Alette exhaled through her mouth. She was exhausted. Audrey looked exhausted too. They stumbled towards each other. Audrey put her arms around Alette's neck and crushed her face into her hair. Alette returned the embrace. She could feel Audrey's shoulders juddering with her steady sobs and the dampness of her tears through her hair and the fabric of her shirt.

"Why did you not transform earlier?" Alette asked her. "When Zelos was pointing his wand at you, when you were in fear of your life, why did you not use your powers then?"

"I could not. I was trying so hard to feel. But you told me to feel anger, and I could not. Or it did not work in the same way."

"So what works for you?"

"For me, it seems to be love. I had to protect you, sister."

Then Alette was crying too. She hadn't cried for a long time – years, perhaps. It felt good. Like the release of her anger when she transformed. She cried for the parents who she never knew; for Storm, who was miles away from her in a strange stable; and for Maneo, the only father she had ever known, who was travelling far away from Essendor and who she would never see again.

A few strands of Alette's hair caught in something at Audrey's neck. Her necklace. She tugged them gently away as she had done so many times when they had caught like that in the chain of her own necklace.

Two necklaces, each half of a whole. They had been apart for so long but they were meant to be together. And then Alette was crying happy tears for she had finally found her twin – the part of her that had been missing for all these years.

CHAPTER FOURTEEN

AFTERWARDS

Audrey

They dried their eyes using starched napkins from the banqueting table. Alette looked a state. Her hair was more tangled than usual; her face was streaked with dirt. Audrey guessed that she didn't look particularly tidy herself. She had worn the same dress for a week, used her apron as a sling for Bramble and torn her petticoat climbing down from the golden tree.

"What do we do now?" asked Alette.

Audrey shook her head. She didn't know. They had never reached this point in the plan. Somehow, against all odds, they had found each other, found Essendor and overthrown the wrongful king. They had claimed their right to the throne but what now?

When Alette had begun her journey, she had planned to travel alone, but Maneo had found her. He had rescued her, helped her. She could not have done it alone. But now it really was just the two of them. There was no one else to show them the way.

Heavy fists pounded on the wooden door. Guards.

Audrey took a deep breath, flung open the doors and greeted three soldiers in full body armour who were pointing lances and swords in her direction. When they saw that the room was occupied solely by a pair of thirteen-year-old girls, they lowered their weapons, confused. They had no doubt been expecting to confront enemy soldiers or another sorcerer rather than two tear-stained adolescents.

Audrey stood back to allow the guards to enter the room. Then she drew herself up and addressed them. "I am Princess Audrey and this is my twin sister Princess Alette."

She did not want the guards to know that she had been crying on her sister's shoulder a moment before. She pretended she was wearing a queen's robes rather than a plain, torn dress and spoke in an authoritative tone, as she imagined her mother might have done.

The guards looked at her and each other in amazement.

"You will not know our names," said Audrey, "for they were never revealed, but we are the twin daughters of Queen Bia and King Elden. We were not murdered alongside them. This was a rumour spread by our Uncle Zelos, who was an evil murderer and a traitor to the kingdom, and who wanted to suppress any knowledge of our existence."

Audrey looked to her sister, as if checking whether she had anything to add. She did not. So Audrey continued addressing the baffled guards.

"Zelos took his own life, as you can see, and now the throne is ours. You will of course want to verify this and we can show you Queen Bia's engraved pendants as proof of our identity. I am sure however that the family resemblance is clear to you all."

One of the guards nodded and bowed low. "Princess Audrey. Princess Alette," he said, nodding to each girl. The others followed suit.

"For now, until our advisers arrive, this news must be kept within the castle walls. Can we count on your discretion?"

The guards nodded.

"Thank you. We will see to it that you are reimbursed for your loyalty. Now, before we do anything else, please arrange for a coach to be sent to the east, to the village of Lullgrove. Find Madam Warner, the miller's widow. She must be told that I, Audrey, am safe and well and that she is to come to Essendor at once. Bring her back in the coach, with as many of her things as she can manage. My cousin will look after the mill. Did you get all of that?"

The first guard nodded again.

"Good. Now go!"

The guards left, the door clunking heavily behind them. Alette turned to her sister.

"Well . . . you sounded just like a queen! Well done!"

And both girls laughed for the first time in a long time.

"Now, I am all out of ideas. We are strangers here in a city that is supposed to be ours – but until my mother gets here we don't know a soul."

"That's not strictly true," said Alette. She looked to Corvus, who was perched on the sill by the open window. He flew over to the banqueting table and rested on the back of a chair.

Alette stroked his head very lightly and he tipped his head to one side. "Corvus, please could you find the Boy River? Search up and down the river banks. He will be there waiting."

Corvus flew out of the window.

"Corvus likes you, doesn't he?" said Audrey.

"And I like him. He seems like a strange, wild thing, yet now I believe he has been looking out for me my whole life. I think he might be my bird!"

And the twins laughed again.

"Are you hungry?" asked Alette.

Audrey nodded. They both looked at all the fine food on the table. Alette selected a chicken leg and Audrey took a bread roll from the bread basket.

The roll was a cloverleaf shape, with three equal segments. It was a favourite shape of Audrey's. Back home, she would make batches of them but her mother would tut and say, "Three parts take three times as long, Audrey. Nothing wrong with a simple round!" Now, as Audrey broke off one of the segments, she wished for a common rounded roll, back home in the bakery. She took a bite, but it tasted of nothing. She chewed one mouthful slowly and left the rest.

Alette also left most of her chicken. "I can't seem to find my appetite," she said. Audrey knew what she meant. She couldn't bring herself to feel hungry here after the scuttling scorpions, the writhing snakes and the poisonous frogs. They were only spells, and the rest of the food was fine, but it was difficult to erase the images in their minds.

The girls pushed their food away, put their arms around each other, and waited.

A TABLECLOTH BUNDLE
Alette

It didn't take Corvus long to track down the Boy River. The guards were told to expect him and he walked straight into the castle and up to the banqueting hall.

Alette and Audrey told him everything that had happened. Berwick's transformation, the journey through the passageway and the great fight with Zelos. They missed out the part about unicorn transformations. Alette had not discussed it with Audrey yet, but she still felt that Maneo was right about keeping their power a secret. It is what their birth mother had done, after all. Given the magnitude of the events, it was a surprisingly short tale. River didn't seem surprised by any of it, even Maneo's betrayal.

"I passed the sorcerer on my way here. He looked like a deer who had thrown off the hunt. I greeted him but he did not reply."

He looked around at all the fineries in the hall.

"I've never seen inside the castle before. I wanted to, when

I was a boy, but there was no chance. Then for a long time I was on Zelos's most wanted list."

"I didn't think you were ever going to set foot in Essendor again," said Alette.

"While that man was on the throne. But he is gone now."

The girls looked around the great expanse of room. "We don't know what to do next," said Audrey.

"I know what you need before anything else, and that's some proper food and proper sleep." River was the right person to call upon. Needs were simple for him. Survival first.

"There is food here. Zelos left it." Alette indicated the spread laid out on the table.

River gave a low whistle. "All this for one person."

"But we can't bring ourselves to eat it. Not here – like this," said Audrey.

River nodded. "Come with me. I know some folk who will appreciate all this. Here, help me."

Between them, they piled the food into the centre of one of the square tablecloths, and tied it in a bundle. They left the bowl of dried scorpions, the soup tureen and the cracked eggs behind on the table.

Then they followed River out of the castle, stopping on the

way to collect Ribston. The orch was waiting in the clearing by the trapdoor.

"I promised to hold my post until you told me otherwise, did I not?"

"Oh, lovely, loyal Ribston," said Audrey, smiling. He asked them question after question until they felt even more exhausted than they were to begin with.

After they had told him the main events, he asked, "What about Berwick?"

It was a good question. The Boy River had not seen him by the south gates. "There was no one there. Maybe he never even went in the first place."

"I suppose he ran off. Now that he is a human again, he does not need us any more," said Alette.

"I never trusted him, even when he was a rabbit," said Ribston.

But Audrey looked concerned. "I hope everything is all right with him. I don't think he would have just left."

"That's because you always think the best of everyone," said Alette fondly. Part of her wished that she could be more like Audrey. She wanted to see the good in people: to learn how to love and trust. Maneo was so cynical and cold. Maybe now that he was gone she could learn to get closer to people.

But now was not the time to think about all this. Now she needed to think about food and rest. The three of them followed River out of the city walls and to the one place where they were certain to receive good hospitality: his mother's house.

THE WILDE'S SUPPER TABLE
Audrey

By the looks of their embrace, Madam Wilde had not seen her son for some weeks. "Oh, my boy! My Boy River! You're safe!" she cried, hugging him. "It is good to see you. Oh, but look at me – we have company. Do excuse me! Please, come in!"

Madam Wilde welcomed them in as if they were old friends.

"I wonder if my friends could stay for supper?" asked River.

"Of course, of course. I have some soup in the pot and an extra potato and parsnip should make it stretch to a few more heads— Colby, get this table cleared and bring out the cutlery!"

A boy who looked very like River, but younger and without the full beard, sighed and did as his mother requested.

"Don't fret, Mother, we have brought some food with us," said River. He swung the giant bundle on to the table and undid the knot in the tablecloth. The food from the banqueting hall looked even more ludicrous in these humble surroundings than it had on the ex-king's table. A whole chicken, cold cuts of meat, cheese, salt, celery, dates and apples. Grapes, bread, some sort of pork pie. Fresh figs, radishes and butter. Half a bottle of wine, complete with silver goblets. An apple rolled the length of the table and plopped on to the floor.

Madam Wilde and Colby stared open mouthed and then Colby picked up one of the silver goblets and mimed drinking from it. He laughed and his mother clapped her hands to her face.

"Where, in the name of the Midnight Unicorn, did you get all that from?"

River smiled and held his mother's hands. "We will explain everything. But first, we must eat."

In Madam Wilde's comfortable home, the food tasted unimaginably good and the company was noisy and fun.

Colby was particularly lively. "You are telling me that these two are princesses? It cannot be! This one looks as if she is fresh from selling cabbages at the market and this one dresses like a stable boy. Smells like one, too."

"Colby! I'm sorry, forgive my brother. One wouldn't know

he was your age – he behaves like an infant and has forgotten his manners."

"Forgotten my manners? Maybe you've forgotten that you said royalty was an outmoded concept and you would never bow down to a soul because of their title."

River's mother put a finger to her lips.

"That may be, but when we have guests at this table they get treated like royalty whatever their rank or station. Now try to be polite and keep your mouth like a daisy at sundown. Shut."

Colby grinned and didn't look particularly chastened. His mother folded a clean white cloth and placed it on the table. She popped a heavy pan on top of it.

"Princess Audrey and Princess Alette, I'm afraid we don't have much to offer but perhaps you would like some fresh soup to complement your meal? It might be nice to have something hot."

The soup was salty and full of flavour and they couldn't stop eating it.

Madam Wilde was particularly interested in the wine. "My, that is fancy. I've never tasted wine before. Do you mind if I do?" She took a sip and grimaced. The bottle was passed around but nobody liked it. Madam Wilde brought through cups of ale, milk and water instead.

Ribston helped Madam Wilde to prepare an apple pie for afterwards. It looked golden brown and delicious. "I don't like to be a Johnny Big Pips but I know a thing or two about slicing apples," he said.

"I am surprised you want to eat them. Aren't they your brothers or something?" said Alette.

"Princess Alette! I should think you would know by now that I am not an apple! I am an orch. An orchard elf. We are knowledgeable about apples and know how to nurture apples, collect apples and prepare apples. We are not apples."

"Aren't you having any, Princess Audrey?" asked Madam Wilde.

"I'm sorry but I can't touch them any more. A bad experience put me off. I am full, anyway."

There was silence for a moment and then Colby spoke. He hadn't said anything controversial for at least four minutes. He turned to Alette.

"So, why are you dressed like a boy?"

Audrey expected her twin to take offence at such a personal question, but she seemed to find it funny. She finished her mouthful of apple pie and grinned.

"These are the clothes I have always worn. Where I come from, there was no use for skirts and dresses."

"When Princess Alette returns to her rightful place at the castle, she will have all the fine frocks she desires. Isn't that right, my dear?" Madam Wilde patted her hand, and Alette grinned again. Audrey tried and failed to picture her sister in a "fine frock".

A knock at the door resounded through the small house. It was not a normal, neighbourly knock. It was a loud, urgent sort of knock that meant trouble.

MADAM TILBURY
Alette

River went to the door. Alette could see from her seat at the table that it was a thin, tired-looking woman. She was propping up a man who was much taller than her. "Please, can you help me?"

"Oh, it's Madam Tilbury. My neighbour. Is everything all right?" cried River's mother, rushing to the door.

Tilbury? Wasn't that Berwick's surname? Audrey called "Berwick!" and they both rushed after River's mother.

Berwick's head was lolling to one side and he had a bandage around his midriff, which was stained an alarming red. River and

Madam Tilbury helped him into the cottage, and laid him on the settle by the fire.

River's mother threw her hands in the air and rushed to get some strips of clean cloth.

Madam Tilbury sat on the floor by Berwick's head and held his hand. She had fear in her eyes. "My husband is dying, I know he is. I hadn't seen him for months and then he came to me in this state. He said Princess Audrey might be able to help us. I don't know who Princess Audrey is or why she should help us. I don't know that he's talking any sense at all but I didn't know what else to do—"

The woman broke off in cracked sobs and wiped her eyes with a handkerchief.

Audrey stepped forward.

"I am Princess Audrey. I think I might be able to help."

Alette and Audrey exchanged a look. Audrey had healed Berwick once before, when he was Bramble. She could make a healing potion now, but no one must know about their powers. They must keep this secret as their mother had done.

Madam Wilde brought in a pail of water and some linen strips.

"Can you please all leave the room?" said Audrey. Madam Tilbury looked at her with wide eyes and then back at her husband on the settle. She looked doubtful. It was true that Audrey was not looking particularly princess-like. Audrey reached for her arm. "It will be all right. We will look after him."

Madam Tilbury was clearly desperate. She left the room with River and his mother.

Alette stayed. "Can you do this, Audrey?"

Audrey nodded. "I think so."

Alette was increasingly in awe of Audrey, who, as she promised, was now able to transform. She created a potion as she had done in the forest by dipping her horn in the pail of water. Alette unwrapped the bandages from around Berwick's waist, dipped the linen strips into the water and cleaned the wound in his side. She wiped away the congealed blood and as she did so, the wound itself seemed to get smaller. Some colour returned to Berwick's pale face. The potion had worked again.

Audrey returned to her human form and smiled at Alette. "He is going to be well."

She sat at Berwick's side. "Are you strong enough to tell us what happened, Berwick?"

"The soldiers found me at the south gate. They recognized me; thought I'd been banished. I tried to hold my post but they cut me down – said I was an enemy of Zelos. I was bleeding so I went home to my family, I haven't told them anything yet. You have saved my life twice, Princess Audrey. I am forever in your debt."

"I am pleased to have been able to help. Can you keep our unicorn secret to yourself?"

"Of course. Your secret will always be safe with me, as mine is with you. I would rather that everyone did not know that I spied for Zelos."

"You should feel no shame. It was not your fault and you have redeemed yourself by fighting for us."

"What shall we do with the potion?"

"I'll take it," said Alette, and threw the contents of the pail out of the window on to the flowerbed.

The girls called everyone back into the room. Madam Tilbury instantly recognized the change in her husband and rushed to his side.

"Oh, Berwick, you are back with us! I cannot believe it. Oh, Princess Audrey, a thousand thank yous." Her whole face appeared changed. "Berwick, I have so many questions for you! Where have you been these past few months? What did that evil king do to you, husband?"

Audrey put a gentle hand on her shoulder. "Perhaps the

questions should wait for a few days, until Berwick has his full strength back?"

"Of course," said Madam Tilbury, blushing and holding her husband's hand.

"For now, is there anything we can get you?" asked Alette.

Berwick looked around at the expectant faces. "Do you know, there is one thing I could drink…"

"Yes?" said Madam Tilbury. "Knowing you, it'll be a tankard of ale."

"… I could just fancy a cup of dandelion tea."

THE OTHERS
Audrey

The girls spent the next few days at Madam Wilde's. Audrey was relieved to be sleeping in a proper bed, and washing in warm water. River did not stay. He was accustomed to sleeping under the stars and felt restricted by four walls and a ceiling. Before he left, they had a favour to ask him.

"You can speak to the animals, can you not?" said Alette.

"I cannot speak to the animals. I just know their ways."

"That's enough. It's just, I keep thinking about all the other spies," said Alette.

Audrey agreed. "It is wonderful that Bramble... I mean, Berwick has been reunited with his family but you heard what he said: there are dozens of them. All wandering out there in the wilds, in fear of their lives. It doesn't matter what they did or didn't do for Zelos; they deserve a second chance. They all have families too."

"Do you think you could somehow send word that the king is dead? Gather together all his spies and bring them here?" asked Alette.

"Would they not be better to left to fend for themselves in the woodland, Princess?"

"No!" said Audrey, shocked. "Many of those poor people committed no crime other than trying to feed their families. Like Berwick. They deserve our pity, not our condemnation."

"Yes. We will help them," said Alette.

Audrey admired her sister's determintation, but she was not sure how they would help these enchanted souls. "How will we reverse the magic, sister?"

"Don't concern yourself with that. If the Boy River can bring them here, then I can manage the rest," said Alette.

*

They gathered together in the nearby woodland. A strange crowd of beasts and birds. Audrey recognized the muntjac deer, the mouse and the squirrel, but there were others besides: an otter, a blue tit, a wild boar, even a snail. River had tried to reassure them but they were still nervous. Zelos had gone back on many promises. They were used to being suspicious.

Audrey and Alette introduced themselves. Explained that Zelos was dead. Explained that they had returned. The animals looked at Alette with wide, trusting eyes. Audrey felt the weight of responsibility and was nervous for her sister. What if she could not undo the magic?

They had discussed it earlier. "I thought that you only knew one spell?" said Audrey.

Alette was vague. "Well, not exactly. I learned a little bit here and there from Maneo."

Audrey tensed. This was the first time Alette had mentioned Maneo directly since he'd left.

"And it's easier to reverse a spell than to cast it in the first place."

Was that true? Audrey wasn't sure. She remembered how difficult Maneo found it to undo the spell that trapped them in the orchard. Audrey had the feeling that Alette knew a little more than she wanted to reveal about spells and sorcery. But now wasn't the time to discuss it.

Alette addressed the crowd. "I ask for your silence while I concentrate."

She lifted Maneo's wand. Audrey shivered at the memory of the last time she had seen it in action. Alette pointed the wand at the group and swept it from left to right, muttering the same spell that Maneo had used to reverse the magic in the woods. It worked. All at once, the animals turned back into people. The smaller animals changed quickly. One second, a blue tit fluttered on a branch, the next a woman with long red hair sat up there. The larger animals took longer: a fox's foreleg became an arm, a badger's stripes slowly faded. They blinked; put their hands to their faces, patted along their bodies, looked at one another. No one spoke.

It was striking then how many there were. Thirty at least, around the number in Audrey's schoolroom back home.

There were women, men, some that looked no older than children. Audrey had placed a pile of cloaks and tunics on the ground to protect their modesty in case, like Bramble, these people were naked, but they all seemed to be wearing something, although some were the humblest of rags. She guessed that they were wearing what they had been on the day of the enchantment.

339

"You are free. We do not ask what your crimes were under the previous ruler. We know that he was unjust and that you were desperate. For us, the slate is clean and any debts are hereby written off. We ask only three things from you. First, for your future loyalty. Second, that you do not speak of us just yet. Not until the news is public. Third, that if you know of any other poor creatures who are still missing out in the woods then send them to us with the assurance of a royal pardon for any past misdemeanours. Some may be lost to us for ever but others are unaccounted for. Every life matters."

The scene began to come to life as the people realized they were truly free. The Harding brothers embraced each other. The boy who had been the muntjac approached Alette approached her and shook her by the hand. "Thank you, Princess Alette."

Then they all returned home to their families.

"Well done," said Audrey to her sister. "Now what are you going to do with Maneo's wand?"

Alette tucked the wand into the pocket of her cloak. "I will dispose of it another time."

Audrey was worried. "No good can come of keeping it. You said yourself that we should leave this sort of magic to the sorcerers. Our power comes from within."

"I will get rid of it. But later. It has been useful today, has it not?"

And Audrey could not argue with that.

THE BEGINNING
Alette

The girls had asked for silence, but word soon got out that the princesses were back. All those people that had been given up as lost by their families returned home with tales of what had happened to them. One told their wife, another their best friend, but soon half the city was buzzing with the news.

Zelos had been an unpopular king. Most knew or suspected that he had murdered their beloved Queen Bia and King Elden. They had submitted to his rule only through fear. Now the princesses were back, seemingly from the dead, and Essendor was quick to embrace them. Happy times could commence again. Alette found Madam Wilde's house quite comfortable. She had never stayed in a family home before and enjoyed the warmth and convivial atsmosphere. She was certainly in no hurry to leave, but after two days, there was another knock at Madam Wilde's door.

"Who can this be? Let's hope it's not another poor soul bleeding from a knife wound. Since you two arrived, I never quite know."

Luckily, the person at the door was in fine physical shape. Her crisp, clear tone rang through the house. "I have been told I will find Mistresses Alette and Audrey staying here?"

Alette didn't recognize the voice, but Audrey instantly leaped up and ran to the door. "Mother!"

TWO RULERS
Audrey

Three days later, Audrey was sitting in her new bedchamber in the south tower with her mother. This chamber had belonged to her birth mother, Queen Bia, and as soon as Audrey saw it, she knew it was the one for her, with the view of the city and the light pouring through the window. Alette chose a smaller room on one of the lower floors.

Today Alette had climbed the steps of the south tower to find her sister. She wore her usual white shirt and soft leather leggings, but today she had her riding cloak draped around her and a travelling bag slung across one shoulder.

"Where are you going?" asked Audrey.

"To find Storm. It has been over a week now. He will have forgotten me."

"Never," said Audrey, and smiled.

"We'll get a coach prepared for you," said Audrey's mother.

"I prefer to travel on my own," said Alette.

"Not any more. You are a proper princess now and you must not endanger yourself or us by travelling alone."

"As you wish." Alette turned and prepared to leave, but Audrey's mother stopped her and patted a seat next to Audrey, indicating that she should sit down.

Since her arrival, Audrey's mother had been looking after them both. The first thing she did was to move them all into the castle. She remembered how a modern royal household should be run. But this could not last for ever. They needed to talk about what would happen next.

"You've done a very good job in reclaiming the throne. I am proud of you. Proud of you both."

Alette gave a wry little smile. Audrey felt for her. Since Maneo had gone, she had no parents left, birth or adoptive.

"Now it is time to plan the next steps. One or both of you may be crowned Queen. Alette, as the eldest, it is your birthright, yet, as twins, it is possible for you to share the throne. If this is what you agree, then we must decide together how it will work. Will you rule together, or on alternate years?"

Audrey looked at Alette. It was her decision, really, as the older twin. But Alette said nothing and Audrey's mother continued.

"You are not allowed to rule independently until you turn eighteen, so you must put together a council to advise you until you come of age. How does that sound?"

Alette shook her head. "I have learned a number of things over the past few days. One is that two queens can never successfully rule together. It won't work. Zelos said it, Maneo said it and I agree. No king or queendom ever thrived under two rulers."

Audrey's mother tutted. "Well, those two said a lot of things. Most can be taken with a large pinch of salt."

She had never been a fan of Maneo and his betrayal had come as no surprise to her. "I always thought that arrogant young man was up to no good. He never smiled properly and he wore his hat too low over his eyes."

Audrey couldn't believe her ears. "And yet you sent me off on a two hundred mile journey with the man?"

"Sent you off? I sent you nowhere at all, young lady. I let

you do what you were set on doing and prepared myself to pick up the pieces should it be necessary."

Audrey laughed. "Speaking of which, we were discussing our future rule…?"

"Yes, as I was saying, maybe they never tried two queens before. There's something to be said for sharing. Six months each. Why not?"

Alette held up her hands. "Please let me finish. The other thing I learned over the past few days was that I don't want to be a queen. I don't even want to be a princess."

"What?" said Audrey.

"What?" said her mother.

"When I set out on this journey, I wanted two things. I wanted to avenge my parents' death and I wanted to find my twin. Now, I have done those things and I feel I can start to live my life. Taking responsibility for Essendor and the kingdom does not come into it."

Audrey nodded. She could understand some of this.

Alette continued. "I don't want to be a princess. Or a queen. I don't want to live in a castle and I don't want to wear fine frocks. I don't want people to bow down to me in the street and I don't want to be accountable for the wellbeing of hundreds of subjects."

"You may change your mind in time," said Audrey's mother.

"I do not tend to do that very often," said Alette.

Audrey smiled.

"The last thing I discovered on our journey is that there is one natural leader among us and one who is happy to step back into the shadows. Only one of us is strong enough for the job of queen. That is the truth as I see it."

For once, Audrey's mother fell silent.

Alette adjusted her travel bag on her shoulder and walked to the door. "Now, I am going to go and recover my horse."

FIVE

MONTHS

LATER

CHAPTER FIFTEEN

QUEEN AUDREY

Essendor was ready for Queen Audrey and she was ready for them. She was becoming known for her kindness, her generosity and, above all, her steely inner strength. Before she was crowned, she arranged for bags of grain to be brought from the east. New life was breathed into the old mill and fresh bread was given to all. She wanted to ensure that the city never knew hunger again. Everyone agreed that the thirteen-year-old queen would make a fairer ruler than her uncle.

A regent was appointed until she came of age. Madam

Warner was the obvious choice. She led an unusual royal council. Ribston Russet and Berwick Tilbury had been fiercely loyal to Princess Audrey from the beginning. They would sit at her side and advise. Some might have thought it strange to see the old king's nanny, a simple peasant and a three foot green orch at court, but if so, then they didn't say so to Queen Audrey's face.

"There is one more person I would like to ask to sit on the royal council," said Audrey.

Madam Warner approved of her choice. "Now, that Boy River is a nice young man. Knows his manners. He always did, you know, even as a boy. I remember when he showed me and a newborn Audrey our way out of the woods. So polite. A credit to his mother."

Audrey nodded. "But I suspect he will say no."

She was right. "I don't know the ways of people," said River. "They confuse me and I am happier out in the wilds with my animals. I couldn't live in a castle or follow the ways of the royal court. But if you need me, I will be there in a flutter of a wren's wing. Just say the word."

The people chose to forego the usual period of royal mourning. Zelos would not be missed. And so, five months later, on a cold snowy day in February, red swallowtail flags fluttered from the castle turrets, bunting was hung in the streets and the crowds gathered in the cobbled courtyard below the south tower to meet their new queen. The freezing temperatures did not deter the crowds. They dressed in multiple layers, stamped their feet and blew on their hands to keep warm. Some things are worth waiting for.

Light, fluffy snow drifted into the courtyard and swirled around the crowds. When Queen Audrey appeared in the arched window, a few snowflakes fell on her rich brown hair and she laughed. The crowds clapped and cheered. The queen was dressed in a simple green velvet dress and her royal robes. The traditional gold crown was locked away in the royal vaults. It was too large for her and too ostentatious for her taste. Instead, the silversmith had fashioned a lighter crown with delicate engraving, set with a single opal. It flashed when it caught the light and perfectly matched the necklace that shone below her throat.

Queen Audrey gave a heartfelt speech, which didn't come from the regent or the council. It came from Audrey herself. She vowed to put the health and welfare of her people at the heart of everything she did. In her reign, wealth would be distributed more fairly across the kingdom and bonds would be renewed with the neighbouring kingdoms. She aimed to restore peace for a whole generation.

The crowds clapped and cheered again for their new queen and for a bright future. In amongst the clapping, a shout went up, from a young child.

"The Midnight Unicorn!"

There was a collective gasp as the crowds looked around. Could it be true? Where? The child pointed behind them, out beyond the city to the fields that lay thick with snow. There on a hilltop in the falling snow, was a dark silhouette of a beautiful creature. Like a horse, strong and proud, but with the unmistakeable shape of a pointed horn on its forehead. Had the people been close enough, they would have seen a white, oval-shaped mark on its face that was never there before.

"The Midnight Unicorn has returned!"

The unicorn stopped, head held high, for a few moments. Queen Audrey raised her hand in greeting. Then, as the snow fell harder, the unicorn galloped away.

Once again, the city would be protected.

And Queen Audrey's would be a blessed reign.

ALETTE

Alette was different to her sister. She made it known that she wanted to lead an ordinary life and the people respected that. She lived in a small cottage on the edge of the city that backed on to the Wilde's home. Madam Wilde looked in on her now and again but other than that it was just Alette, her horse Storm and her strange pet raven.

She was known only by her given name– no title – and soon her neighbours almost forgot that she had ever been a princess. People often remember only what they choose. That was just the way Alette liked it. That first autumn at Essendor she worked hard to bring in the potato harvest. She helped with the hedge cutting as the cyclamen bloomed and she danced at the wintertide festival with the rest of them.

Some said she was a sorcerer, like her uncle had been. A good sorcerer, of course, but still someone who knew magic. She did not say a lot, she kept herself to herself and was a slightly mysterious figure.

Alette did not practise magic or chant spells, but she did have at least two secrets from her neighbours. One was a light black wand, which she kept well hidden. She didn't use it. Her days of practising spells were behind her. Still, she could not bear to throw it away. It might be of use one day. So it stayed wrapped in linen and packed in a box, in a hiding place that only she knew.

The other secret was one that she had kept for almost her whole life. It was as much a part of her as eating or breathing. But for the first time in her life it was a secret that Alette could share with someone who understood. Had they wandered into the forest on a clear evening at midnight, then Alette's neighbours might have discovered the second secret. They would have seen not one, but two, twin unicorns turning nose to tail in the dappled moonlight.

THE END

Alice Hemming
Q&A

DID YOU LIKE FAIRY TALES AS A CHILD?

Yes. I have always loved fairy tales. My favourites as a child were the Hans Christian Andersen tales, especially "The Snow Queen", "The Little Match Girl" and "The Little Mermaid". All quite sad stories!

WHAT DO YOU LIKE ABOUT FAIRY TALES AS A GROWN-UP?

I love the endless possibilities for interpretation and reinvention.

WHAT IS YOUR FAVOURITE FAIRY TALE AND WHY?

I enjoy discovering less well-known fairy tales, and my favourite of the moment is an old fairy tale called "The White Cat", from *The Blue Fairy Book* by Andrew Lang (1897). A king sets his sons a series of tasks in order to distract them from taking over the kingdom. One task involves finding the tiniest, prettiest dog in the kingdom, which is eventually discovered lying on a white cushion inside an acorn. When the prince lifts the acorn to his ear, he hears a tiny "bow-wow!"

WHAT IS YOUR LEAST-FAVOURITE FAIRY TALE AND WHY?
"Hansel and Gretel". Because it's really scary. The bit where the witch wants to pinch their fingers to see if they are fat enough for the pot is horrific!

IF YOU COULD CHANGE ANYTHING ABOUT A
WELL-KNOWN FAIRY TALE, WHAT WOULD IT BE?
It is hard to ignore the fact that women get a bad deal in many of the well-known fairy tales. It has been pointed out that Sleeping Beauty is one of the worst offenders in that she spends ninety per cent of the story asleep and is kissed without her permission. But I like the imagery of the story – the sleeping people and the thorn-covered castle – so I would like to write a version where she somehow influences the story despite her deep sleep.

WHO IS YOUR FAVOURITE FAIRY TALE BADDIE?
Hans Christian Andersen's Snow Queen, with her icy beauty, cold heart and frosty kiss!

WHAT ADVICE WOULD YOU GIVE TO A CHARACTER IN A FAIRY TALE?
DON'T OPEN THE DOOR. DON'T EAT THE APPLE. DON'T TOUCH THE SPINDLE. But they always do. Sigh.

FAIRY TALES USUALLY TEACH US LESSONS OR MORALS. WHAT WOULD YOU LIKE READERS TO LEARN FROM *THE MIDNIGHT UNICORN*?
Appearances can be deceptive. The strongest people can come across as quite quiet and shy, just as people who seem confident can be hiding vulnerable natures.

IF YOU WERE JACK, WOULD YOU HAVE TRADED YOUR COW FOR JELLYBEANS?
No, but I could be tempted by chocolate buttons.

IF YOU WERE HANSEL OR GRETEL, WOULD YOU HAVE
GONE INTO THE GINGERBREAD HOUSE?
Yes, probably. It's so pretty! And made of gingerbread. But –
eek – bad move!

IF YOU WERE SLEEPING BEAUTY, WOULD YOU HAVE
TOUCHED THE SPINDLE ON THE SPINNING WHEEL?
Again, probably. I'd like to be able to spin … zzzzzz

IF YOU WERE ALADDIN, WHAT WOULD YOU USE THE
LAMP TO WISH FOR?
A tiny, pretty dog on a white cushion inside an acorn, of course.

Acknowledgements

Thank you to…

All those at Scholastic who made this book happen, especially Fiz for your guidance, encouragement and unswerving belief in me.

Mum and Dad for passing on a love of stories, books and language. And for the unicorn stress reliever.

Paul, for your constant support of my work. Any evil brothers in this story are entirely fictitious.

Jodi and Louise, the best writing buddies ever. Stream On.

Amanda and Tracey, my very own Audrey and Alette.

Ruth. I strongly suspect you have hidden unicorn powers.

Tom G for a shared love of fairy tales. I may have stolen an anecdote from you and Maja but you'll soon be far too busy to notice… And Kieran—when are you going to write a book?

Sarah, who has made me laugh since I was eleven. I think we've ticked off the last set of life goals. Shall we plan the next ones?

Caroline, Naomi, Rebecca and Kate, for timely coffees and support.

Em and Sarah for walks, talks and elves in July.

Joss, Claire and Norie for always understanding and being there.

Shishi, for Bramble inspiration and research.

And to the three people who helped my heroes across the bridge, named the horses and put out the bins. Simon, Clara and Tom, I couldn't do this without you. Ready for the next one?